Class No. F
Author. MARSHALL

LEABHARLANN
CHONDAE AN CHABHA

D0716296

- 4 SEP 2000

1. This book may be kept three weeks.
   It is to be returned on / before the last date
   stamped below.
2. A fine of 20p will be charged for every week
   or part of week a book is overdue.

1 FEB 1997		

CAVAN COUNTY LIBRARY

The Chequer-board

Sybil Marshall

Cavan County Library
Withdrawn Stock

PENGUIN BOOKS

PENGUIN BOOKS

Published by the Penguin Group
Penguin Books Ltd, 27 Wrights Lane, London W8 5TZ, England
Penguin Books USA Inc., 375 Hudson Street, New York, New York 10014, USA
Penguin Books Australia Ltd, Ringwood, Victoria, Australia
Penguin Books Canada Ltd, 10 Alcorn Avenue, Toronto, Ontario, Canada M4V 3B2
Penguin Books (NZ) Ltd, 182–190 Wairau Road, Auckland 10, New Zealand

Penguin Books Ltd, Registered Offices: Harmondsworth, Middlesex, England

First published by Michael Joseph 1995
Published in Penguin Books 1996
1 3 5 7 9 10 8 6 4 2

Copyright © Sybil Marshall, 1995
All rights reserved

The moral right of the author has been asserted

Extracts from the Authorized Version of the Bible (The King James Bible), the rights in which are
vested in the Crown, are reproduced by permission of the Crown's Patentee, Cambridge
University Press

Every effort has been made to trace copyright owners for permission to reproduce quoted material.
If there are any omissions the author and publisher would be happy to rectify them in future
editions

Printed in England by Clays Ltd, St Ives plc

Except in the United States of America, this book is sold subject
to the condition that it shall not, by way of trade or otherwise, be lent,
re-sold, hired out, or otherwise circulated without the publisher's
prior consent in any form of binding or cover other than that in
which it is published and without a similar condition including this
condition being imposed on the subsequent purchaser

CAVAN COUNTY LIBRARY
ACC No. C63113
CLASS NO. F
INVOICE NO. 3429
PRICE £5.99

In memory of my two much-loved nieces,
Rachel (1935–1944) and Carole (1945–1995)

'Tis all a Chequer-board of Nights and Days
Where Destiny with Men for Pieces plays:
Hither and thither moves, and mates, and slays,
And one by one back in the Closet lays.

The Rubáiyát by Omar Khayyám

Contents

Felo de Se

They were all quieter than usual, subdued by shock and distress. Gardner, their host, sat far back in his armchair, his face in shadow. Beckett drew the large square Victorian ash-tray towards him, and tapped his pipe into it. The reeking dottle fell on to the motto inscribed on it. 'All is vanity', it said. He beat the smouldering ash with the bowl of his pipe, and looked towards the window, where Trefor Lewis stood with his back to them, restlessly jingling the coins in his pocket.

'I suppose there's no doubt that it was suicide?' Beckett asked of Lewis's back.

The doctor turned and came to the fire. 'None at all. He had been out shooting all day, and was cleaning the guns in his study, and five minutes before young Harry had been there with him, admiring them. Double-barrelled Purdys – but of course you know. Then he put the end of it into his mouth, and pulled the trigger. I know!' He grimaced, and turned back to the window, unwilling to pursue the matter further.

'But *why*?' Beckett insisted. 'I can't take it in, if you know what I mean. My mind won't reach to it, or accept it. I've known Johnnie since we were kids at school. He was my nearest neighbour, and my best friend. I was best man at his wedding. We've shot and fished and played golf together for more than forty years. If any other man knew Johnnie well, it was me. I could swear he had no cause to do a thing like that.'

Gardner spoke from the shadows. 'Sit down, Trefor, and try to relax. He was your friend, too, and you've had the worst of it.' His voice was calm and soothing, that of an old man who had the serenity of those able to choose the time to stop fighting the current of events, and to go gently with the stream. He was as distressed by his old friend's sad end as any of them, but he had been the county coroner for many years before he had retired, and suicide was nothing new to him.

'Help yourself to another whisky,' he said, as the doctor at last sat down.

'Another Johnnie Walker?' said Lewis with bitter irony. But he filled his glass all the same, and sat down at last.

Stone sat twisting his glass round and round in his fingers, staring at the amber liquid in the glow of the firelight.

'George says he could swear old Johnnie had no cause to do away with himself,' he said. 'But how can anyone be sure? Nobody knows, really, what goes on in another person's life from day to day. I mean, I can imagine circumstances that might make me consider it, though I'm not a suicidal sort of chap by a long chalk. If Trefor, for instance, were to tell me that I had all the symptoms of some awful disease that would in time turn me into a helpless invalid dependent upon paid attendance for the rest of my life, I simply couldn't face the prospect.'

'You warn me not to tell you the truth,' said the doctor. Major Stone was a military man reaching the end of a distinguished career that had prevented him from marrying, and he had no near relations. 'Of course I can't, and shan't, discuss Johnnie as a patient, but I shall be testifying at the inquest that he was just about the healthiest specimen for his age in the country.'

'Money, then?' persisted Stone. 'Family squabbles? Eternal triangle?'

George Beckett snorted. 'I imagine that when his will is published it will prove he wasn't short of the price of a bottle of whisky,' he said. 'He must be one of the wealthiest as well as one of the healthiest men in these parts. As for your other suggestions – they're ludicrous. Since he and Susan met when they were twenty, they've never been interested in anybody of the opposite sex except as friends. It was such a complete, happy marriage that it washed off on their children. The entire family was – wholesome, if you know what I mean. The tensions most folks have just weren't there. I've envied Johnnie his home and family life many a time. Mine has been happy, too – but not in the same way. He had everything.'

'And yet tomorrow, at the inquest, they will bring in a verdict of felo de se. Self-destruction. And no doubt to make things easier for Susan and the family, they will add "while the balance of the mind was disturbed". It's the only possible verdict.' The old coroner spoke with the authority of experience.

Beckett's jaw took on a belligerent jut. 'And what does *that* mean?' he said. 'That Johnnie Walker was off his rocker? That's simply monstrous! A saner man never lived.'

'Neither did he,' said the doctor. 'That's what it's all about.'

'Don't you dare joke about it,' said Beckett, angrily.

'I wasn't,' replied the doctor. 'In fact, I was agreeing with you. If there had been any physical reason for him suddenly to have lost his reason, I should have known. And as a friend, as well as his doctor, I shall have to say that Johnnie and psychological hang-ups just didn't go together.'

Gardner sat forward, anxious to soothe and prevent wounded spirits seeking relief in asperity.

'What is a psychological hang-up, though? It's a convenient phrase, but it doesn't tell us anything, really. We say "while the balance of the *mind* is disturbed". "Mind" connotes the power of reason, and to say a man has lost his reason means he's mad. But you don't have to be mad to allow emotion to overpower reason, or to stop it functioning for the split second it takes to pull a trigger. It would be much more to the point to say "while the balance of the emotions was disturbed". The French understand that. They allow for "*crimes passionnels*". In that respect there's no real difference between suicide and murder. A man can turn uncontrollable passion against himself as much as against another person. The stronger, the more normal a chap is in the ordinary way, the more he is likely to be able to keep powerful emotions in check, sometimes for a lifetime. But if then some apparently trivial thing jolts him, the control snaps. It may be that the constant need to control some powerful emotion over a long period has in itself worn a weak place in the chain. Then there's tragedy.'

They knew that he spoke from years and years of experience, and were silent, trying to fit his abstract reasoning to the case in point.

'But what emotions?' said Stone at last. 'George has practically ruled out love and hate in the case of old Johnnie. Trefor has ruled out fear. What others are there strong enough to cause a man like Johnnie to snap?'

'Ah − that's the mistake so many people make, especially juries. There are other emotions quite as powerful as hate and fear, if not so dramatic. What about guilt? Or terrible grief? Or remorse, eating you like acid year after year after year?'

'Well, it seems to me that guilt must include fear,' said Stone.

'Not always, I think,' said Gardner. 'It may not be criminal guilt, and it may be terribly mixed up with grief. But perhaps remorse is the most wearing of all. I remember a case, many years ago − would you like to hear it?' He paused, being a modest man and a courteous host. His guests were only too glad of anything that would take their minds off the immediate present.

'Fill up the glasses for me, Trefor,' he said, and waited till it was done.

'It wasn't one of my cases as a coroner, you understand,' he began. 'In fact, it happened while I was still a student. My father was a country solicitor, deep in rural Kent. We lived in a little village, though he practised in the market town a couple of miles away. Used to travel on horseback, or in a little horse-drawn trap. Seems incredible, doesn't it? As usual, the village was made up of two kinds of people: the farmers and their labourers, mostly indigenous, on the one hand, and the few professionals on the other − parson, doctor, lawyer, with the schoolmaster on the edge of both groups. The village was dominated by the church, a huge and beautiful building, and by the Hall. The living was a particularly good one, in the hands of a family of aristocratic landowners. The Hall was one of their many seats, and its present inhabitant was a son of one of its minor branches – Canon Lancelot Crowle-Tibberton. He had gone into the Church when young, and made his mark. But I think he had come into money, and with the living and the Hall at his disposal, he was far more of a squire than a parson. He retired from active service, so to speak, at the age of fifty or so, and gave himself up to his great passion, which was the study of old silver. He put a curate into the huge, rambling old rectory, and left the cure of the souls to him.'

Gardner paused to take a sip from his glass. 'He was a typical aristocrat cleric, in looks and manner. You don't see them nowadays, of course. Parsons either creep about in their dog collars looking like apologetic poor relations, or stand at public bars with a pipe in their mouths and a pint in their hands trying to be one of the boys. Crowle-Tibberton was representative of many of his time. Tall, thin, ascetically handsome, proud and aloof. My father did some of his minor legal business, though I believe the family trust was looked after by a London firm. So he saw Pa frequently, and to some small degree made a friend of him, though he despised him. He told him so – to his face. He explained that Pa was not a gentleman. There were three criteria of a true gentleman, in his book: you came from an ancient family, as he did; you went to Oxford or Cambridge, as he had; and you travelled the world when young, to give you perspective, as he had done. Pa qualified for none of them. It wasn't very likely that Crowle-Tibberton had many friends. But he did have a family – a nice if subdued wife, and four children, all grown-up, of course, by the time I'm speaking of. And he had his interest, and his collection of silver.

'He really was a connoisseur, and an expert. He had made himself a name as an expert that was known the world over, by a paper he had written for some learned journal about seventeenth-century table silver. He was consulted by other experts – museum curators, and folks like that – all over the place. He would tell my pa with pride when such a thing happened, and show him any new additions to his magnificent collection.

'I hated the fellow, as a child, and never stopped to be ignored or dressed down if I saw him in the distance. I'd just finished at Cambridge and moved in as a junior partner here when it happened. I wasn't married then, of course, and still made my base at home for holidays and weekends, and so on. The Canon made it his business to take the services on all the main festivals. So there we were, that beautiful Easter morning, sitting in the sunlit church waiting for his reverence to honour us with his presence. He was late, and came in down the aisle still wearing his overcoat over his cassock and disappeared into the vestry. The organist was playing – voluntaries, I believe they're called, one after the other. The curate sat with the choir boys, willingly playing second fiddle. It had all happened so many times before: Crowle-Tibberton liked the power he had, to keep people waiting for his presence, I think. But he usually robed very quickly and once he'd arrived the service would get under way. After about ten minutes, the curate tapped on the vestry door, but there was no answer, so he opened it. Crowle-Tibberton had cut his own throat. He had, apparently, put on his vestments and picked up his notes, ready for the service. But the verger said at the inquest that from custom dating a long way back, a quill pen was always kept in a drawer for those who wished to sign the marriage register, and beside it an ancient silver penknife, very sharp. "Suicide while the balance of the mind was disturbed", of course. But the affair intrigued and fascinated my pa and me. We couldn't let it alone, and between us we made out a case to account for it – the snapping of the last strand of control that had caused him to commit two of the worst crimes in the Church's book, suicide and sacrilege.

'About ten years previously, he had had to engage a new curate when the one he was used to died suddenly. Crowle-Tibberton wasn't a man who liked opposition. He was fair and just in his dealings, but if he had a real vice, it was pride. He liked things his own way, so he naturally chose as his helper a good, hardworking, but humble and meek man. The new curate, Cradley, was all those things. He was about forty, big and handsome in a gentle way, and very pleasant. He had a wife who looked as if a good puff of wind would blow her away, though she was bright and cheerful and energetic and shouldered the work of a curate's wife as to the manner born, which I believe she was. Her father had been a country parson who had died young. She knew all about poverty the hard way. They had three young children, and in spite of being very poor, always gave the impression of being happy and contented. I soon found out that to boys of my age Cradley was everything that Crowle-Tibberton was not. He knew all about fishing, for instance, and was never too busy to help. If I got into difficulty with my Latin homework, it wasn't to Pa I turned, but to Cradley. I'd go round to that great barn of a vicarage, and find him with his sleeves rolled up making bread, while Mrs Cradley ran the Girls' Friendly Society in the next room. And he'd take me through my prep, while he kneaded the dough, and I'd take care to make it last till the first loaves came out of the oven. There's nothing to touch homemade bread still hot, butter or no butter. There was no butter there – they couldn't afford to give it away. He explained many a time that he made bread for the family because it was cheaper, not because he really wanted to waste his time doing it. They must have been very, very poor. He used to knit for the children, as well, I remember. Carried a sock on four thin needles round with him, and turned the heel while he visited what were called "the poor" of the parish. Well, he seemed the ideal sort of chap for Crowle-Tibberton to lord it over. My pa happened to be present when the Canon got what seemed to him – Pa, I mean – to be an unwelcome surprise with regard to his subordinate.

'As I said, if Crowle-Tibberton acquired a new piece for his collection, he usually sent for Pa to go up and see it, and arrange the insurance on it. He had just come by a most beautiful little early seventeenth-century salt, and was overjoyed with his new acquisition. It had put him into an unusually relaxed and pleasantly expansive mood. They were in his library, where the collection was also kept, and he had taken out from the display cabinets some of his other choicest pieces, and ranged them with the new one on the top of a beautiful refectory table set below a window where they got the full benefit of light. They stood admiring the stuff when the maid announced Cradley's arrival, saying he needed to see the Canon rather urgently.

'Crowle-Tibberton put down the little chased bowl he was holding, and turned to her. "Show him in here," he said. The maid, according to Pa, looked utterly astounded but all she said was, "Yes, sir", and a minute or two later Cradley's mended boots carried him across the threshold of the Canon's holy of holies for the first time. The apology for intrusion he had started to make died on his lips, as the saying goes, when he saw the silver. He moved towards it like a man in a dream, and stood looking down on it with an expression both rapt and knowledgeable at the same time. His normal composure seemed for a moment to have deserted him.

'"My sainted aunt!" he exclaimed – that was the nearest he ever got to an oath, I believe. "What a sight! What absolutely exquisite pieces! May I please hold that one a moment?" and he pointed to the bowl the Canon had just set down.

'The Canon put it into his hands, and perhaps for the only moment in the whole of their relationship they were absolutely at one.

'"You know something of old silver, too, I see," said Crowle-Tibberton, in a voice he had rarely used before to poor Cradley. The curate shook his head. "No, I know absolutely nothing," he said. "I just love it. If I had the means and the time, I should make it my business to know about it, but of course that's impossible now."

'The Canon was curious. "How did you come to be interested in it in the first place?" he asked.

'The curate smiled ruefully. "Oh, that's easy. My grandfather had some very beautiful pieces he had collected during the eighties and nineties, and when I was a little boy he used to show me them and let me hold them and tell me tales about them, putting them into historical perspective, you know. I was fascinated. I adored him, and the silver. Looking down on that collection just now was like being transported back to my childhood."

'"What happened to it, then?" asked the Canon, the collector's avid gleam in his eye.

'"Oh, Grandfather fell on very hard times, and had to part with a lot of it. Then he died, and it was split up amongst the family. My cousin, who was head of the family, got a good deal of what was left, and I had the few pieces Grandfather knew I had loved most. I think he hoped the time might come when I could add to it again." He laughed, ruefully. "Some hope! My cousin had no real feeling for it, and just at that time some expert wrote an excellent paper about seventeenth-century table silver. My cousin read it and cashed in on it. I've forgotten the chap's name who wrote the paper – a double-barrelled name, I feel sure, and I ought to remember." He screwed his face up in an intense effort to bring the name back to memory, and Pa let out a chuckle that let the penny drop. The curate turned towards his superior with a look of awe and admiration. "Oh course – it was *you*, sir! Crowle-Tibberton. I simply never connected the two. How wonderful! What would my dear old grandad have said if he had known it was my good luck to work for someone who had really studied the subject." He was beaming, his normal humility quite forgotten. But Crowle-Tibberton was basking in his admiration, and did not seem to mind the sudden unwonted social ease of the moment.

'Then poor Cradley made his unwitting mistake. "I've often wished my cousin hadn't been quite so hasty in selling," he said. "You see, he had all the pieces that were family pieces – stamped with the family crest, many of them, quite unique, I believe. He was older than I, and it happened while I was up at Oxford – not that he would have consulted me, of course. The family had drifted apart a bit, because my father had been a missionary and we had spent all my youth travelling from one heathen spot to another. Very broadening experience, of course, but hardly conducive to family unity. My father died on active service, so to speak, in the West Indies, and my mother brought all my brothers and sisters back. It was a terrible struggle for her. Most of my legacy from Grandfather went bit by bit for the pot. Some of it was sold far too cheap – I know that now. But at the time I was just thankful I had something I could contribute."

'My pa told me often that it was like watching a well-acted play. He said Crowle-Tibberton's expression changed during Cradley's artless recital, from benign interest to cold, proud chagrin, and searched in his mind for what the innocent curate had let drop to cause the sudden change of mood. Pa used to grin quite wickedly when he recalled it. You see, in that one little speech, Cradley had given proof that in spite of his broken boots and darned cassock, he fulfilled all Crowle-Tibberton's criteria of a gentleman, those my father had so signally failed in. The Canon had chosen his humble curate without looking into his antecedents. Now he faced a future knowing that socially his subordinate was his equal. He had to find a way of taking the curate down immediately, before this *bonhomie* insinuated itself permanently into their day-to-day relationship.

'"I expect your cousin did quite well out of his sale," he said, coldly. "You say your grandfather collected most of his stuff in the eighties and nineties. Alas, I fear that anything that changed hands during that period must be suspect. It was the great age of the faker. There were workshops, in France particularly, where craftsmen spent their time and skill faking antiques of all kinds – medieval church pieces, armour, swords and daggers, enamels and silver. Anyone other than an absolute expert could have been utterly fooled. I really doubt if your family lost anything of historical value."

'Poor Cradley was looking abashed, embarrassed, and a bit put out. But he remembered who and where he was, and accepted the rebuff and disappointment with his usual humility. He opened his mouth to speak, but not before Crowle-Tibberton, all icy pride, had said, "Mr Gardner and I have business to do. What was this urgent matter you wished to discuss with me?"

'"Oh, of course – I do beg your pardon! I expect you are quite right, sir – after all, you are the expert, and my grandfather was only an amateur. I'm afraid my wife has not been at all well during the last few days, and she has just had to go to bed. I fear she will simply not be able to take the Girls' Friendly meeting tomorrow evening, and I have a confirmation preparation. My wife wondered if one of the Miss Crowle-Tibbertons would possibly stand in for her?"

"I don't think that will be possible. I'm sure they all have previous engagements. Tell Mrs Cradley to cancel her girls' meeting. I don't think it at all important."

'He turned back to Pa, and Cradley, flushed and for him quite angrily distressed, was dismissed. There was nothing he could do but to say goodnight, and withdraw.

'"That is the worst of amateurs," said Crowle-Tibberton as the curate's footsteps died away down the hall. "Every goose they hatch is a swan. They forget how rare the phoenix is – or was."

'Mrs Cradley's indisposition turned out to be another pregnancy, and from the beginning things did not go well. She was soon up and about, doing all her usual work and duties, but even I, as a child, could see that all was not right. Cradley himself bore as much of the extra burden as he could, and still seemed to have time and patience for anybody who wanted or needed him, though he looked less serene than he had done previously, and whenever it didn't interfere with his duties, he had the other children with him. There was little time for talk or discussion of a social nature with him.

'The poor woman had a terribly difficult labour, I believe, and after about two days and nights gave birth to a little girl – a beautiful child in every respect except that her right hip was dislocated and the leg deformed.'

Gardner paused, and stared into the fire while he lit another cigar. When it was going well, he took up his tale again.

'I think we forget what it was like for people like Cradley before we had the 1948 National Insurance Act, and the Welfare State,' he said. 'The nearest hospital was twelve miles away. The only person with a car was Crowle-Tibberton. Even the doctor didn't buy one until his horse died in the shafts one night. The war was over – the first one, I mean – and things had changed in towns, but deep in the countryside as we were the changes were only just beginning. The child went into hospital, but there was little they could do. It was obvious that she would always be a cripple. Mrs Cradley got about again, but she grieved for her baby, and never seemed to pick up. They got little Frances home when she was about six months old, and Cradley rigged up a kind of rucksack so that he could carry her about with him, and so relieve his wife of a bit of the care of her. But it was quite obvious that Mrs Cradley was going downhill fast. "Consumption", as it was called then, was in every line of her. The ladies said she was "going into a decline". It wasn't uncommon. What she needed was rest, and comfort, and good food. There was none of them at the rectory.

'My pa was very worried about the situation, but apart from sympathy there was little he could offer. Cradley was one of his own class. Anything that smacked of charity was out of the question. Then he hit on a plan. My school work wasn't bad, but it wasn't up to Cambridge standard, and Pa had set his heart on me going there. My classics master had suggested that I needed extra coaching in Latin. Why shouldn't Cradley coach me, for a proper fee, as he had done so often in the past for nothing? Pa put it to me, and I was all for it. So we set off to walk to the rectory, and to see what Cradley himself thought of the idea.

'Of course, he knew quite well what had prompted the suggestion, though my need of him was genuine enough. His relief at the thought of the bit of extra money was pitiful – but no more so than the pride that made him want to refuse, or the humility and love for his wife and family that beat the pride down. He accepted, and squared his shoulders like the man he was as he turned to face Pa again.

'"I shall not hide my gratitude," he said, quietly. "I'm afraid I'm not going to be able to keep my wife long. I'd like her to have what comfort she can while she's still with us."

'My own mother had died when I was young, too. Pa knew what Cradley was going through — though we hadn't been in poverty, thank God. The two men understood each other.

'"Will you regard me as a real friend, and call on me if you need to?" Pa asked, adding hastily, "You could always have the fees for coaching this young dunderhead in advance, you know."

'Cradley looked his gratitude, and Pa ventured further. "I don't want to pry — but have you managed what little Frances and Mrs Cradley need so far?" It was a delicate way of asking him if there were any debts that could be discreetly paid off.

'Cradley smiled. "You are too transparently kind, Mr Gardner," he said. "I have managed. You were there, at the Hall, when I told Mr Crowle-Tibberton I still had a few bits of antique silver left. He asked to see them, and in spite of what he had said, he pronounced most of them to be quite genuine — 'right', I think, was the curious word he used. He offered to buy them all, but I did not want to part with anything I didn't really have to. So I sold them to him one by one, and I must say he was generous — most generous. It has made all the difference."

'"And they are all gone, now?"

'"No — I still have three or four pieces left. I'm trying not to part with them yet. I have a desperate sort of hope that, somehow, something may happen to turn the tide for Elsa. If I could raise enough money anyhow to get her to the mountains for a month or two, or even to a good convalescent home by the sea, where she could have rest and good food, I still have faith enough to think she might be saved. So I have withheld three of the most valuable bits. The Canon would buy them, I think, but he advises me that I might get more if I let one of the big auctioneers in London deal with them. Would you like to see them?"

'He had cheered up considerably during this talk, and went off to fetch the silver, humming to himself. He came back carrying a small box with a padlock. Inside it were four bundles wrapped carefully in green baize. He unwrapped them and stood them before us. There was, I remember, an exquisite little Georgian teapot that would have held about one good cupful, its lid made of five silver oak leaves, and its knob a perfect little acorn. Another bundle contained a set of silver carving dogs – except that they were lions, each with its paw on its kill, an antelope in one case and a zebra in the other. Then there was a christening mug with a name engraved on it. The fourth package Cradley did not unwrap at first. When my pa had duly admired the pathetically beautiful remnants of past affluence, curiosity overcame me.

'"What's in the other bundle?" I said.

'Cradley picked it up, turning it over ruefully in his hands. "This is the piece I've been putting my real hope in," he said, "though it is the one piece I promised my grandfather I would never part with. It has both a story and a sort of family connection. But alas – it is the one piece I have that the Canon says is not genuine. It is a clever fake, and practically worthless. So I shall keep it, of course, for old times' sake." Then he slowly unwrapped from the baize a little oblong box of tooled leather. You could see it had once been a rich red, but it had darkened a bit here and there. Pa and I were fascinated by the first glimpse of it. At one end there was a pair of delicate gold clasps, and when Cradley undid them, the end of the box lifted back on tiny hinges. The inside of the case was crimson velvet, looking nearly new, and from the depth of the box – the length of it, actually, if you see what I mean – there stuck up two handles. Cradley pulled gently, and drew out a knife and fork. Do you know, I can still feel the prickles down my spine, after all these years. I have never, before or since, seen anything so exquisitely beautiful. The handles were of pink agate, with mounts and little bands of gold filigree. The end of each was finished with a sort of knob, a bit like the pommel of a sword, made of gold, with a dolphin curved over it, head on one side and tail on the other. The sides of the knob were flattened and had tiny insets of enamel work – three gold lilies on a blue field one side, and a black eagle on a gold field the other. They were absolutely breathtaking. The blade of the knife was quite ordinary, though both were a bit on the small side, and the fork simply had two sharp little prongs – silver, of course.

'Cradley was holding them ruefully in the palm of his hand, turning them over.

'"See – the lilies of France on one side, and the eagle of the Empire on the other. And the dolphin. Unmistakeable. Too unmistakeable, according to the Canon. It's their very excellence that damns them. According to him, this was the mistake the most skilled of the forgers made. They overdid things. The Canon says that even if by a millionth chance such a set as this could have survived, and by a billionth chance come into my family, it could not be in this sort of preservation. Nor would it have been likely to bear the arms both of France and the Empire. It's simply overdone. Worth nothing except as a clever fake, and for what it is, knowing that it's a fake."

'Pa was absolutely goggling. "My dear chap!" he said. "Just supposing it had been genuine!"

'"Just suppose pigs could fly!" said Cradley, putting the beautiful things into my hands.

'"What does it mean, then?" I asked. "These arms, I mean. What is it faked to represent?"

'Cradley ought to have been a schoolmaster. He couldn't resist passing on information, and even in this situation his interest took over.

'"Such little sets of personal cutlery as this were quite common I believe, once. People simply carried their own table irons with them. The rich and the great had theirs specially made, and marked with personal insignia. I told you there was a story with this, though in the light of what I know now, I suspect my grandfather simply used my interest in this exquisite little set – you can see it was in fact made for a child – to teach me some French history. He always told me tales about the people who could have used his silver when it was new, and what was happening at the time, and so on. But only with this did I ever gather that it was supposed to be a true story. No doubt that was because I wanted it to be. According to the tale he told, one of my ancestors was an envoy who was sent on a mission to France. Louis XIV was at Versailles. He kept the Cradley of the time hanging about there for days, awaiting an audience, while he supervised the installation of a new fountain. Apparently he loved doing actual manual work himself, and would take a hand, getting in the workmen's way and infuriating his architect by insisting on changes of plan. If he felt like it, he would send for meals there where he was, and picnic – if such extravagant fare as he had could be given such a common term. One thinks of a picnic as egg sandwiches and an apple! Anyway, it was on such an occasion that my ancestor, it seems, encountered him at last. He had his little son with him, the dauphin, who was then a toddler. And the toddler was using his very own little personal set of table wear, except that it was the one that Louis XIII had had specially made for the present king when he was a baby. Well, according to the story, the little boy suddenly flung the box, with its contents, into the fountain, and promptly fell in after it. The Cradley who was there jumped in and hooked him out – there was no danger, really. But King Louis had been frightened, all the same, and after the child had been whipped away to be reclothed, my ancestor found himself still holding the little dauphin's cutlery. In his gratitude and relief the king insisted that he should keep it as a memento of the time he had saved the life of the future king of France. Gross exaggeration, of course – there had never been any crisis, and there were hordes of other folk about in any case. Cradley happened to be the nearest. And of course that little boy never was the king of France. When Louis XIV died, it was his great-grandson who succeeded. But it's a good story, isn't it? Grandfather probably ought to have been a novelist. He always could tell a good tale."

'Pa took the exquisite things from me, and had a good look at them. Then he gave them back to Cradley.

' "Have you ever thought of having them properly examined by an expert?" he said, unguardedly.

'Cradley laughed. "Where? The V. and A.? Sotheby's? The Goldsmith's Livery Company? Apart from the fact that I couldn't afford their services, what would they do? Give their own guarded opinion on it, and then send it to the acknowledged expert on antique table-ware – Canon Crowle-Tibberton! His considered advice I have already had, for nothing. But he is quite, quite sure about it. So really, there's no more to be done. I'm very, very fond of it, and when these three have gone as they probably will have to go, it will be the only thing of Grandfather's I shall have left. There's a tiny corner of me that is glad it's only a fake – though it would have gone tomorrow if it would give Elsa the least bit of a chance." He sighed, and put the box back in its baize. After our excursion to the glories of Versailles we were suddenly pitchforked back to the present, and the bare old rectory with all its problems.

'We left soon afterwards, and for the rest of the spring and summer I went regularly to Cradley for coaching. He was a very good teacher, and I owe it to him that I went up to Cambridge in the autumn. Mrs Cradley had rallied a bit with the good weather, and the gloom had lifted quite a lot. Once I was up at Cambridge, I'm afraid the affairs of the village curate didn't occupy me very much, though I saw him when I went home, and Pa kept me up to date with the news. It was during the next winter, which was pretty severe, that Mrs Cradley was suddenly taken worse, and died. When I went home for Christmas, Pa insisted that I ought to go up to see him – Cradley, I mean. Pa went with me. He was calm and resigned, but stunned, doing things mechanically but without really connecting. He talked freely of his wife, and of his children and their future prospects. He couldn't continue where and how he was, without his wife.

He could not afford the necessary help with the children, and would certainly never marry again.

'"Desperate diseases require desperate remedies," he said. "I have made up my mind what I shall do. I propose to go back to missionary work – in the West Indies if possible, taking the children with me. I know the life there. It will be good for us all. I have a hatred now of this wretched climate. It was that that killed Elsa. If only I could have got her away, before it was too late."

'He paused, as if he was considering whether or not to go on. "Just before the end, the Canon came to see me. He offered to buy the dauphin's little set from me, for £500. I could have sent Elsa to the south of France for that! Of course, he did it out of the goodness of his heart. He knew it wasn't worth anything like that."

'"But it was already too late?" said Pa, gently.

'Poor Cradley's smile was agony to see. "It was certainly too late," he said. "There had been a dealer at the door a couple of weeks before, when Elsa was having her first relapse. He offered me £50 for it, and I took it. Fifty pounds was an absolute godsend, just at that time. But I'm sorry, apart from the money, that the Canon hasn't got it. He really was very disappointed when I told him what had happened.

'"'My good man!' he exclaimed. 'What an incredibly stupid thing to do with a piece like that, to sell it at the door.'

'"But I reminded him that I knew it was only a fake – he had said so himself. And a bird in the hand—"

'We shook hands with him, and left. The last I saw of him was as he stood at the door to see us off, with little lame Frances on his arm. By the time I came home for the Easter vac, he had gone, and a new curate had taken his place, a very different sort of man.

'So time went by till I was in my final year at Cambridge, and we come back to the Easter morning, three years later, when Crowle-Tibberton cut his own throat in the vestry. Just as with dear old Johnnie, everybody was wondering what on earth had caused him to do it. Pa had a lawyer's inquiring mind, and so had I. We couldn't let it alone.

'Then one day, Pa found a clue to the mystery, in a six-month-old copy of *The Times*, of all places. It was a report that a dealer was offering for sale a unique piece of antique table silver, reputed to have belonged to Louis XIV when he was a child. The French were very interested in it, as a national treasure, if its provenance could be proved. But expert opinion was absolutely at loggerheads about it. On one side there were those who said it could not possibly be genuine because it was too good. On the other were those who, by patient research and comparison, said it was simply too good, too right to be a fake. If genuine, its value was some £10,000 – a fortune. If a fake, perhaps £200, for the interest of it, and the chance. The report closed by stating that the world's most renowned expert on antique table silver, Canon Raymond Crowle-Tibberton, had been consulted, and had given his considered opinion that it was a fake.

'We felt we were on to something, but we didn't know what. We recognized the object, of course. So Pa went on following the matter up. I had other things to do – I'd just come here, and met Anne. Crowle-Tibberton was dead, anyway. Then Pa came up with something else. Just before that Easter, *The Times* carried another report about the matter. A French millionaire collector had bought the little set, for £10,000, utterly convinced it was genuine – as of course it was. Crowle-Tibberton had known it was, all along. In the first instance, he had coveted it with all the passion of a true collector's soul – but even with his wealth he couldn't have paid what he knew it was worth. When poor Cradley was in such desperate need, he tried to make amends by offering him about ten times its value as a fake, but was hoist by his own petard.'

'Make amends!' snorted Beckett. 'He was still going to steal the thing, virtually. He knew what it was really worth.'

'But he gave his opinion on it, officially, the second time,' objected Stone. 'He still said it was a fake, in spite of informed opposition. What proof did he offer?'

'None, apparently. That was where the other side eventually scored. He could only offer a sort of negative evidence. They offered positive comparison with other existing pieces, and authenticated the use of personal insignia, and so on. But he couldn't then admit that he was wrong, could he? Admit to the world that he had made a wrong judgement? Where would his reputation as an expert have been? He was a proud man in all ways, but in none so proud as that of his self-made reputation.'

'But he was proved wrong,' said Trefor Lewis.

'Yes, but he could honestly say that it was still his word against another's. The French millionaire simply had the cash to back his hunch. That he had paid £10,000 for it didn't make it waterproof genuine. It only swayed the balance, though no doubt it contributed to Crowle-Tibberton's end. But the real reason for his suicide was remorse. He had done Cradley out of a fortune at a time when a pound meant life or death to him, pretty nearly. If he hadn't wanted it himself, or if he hadn't resented Cradley having it, he could at least have given it some chance of being genuine, and left it to others and to the vicissitudes of the antique trade. A thousand pounds then would have changed Cradley's whole future – and poor little Frances's. No doubt he had carried that remorse with him every day of his life, after Cradley told him he had sold it. Not *guilt* – I stress that. There's still no *proof* that the thing ever belonged to Louis XIV or anybody else of importance. It still might be a fake. What Crowle-Tibberton had to face was the knowledge that his own acquisitive spirit, and his pride, could have been subordinated to a Christian desire to try to help a fellow man in trouble, and they weren't. He wasn't a bad man, or a mean one. His vice was pride. And he was a Christian – a good one, I should think, by most criteria. That's exactly why he had a conscience about it. He couldn't forget it, and was slowly eaten away by remorse. Then, that Sunday morning, he broke his fingernail in his haste to get into his vestments. He remembered the little silver penknife, and reached for it. But the size of it, and the feel of it in his hand, were too much for him —' Gardner's voice trailed into silence.

'And Johnnie?' said Beckett. 'We shall never know what it was that caused him to do what he did – but I swear it wasn't anything like that swine Crowle-Tibberton.'

'I have my own theory, for what it's worth,' said Gardner, slowly. 'Johnnie shared everything with Susan – every joy, every sorrow, every success, every trouble. But there was one thing in his life no woman could share – his love of his ship and his grief when she went down in 1942. He was one of the few survivors. He grieved for her, and his shipmates, in solitary silence for forty years. Then, on the morning of Thursday last week, the news came of the sinking of the *Sheffield* in the South Atlantic. It was all it needed. The gun was in his hands when he turned the radio on.'

Half Measure

When the news that Joe Dunnett was going to get married leaked out, it ran round the village like fire through stubble. From cottage to cottage it leapt across dykes, greeted with stunned ribaldry by the men and unconcealed indignation by the women. They hadn't expected it of him. Not one of the women could take credit for 'seein' which way the wind was a-blowin', like' and putting two and two together. They felt affronted that something so long taken for granted by them all should suddenly be altered without their knowledge or consent. Hadn't every one of them known Joe since he was 'a poor little ol' bor all'us a-wandering the fen by hisself, taking no notice of nothing nor nobody only wild animals and such, specially 'osses?' However did he come to get in with *her*? Right under their very noses, and yet they hadn't seen it coming!

The men, gathered in the pub, had different reasons for their comment. 'What's she arter?' said Bill Townsend, taking off his cap and scratching his head. 'She's a widder, ain't she? 'Tain't as if she were a old maid with a lot to find out!'

'She wou'n't find a lot out from Joe, anyways,' said Tom Tilley. 'Arter all, Joe ain't above 'alf a man, is 'e?'

'Well, I dunno. I dessay it's accordinlie to which 'alf she's arter. I am 'eard tell as folks as ain't got much up top in their 'eads make up for it down below. But I dunno. Pre'aps it's just 'cos she is a widder. What you never 'ave, you never miss, they say, but pre'aps she does. I jest 'ope for Joe's sake as she wou'n't be disapp'inted. She ain't the sort o' woman to take being disapp'inted layin' down, from what I'm seen of 'er.'

'Tha's just 'ow she will hev' to take it, bor!' said George Roberts, surprised at his own wit when the others greeted this

22

sally with a loud guffaw that needed several long swigs of beer to extinguish it.

Tom set his mug down looking thoughtful. 'Yew can't be sure,' he said. 'Yew can't be sure o' nothink. I reckon as all on us may be a-looking at this 'ere arse-forrard, like. Being as she is a widder, she's pre'aps 'ad as much o' that as she wants. Pre'aps it's because Joe is only 'alf a man as she's arter 'im. What's she got to lose? He's got three acre o' land all 'is own, and a cottage on it, and no family to interfere. He got the lot when all 'is brothers got killed one arter the other, and that fly-by-night sister of 'is'n went off with a feller from Austrailie, and were never 'eard on no more. There wern't nobody else for 'is mother to leave nothink to. He got it, fair and square – old Mr Pope see to that. Pre'aps she ain't daft at all, takin' up wi' Joe.'

The silence that followed indicated that they were all now considering the matter in this new light.

'Does anybody know anythink at all about 'er?' asked Tom. 'I mean, we all know as she come here from somewheer up north, 'cos o' the way she talks, like; an' by what she tells folks, she's a widder-woman whose man got killed at Dunkirk – but Liza Potts at the post office told my missus as she don't draw no widder's pension nor nothink. More'n that, nuboddy knows.'

Bill shook his head. 'Ah, she's a queer 'un – well, so all the women say. My missus were in the shop one day soon arter she fust come 'ere when she went in for a packet o' fags. The women as were there passed the time o' day with 'er, trying to be friendly, like, and they asked her a few questions about 'erself. Seems she took the 'ump proper, and made it plain there and then that she wern't a-going to be ketched into neighbouring wi' any on 'em. So they let 'er be, since then. Well, they cou'n't do no other, could they?'

'Young Charlie Abbot, what works along of 'er down at Pope's Farm, don't reckon a lot to 'er,' said George. 'I arst 'im 'ow the new land gal were a-shaping, and bor, yew should ha' 'eard 'im laugh! "Land gal did you say?" he says. "She ain't no more a gal than I am. Thirty-five if she's a day!"'

'Well, Charlie can't be more'n fifteen hisself,' Tom said. 'You 'ave to make allowance for that. Old enough to be his mother!'

George agreed, but went on with his tale. 'Charlie were a-gooin' by the look of her,' he said. 'She look a dang sight more like a man than a gal, accordin' to Charlie. He'd got it wukked out as she were a man in disguise, so's he could be at work as a Land Army gal instead of heving to go to fight.'

'They'd ha' found out,' said Tom, looking worldly-wise again. 'They hev 'em all stripped naked, so I'm heard. But young Charlie's right. She do hev the look of a man, and she's bigger than a good many men as I'm knowed in me life. That I'll own.'

'Ah! Looks as if she's bin chopped out with a shovel,' George put in. 'Specially her face!'

'Pre'aps she's one o' them as ain't properly neither one thing nor the other – don't they call 'em moffradites, or something?' This from Bill. They all gazed speculatively at him, weighing up this new thought.

'Tha's just about the size on it, Bill,' Tom said at last. 'That would account for this 'ere news about her marrying Joe. Wheer there's a Jack, there's a Jill. I reckon you're hit the nail right on the 'ead, Bill.'

'I 'ope as how Joe knows,' said George anxiously. 'So as 'e ain't the one to be disapp'inted, like. How much do yew reckon he understands about anythink like that? Can't ha' got to twenty-five without finding a few sich things out for 'isself, can 'e?'

'I don't see 'ow,' said Tom. 'Simple he may be, but Old Pope let him work on the farm with the 'osses from the time as Joe's father died. He must ha' bin about up there when the stallion come round, surelie? Besides, now I come to think on't, he keeps pigs hisself, don't he?'

'My missus'll know,' said Bill. 'Arter all, we lived up the Cut-Dyke Bank cluss to 'em till arter his mother died. But we flitted when Joe were about sixteen, an' we ain't seen nothing of 'im since. Come to think about it, tha's why we are all so took-aback now! We're all knowed him since he were born, but since 'e growed up there ain't one on us as is had more'n half a dozen words with 'im from one year's end to the next. He never comes down this way, and nuboddy ever goes up the Cut-Dyke Bank as I know on. If Joe goes out at all, it's uvver the Cut-Dyke to Pope's Farm. We can't none on us lay claim to 'im belonging to us. We ain't bothered about him, and 'e ain't bothered about us. So it's none of our business now, as I see it. But I bet my missus won't see it like that. She'll say as we ought to ha' bothered with 'im a lot more, seein' as everybody knows 'ow he is, like. But it's too late now. Poor ole Joe! It's 'ard enough for him to ha' bin born as 'e is, without gitting mixed up wi' a furriner as pre'aps ain't a proper woman at all. That family never did hev no luck though, no'ow. Got a sort o' curse on 'em all, I reckon.'

Tom had come near to the truth. Joe's father, a typical fenman, had started off well enough, having inherited a three-acre smallholding with a two-roomed fenland bungalow on it. The dwelling stood below the high bank of 'the Cut-Dyke' in as isolated a spot as it was possible to find in that bleak landscape. Being on the village side of the twelve-foot-wide cut it was technically in, but not of, the scattered hamlet around the pub and the chapel. As the other cottages along the bank had been vacated and allowed to crumble, the Dunnetts had been left without neighbours. But there in his two-roomed home Joe's parents had raised three boys and a girl. Three acres was not enough to support them, so Joe's father had worked for a farmer, and as the boys left school, each turned his back on 'th' ol' fen' and found employment in the nearest town – thus making themselves available for call-up and death in the Great War. Then their sister climbed out of the window one night and was gone with a soldier. Joe Dunnett, senior, had little left to live for – until, after nineteen years, his wife 'fell' for what she and all her friends called a 'change child'. Though a bit worried, because his wife had already passed her fiftieth birthday, the news cheered him up – till the boy was born. The child had a hare-lip and a cleft palate and a very frail hold on life; before he had even begun to make the strange noises that ever after had

had to serve him for speech, his father, apparently lacking the will to live, had succumbed to the outbreak of Spanish flu in 1918. Mother and baby were left to face the world together, isolated in all sorts of ways from what society a fenland community offered between the wars.

Joe's mother had been bred to hard work, and had met hard sorrow with a stoic's heart. She worked the smallholding herself, with the help of the farmer whom her husband had served all his life.

'Old Pope', of Pope's Farm, was an anachronism who loved his land for its own sake more than for what it did to his bank balance. Dunnett had been a good workman to whom he had often lent horse and plough to use on his smallholding; when he died, the farmer had seen to it that a man went with the implement to do such work as the widow could not do herself.

With that amount of practical help, she got along; only she could understand and interpret the string of nasal vowels which were all that her little boy could utter. So, living where he did with no one but his work-worn mother, and unable to communicate with any other, he had no playmates at all. He did not miss what he had never known; he roamed the dyke-sides gathering wild flowers, and while very young acquired a rapport with other wild and speechless creatures, and for horses he developed a consuming passion. It was only on very rare trips with his mother to Pope's Farm that he had any chance to indulge it, because the farmers and smallholders of the hamlet soon 'hauxed 'im off' if they found him wandering near their stables. It didn't do to let the village idiot loose in any farmyard, and as such Joe was regarded by everybody, on account of his looks and his inability to communicate.

When he had to go to school, the old-fashioned 'governess', nearing retirement herself, took one look at him and put him down as uneducable, and that was that. The other children did not include him in any of their games, not because of any cruelty or discrimination on their part, but because he had no wish to join in. He didn't know how, so he just stood and watched and wondered and longed for it to be 'home-time' again. As he grew older and stronger, he was useful to his mother on the land, and was absent from school as often as he was present. Both the teacher and the attendance officer looked the other way.

He left school officially when he was fourteen, and his mother took him to see her only true friend, 'Old Pope'. She was already sixty-five, and beginning to worry a great deal about what would happen to Joe when, inevitably, he would be left alone. Mr Pope gave him casual labour on his farm when his mother didn't need him at home. But there had been more to his mother's visit than that; she had charged her only friend with instructions for her own funeral, told him where to find the money to pay for it to prevent her having to be buried by the parish, and requested him just to keep his eye on Joe. He promised to do all she asked, and she went home comforted to do what was in her own power to make the boy as independent as possible. She encouraged him to learn how to cook, wash, clean the house, and do the gardening. The cottage garden became the joy of his life, next only to his menagerie of wild things, most of them rescued by him when injured, brought home and cared for, and released when restored.

When his mother died, just after Joe's sixteenth birthday, he accepted it as he had accepted everything else, with quiet resignation. With almost her last breath, his mother had told him to 'keep hisself to hisself, and go to Mr Pope if he needed help real bad'.

Freed from his mother's fear of poverty, he took in more land to enlarge his garden, and built sheds for his many pets, which by this time included a tame otter that came and went as it wished, a barn owl with a broken wing, a couple of ferrets and a fox cub he had picked up almost mauled to death by farm dogs. Cats and kittens abounded, and a variety of wild birds, kept in cages for their own safety till they could fly again, though some, like his favourite hen chaffinch, chose to stay around where she could come to his call and sit on his shoulder or peck food from his lips. All in all, Joe was as happy a man at twenty-five as anybody in the fens. What only he himself and Old Pope knew was that he was not, and never had been, short on intelligence.

But if you give a dog a bad name, you may as well hang him and be done with it. At the age of sixteen, when he was left an orphan, his appearance did nothing to help him. Apart from his facial disfigurement, he looked the part he had been allotted in other ways. He was more than six feet tall, with a loose, gangling body and huge extremities. His neck was so long that he appeared to have suffered at the hands of an inexperienced hangman, and was topped by a round bullet-head thatched with dark, straight, shaggy hair, the extra long neck making his head so far away from the rest of him that it seemed incongruously unattached.

The local vicar, and the newly appointed and self-important schoolmistress, laying their heads together just after his mother died, came to the conclusion that it was their duty to see that he was found a place in a home. They reckoned without Old Pope. Their officious attempts at interfering charitably were defeated, and with clear consciences they forgot him. So did everybody else – until the startling news broke that he was going to get married.

Ivy Ward was also an orphan, who had been brought up in a children's home on a bleak moor outside a shoddy little Yorkshire town. When turned out from there, she had worked in a shoddy mill till picked up one night by a soldier from Glasgow. He bought her a ring and she served all his needs till he was posted, and made no demur when he suggested she should follow him into East Anglia. From there he was drafted to France, and it was only after the Dunkirk débâcle that he stopped sending her enough to live on. He had been killed on the beach, leaving a widow and four children in Glasgow. Well – there was no shortage of other men on the lookout for a willing partner; as the country adage has it, 'a hungry dog will eat any old bone.' But not all of them were generous, and she had to live. The Land Army needed strong women, and that she certainly was. Fate landed her at Pope's Farm just after Old Pope died, and his son took over.

She was thirty-five, strong, healthy, with an eye open for the best chance. Her body was tall, with flat planes and hard angles; her face had the same characteristics, as George had noticed. It might have been carved from millstone grit, as far as any softness in it went, and her head and her heart were as hard as her face. Life so far had taught her to 'look after hersen', first, last and always. Privation from early childhood had caused her to grab what she could, but always to secrete a bit of food somewhere in case there was none tomorrow. She was as mean in spirit as she was unprepossessing in face and figure.

She liked her job on the farm, except for the fact that there were no males other than fifteen-year-old boys and old fen tigers. She couldn't make any more sense of their fen twang than they of her Yorkshire speech. Communication was therefore kept to the absolute minimum. She was found to be capable, and could soon handle a tractor as well as a man; but she had an Achilles' heel – she was terrified of horses, and while Old Pope had lived, the farm had been famous for its continued use of huge Suffolks.

It was when she was attempting to harness a young Suffolk one day that things went wrong. She was lifting its collar to get it over its head when her fear communicated itself to the horse. It laid back its ears, rolled its eyes, and moved backwards so that the collar instead of going over its head caught it a sudden, unexpected blow. It reared, then, on its massive hind legs, missing Ivy only by inches as it came down again with one of its forefeet through the fallen collar. Ivy screamed, a string of high-pitched, terrified Yorkshire curses – and Joe appeared as if by magic from somewhere. His concern was for the horse, not for the frantic woman, of whom he took no notice whatsoever. As soon as he reached its side, the horse lost its rage and its fear, and stood docilely while he extricated it and proceeded to harness it to a cart while she was still recovering her breath.

The horse nuzzled Joe's face as he held its bridle, murmuring a sort of nasal drone into its ear. Ivy approached with caution to take the halter from his hand; he wanted to tell her that Prince would be quiet enough now, but he was abashed by her hard, contemptuous gaze. When at last he murmured something, it was quite unintelligible to her; and when she replied with a belated word of thanks, it was just as unintelligible to him. She moved away, leading the horse. It was not an auspicious beginning.

Nevertheless, it made an impact on both. Ivy had found that Joe was not the idiot she had been led to believe; Joe, who had rapport with all frightened creatures, had understood her fear, and in his own solitude understood hers, in this strange fenland world where she was such a misfit. He was sorry for her in a way he could not have expressed, even if he had been able to enunciate the words.

He was recalling the incident the next Saturday afternoon as he sat fishing on the bank, and looking up, saw her approaching. She did not know what to do with her own time in this bleak flat wilderness of a place, but she was restless when not active. She had never walked the Cut-Dyke Bank before, and had taken that route out of idle curiosity to see where her rescuer lived.

She was not one to be embarrassed. She stopped, and spoke, and received some sort of reply. She sat down beside him, much to his chagrin, and started a conversation. Perhaps it was the strange fascination of not being able to understand each other that kept them there till teatime, when Joe packed up his gear and prepared to go home. Ivy strolled along beside him. She was surprised to find his tiny home, which she had envisaged as nothing more than a tumbledown hovel, so pretty, so neat and tidy, so well-kept and cared for. She said so, and was understood. Joe was flattered into asking her in for a cup of tea, to see it from the inside. It surprised her more than the outside, as did Joe's handiness with everything he did. By the time the tea was made, they had both turned the key to interpretation by listening to the other's intonation. It was a unique experience for Joe to have anybody at all inside his little living-room. To Ivy, it was the germ of a plan to ensure her own future. She knew he would bolt like a scared rabbit if he suspected her interest; but a rabbit stands little chance against a stoat.

A few discreet inquiries soon put her into possession of the facts that mattered. What if he was supposed to be a bit soft in the head? She didn't intend to produce any children – she knew a thing or two in that direction. She did propose to have a home, and security. She could work on his land and help him make money; and she could give Joe what he had never had, and what none of the girls with whom he had gone to school would have ever considered doing. So she set to work to woo him, craftily keeping her visits to the cottage secret.

It was after she had somehow manoeuvred Joe into bed with her that she proposed a lasting union which she pointed out to him could only be advantageous to them both. Joe was overwhelmed by his first and only experience of sexual intercourse – which is just what she had intended. But when he wanted more, she declined – unless a wedding ring and a proper marriage came first. That was her fiat, declaring which she banged the door and left him to think it out, staying out of his sight for a week.

He was lonely for the first time in his whole life, uneasy and restless. He was reluctant to accept her proposal because of his native wit and fenland caution. If only old Mr Pope had still been alive, to be asked what to do about it. Joe brooded behind the plough, and among his flowers, and as he fished, or tended his menagerie. Had he ever known any woman other than his mother, he would have seen that his case was hopeless. He had no knowledge or experience to help him, and when Ivy had made all the necessary arrangements for the ceremony, she let the news out long enough before the appointed day to stun the village, but not long enough for anybody to interfere. Joe was taken to be married as inertly on his own part as he might have been taken to be buried, and not a finger was lifted to save him. Ivy had become Mrs Dunnett.

Joe accepted his changed circumstances with the same resigned
fatality with which he had accepted his disfigurement, his inability to communicate and his previously enforced solitude. His
marriage at first gave him both satisfaction and doubts; but he
went along with Ivy easily, because he was unused to argument.
She played her hand coolly at first, but her hard-headedness and
the avarice bred into her by nature as well as by her deprived
childhood soon asserted themselves. She could no more help
herself than Joe could cure his own cleft palate.

It was dumplings that caused their first row. Wartime rationing bit deeper and deeper, but Joe's rod and line, as well as his
gun, kept them well supplied, even though the pigs they fed at
the bottom of the garden could no longer end in their own
pork-pot, by law. Joe had been in the habit of making himself a
rabbit stew most weeks; one rabbit with enough onions and
dumplings would feed him for three days. Now there were two
of them, one rabbit had to stretch further, but dumplings
flavoured by it could still make a good meal. As all country
people said, 'What don't fat, fills.'

He looked down at his plate when Ivy slapped it before him –
she was not the same sort of cook as his mother or himself. One
front leg of a small rabbit and a few skinny ribs, a swill of pale
thin gravy, some strands of barely cooked onion, and two hard
little dumplings. He held up four fingers, and pointed to the
dumplings. 'I wa' four,' he said.

'Tha'll hev two, an' be satisfied, from now on,' she replied.
'Tha knaws reet well there's a war on!'

Joe was disgruntled as he had rarely been before. He argued.
Why? Were they short of flour? Lard? No? So why could he
only have two dumplings when he was hungry?

''Cos tha never knaws what t'future may hold,' she said.
'Allus keep a bit put by fo' t'next day – that's my motter. Tha'
allus ate twice as much as is good for thee. Tha can save thy
breath, 'cos thee'll get no more from now on.' And that was that.

To do her justice, she worked quite as hard as he did, and ate
no more; but rationing and other wartime restrictions provided

her with an excuse to put into practice her native streak of 'carefulness' and bolstered her ingrained avarice. Having the sort of security which in the past she had only dreamed of had set up in her the miser-syndrome. What she managed to save was never enough. When she had scraped a few pounds to 'put by', her one aim was to make it more. She scrinched and saved, and Joe suffered. He grew thinner, and communicated with her only when forced.

They reached another milestone when it was she who decided what should be set on Joe's land. Their aims were different: he knew what it meant to keep the land 'in good heart', and his plan was to make it supplement their table as well as making it pay for the work they put into it; her aim was to grow things she could sell for cash on the black market if necessary – and bank the money. He was no match for her, so she had her own way. As he watched her thrusting her gaunt legs into her Land Army breeches, he knew that from now on it was she who would wear the trousers, metaphorically as well as literally. Well, he was used to accepting fate.

She knew it too, and planned accordingly. His garden was too big; wasn't he ashamed of growing flowers when every inch of land was needed for food? His rose bed became a cabbage patch, everything it produced finding its way to market. She said she never had liked cabbage.

He spent too much time fishing. Especially Sundays! With labour so scarce, pay was time-and-a-half for casual labour on Sundays. He argued, this time, that the fish he brought home for the pot cost nothing.

'Tha may like the muddy-tastin' stoof tha brings 'ome,' she said, 'but Ah doan't. An' what's more other folks doan't, so I can't sell 'em. It's just bloody waste o' thi time, setting there gawpin' at nowt. Tha'll go t'work one Sunday, and fish t'next. It's all arranged. There's no more to be said.' And there wasn't.

When Joe got home from work the next Sunday, and went out to feed his pets, all were gone except one young tom cat. The injured wild had been turned out to fall prey to the first predator; the ferrets had been sold. The otter would survive, perhaps. Joe did not dare ask what had happened to the fox and the owl. She had hated those worst of all. That somebody had disposed of them at her request was all he ever found out.

'Nasty, mooky, stinking things,' she said. 'Nobody in his reet mind'd expect a decent woman t' share 'ome wi' ferrets and foxes and such. But theer, tha never were in thi reet mind. I knaw that now!'

He was too heartbroken about his pets to care about her jibe at him, but cowed as he was, he asked her why she had bothered with him in the first place.

''Appen I thowt I could mek a man o'thee, instead o' the 'alf-job thi' moother made on't,' she snapped. ''Appen I still can, now there's nothing left for thee to fool thi time away on. Waste o' good brass, letting thee keep 'em as long as I 'ave. What they ate cost brass as we could ha' put by for us old age.'

Joe said nothing. There was nothing to say. He still had the four Suffolk mares at the farm that were his special charge. She couldn't rob him of those. So he lavished all his love on them, and poured out his marital woe into their receptive ears.

The stables at the farm were his refuge. Even though she was there, her fear of the horses kept her away. He took longer to bait and groom the mares than was ever necessary, especially in the evening, because it put off the time when he had to return to Ivy. He polished brasses and leather as they had never been polished before. For an hour or two every day, Joe could still be happy.

Time, though, is the real dictator. The war ended; farmers who had made money as they had never done before had been affected in the same way as Ivy with never having enough. When agricultural implements no longer had to be more or less raffled for, they bought what they needed, and made changes. Old Pope's son gave up the farm to his son, who had been to an agricultural college; and the first thing he did was to decide to get rid of the Suffolks. He had no use for the sentimental twaddle that his grandfather had felt for the land or the animals on it. The young horses would find other buyers; the four old mares would end in the knacker's yard.

Waiting for the end was cruel. Joe's cup of bitterness had overflowed at last. His gaunt frame grew thinner, his eyes more prominent, his neck even longer. He lost what appetite he had for Ivy's ill-cooked meals.

If Ivy noticed, she said nothing. She had no worries at all. She had security; she had made herself the boss. Their bank balance, now in joint names, would have astonished Joe if he had ever been privileged to see it. When Ivy said, 'What's thine is mine,' she meant it quite literally. The only time her rocky face ever shifted into a smile was when she contemplated how much she had managed to get put by since she had married Joe. The Land Army, as such, was disbanded, but her job was secure. Joe's wasn't. When he suddenly developed bronchitis, she left him in bed and went to work as usual. Next day he was so much worse that she grudgingly agreed to send for the doctor.

'Tha'll hev to let him in thi'sen,' she said, before she left him to go to work. 'Tha's reet enough, if thi pulls thi'sen together. Nowt wrong wi' thee, only moonin' over them bloody old mares.'

As it happened, there was something in what she said. The local GP had not been down the Cut-Dyke Bank for a very long time, but he had been present at Joe's birth, and had signed the death certificates of both Joe's parents. Like most of his kind, he knew a great deal more about most of his patients than could be found out from reading their medical records. He knew quite well that Joe's cleft palate had no effect on his intelligence, and had gone out of his way to point the fact out to the teacher when Joe first went to school. But the war had been hard on country doctors, especially those like himself who were growing old at their job, and because he was so grossly overworked he had taken his eye off Joe. Patients who are never ill don't occupy much of a rural doctor's thought.

Dr Grove had to leave his car at the top of the Cut-Dyke Bank, and walk almost a mile down the bank. He was quite used to having to let himself in to a fenland cottage swept and garnished against his visit as it might have been for royalty. As he walked, he regretted his neglect of Joe in recent years; he remembered the time when he had often encountered Joe roaming alone and held up a cheery hand in greeting, or, if he was not in too much of a rush, had stopped his car to have a word. The result had almost always been that when he went back to his car after a visit somewhere else, there would be a big pike or a couple of rabbits on the back seat. He recalled now how long it had been since such a thing had happened; perhaps Joe had been sick for longer than he knew.

Acting on the orders he had been given, Joe had got up, and was sitting, dressed, in his old wicker chair when the doctor opened the door to let himself in. Joe had just been making up the fire, and was wheezing badly from the effort in the smoky atmosphere, gasping for oxygen that wasn't there. The doctor took in the situation at a glance, and ordered him back to bed so that he could examine him properly.

The experienced doctor was only too well acquainted with meeting inarticulate ignorance on even the most ordinary medical matters, and had long ago discovered that asking questions was no help at all – they only produced long irrelevant tales of no consequence whatsoever except that of wasting his more than precious time. Though by no means a loquacious man by nature, he had nevertheless developed a method of forestalling this tendency by doing all the talking himself, and watching the patient's reactions for clues. In the case of his present patient, this method also saved him from having to try to interpret any answers he might get. So he began his examination, talking all the time except for the few moments he was listening to Joe's chest. Then he whipped off the stethoscope, and sat down on a chair by the side of Joe's bed.

'Now, my boy, what's all this about? Don't tell me you caught a cold getting wet through! You've been wet through as many days as you have ever been warm and dry. Always out, roaming the fen in all weathers, falling in dykes or wading in to get flowers, since you were britched – besides working out in the rain from morn to night with only a sack over your shoulders. Isn't that so?

'But you're too thin, my boy. Try eating a bit more, for a start. Rationing? Come off it, I know better! What's happened lately to my treat of a stuffed pike? Things changed, have they? Don't care so much for fishing as you used to, since you got married? Better things to do at home, eh? Well, we'd better do something to get rid of this cough, somehow. Can't have you being too short of breath to carry out your duty as a husband . . .' and so on, all the time watching the effect of his words on Joe's expressive face.

He left a bottle of medicine, and walked back up the bank to his car very thoughtful and even a bit anxious.

At suppertime he shared his worries with his wife, as he was wont to do. 'There's nothing much the matter with Joe,' he told her, 'but he seems not to care about anything. Nobody can do much for a patient who won't help himself.'

'Have you seen his wife?' she asked.

'What's that got to do with it? I didn't see her today, because she'd gone to work. I suppose I shall have to consult her.'

'I meant what I said,' Mrs Grove replied. 'I meant have you ever seen her? Perhaps Joe is taking the easy way out. She's a tough nut, by all accounts. Too much for a simple chap like Joe Dunnett.'

The doctor called at Pope's Farm next day, and spent a few very enlightening minutes with Ivy. Then he went into the house to have a glass of whisky with Young Pope, before setting out to trudge down the Cut-Dyke Bank again.

His patient was no better; in fact, if anything, the feverishness was worse. Dr Grove began his searching prattle, watching Joe's glittering eyes.

'Saw your missus down at the farm this morning,' he said cheerfully. Joe closed his eyes wearily, and made no attempt to answer. The doctor applied his stethoscope, listened, frowned and removed it. Putting it away, he glanced over his shoulder, and saw Joe's eyes now wide and intelligently open.

'I had a drop of Scotch with the boss while I was there. He told me all about his plans to mechanize the farm. Sold all his Suffolks, he tells me. I don't know what his grandfather would have thought of that!' A look of such pain crossed Joe's distorted face that the pieces of the doctor's jigsaw puzzle fell into place.

'My old friend Mr Pope will turn in his grave the day they go,' he meandered on. 'Seems there's a farmer over Ely way who is as crazy over the big horses as the old man was. He's bought the lot.'

Joe was sitting up in bed, gasping and uttering some question over and over again. The doctor pushed him back on to his pillows, and held him till the paroxysm was over, trying to interpret the intonation of what he knew to be a question. Then the penny dropped.

'Took the whole lot,' he said again. 'Apparently there are four old mares past breeding that Young Pope had marked for the knacker, but this chap at Ely couldn't bear the thought of it, so Pope just threw them in with the deal. They're going to live in clover – quite literally, I think. Life without work in some daisy-covered meadow down by the river somewhere. Lucky things. It's time I was put out to grass, as well. I wish some rich man would set up a place for worn-out doctors.'

Joe lay back, exhausted by the fit of coughing, but with such an expression of relief and joy on his face that it did not surprise the doctor in the least to see tears sliding on to the pillow. He repeated every detail of his conversation about the horses that he could remember, knowing now the cause of Joe's apathy even if he had no cure for it. But every scrap of information he could offer might be of some help.

'Name of Welch, I think Pope said. Another nutter about Suffolks, like Old Pope. Made a lot of money in the war, and spends it on his favourite hobby. Ah, well. There's no accounting for people's tastes, is there? I once had a patient who had nothing to eat but Shredded Wheat for about five years! Seemed to suit him, so I didn't interfere. He was as strong as a horse on it. Keep taking the medicine. Tell your wife to let me know if she needs me to come again.' He was pretty sure that Joe would now recover quickly, which in fact he did. He went back to work the next week, by which time all the horses had gone.

Nobody considered that Joe would be able to use machinery; without the horses, there was little for him to do. When he was told so, it was almost a relief, because wherever he went there were reminders. The harness room with its nostalgic smells was more than he could bear, and he took his dismissal with the same apparent lack of feeling as he had always taken everything else. But in his heart, there was rejoicing. Ivy was a full-time worker at the farm, which meant that he could have his house and his land, and best of all, most of his time, to himself again. He made plans, and began to carry them out.

One Sunday morning, he got up early and was gone before Ivy missed him from her side. He went across dykes, drains and fields with unerring instinct till he could see the pile of Ely against the pearly sky, and by ten o'clock was on Welch's farm, in a meadow that sloped down to the river. And there, sure enough, were his four old friends, along with two others. The mist still clung to the willows, and with eyes blurred by tears he failed to notice the stocky, middle-aged man who leaned quietly against one of the trunks, a gun at his side. Joe stood still for a minute or two before whistling through his teeth – a long, low sound that carried far. Four great heads were raised, and eight ears cocked expectantly. Joe repeated the whistle, and the four horses turned, facing towards the direction of the sound before starting to plod curiously towards it. When Joe whistled the third time, Old Petal broke into a heavy trot, and the rest followed.

The watcher under the willow tree gave no sign of his presence there as Joe fondled the velvet muzzles one after the other, pulled the cocked ears, rubbed the huge necks and slapped them caressingly. From his pockets came carrots and apples and lumps of sugar, 'stolen' from Ivy's 'put by' store. When his pockets were empty, the mares still stood round him, now in their turn nuzzling him while he poured out a stream of endearments in the sing-song terms he reserved only for other dumb creatures. When the farmer who owned the horses drew near enough, still unobserved, to hear the consonantless speech, he looked for explanation of it to Joe's face, pressed now against Old Petal's cheek, and saw that it was wet with tears. He didn't know who Joe was, but there was much he did know – and understand.

He went forward without speaking, and joined the group, taking from his own bulging pockets apples and chunks of bread, and slipping them beneath the mobile velvety lips in turn. Joe had snatched off his cap and dried his eyes on it, standing there abashed, embarrassed, almost afraid. The farmer emptied his pockets before giving any attention to Joe. Then he looked him straight in the eye. Joe returned the glance without flinching, and in that moment found a friend.

'Come far?' asked Welch.

'Ah.'

'From Pope's?'

'Ah.'

'Walked? It must be every step of eight miles, as the crow flies.'

'Ah.'

'Walking back as well?'

A nod. 'Ah.'

'And it is worth the walk?'

Joe looked at the meek, strong but ageing friends he had come to see, and then up at the man who had saved them and led them to this paradise to graze out their days in comfort. His long-breathed-out reply, and the look of gratitude he cast on the farmer, said all that his tongue could not make plain.

'A-a-a-h!'

'Come whenever you like.'

'Ah! Ang oo!'

'What's your name?'

The reply being completely unintelligible to Welch's ears, he tried again.

'Can you write?'

The swift though instantly suppressed expression of hurt indignation that crossed Joe's face told the soft-hearted farmer more than any string of words could have done.

'Ah!' said Joe, this time in forceful affirmation of his nod.

Welch produced a pocket diary and its tiny pencil, and held it out to Joe, who filled a page with his childlike script.

'Telephone number? In case I should ever need you?'

Joe didn't believe in the possibility of such an occasion, but he would do anything to oblige a man who loved horses enough to keep four which were no good to him. Laboriously he wrote down the number of Pope's Farm, with 'Pope' beneath it.

'Work there?'

The gesture that took in the horses, the sad look, the shake of the head, told Welch what the situation was. Joe spoke. 'Wife does,' is what the sounds meant, and to the surprise of both men, it was understood.

'Live close to Pope, then?'

Another shake of the head, a pointing finger, and three fingers held up.

'Three miles away from the farm.' It was no longer a question, but a translation. They could communicate. It was the balm of Gilead to Joe's wounded and lacerated spirit.

'I'll see you again?' asked Welch, holding out his hand.

'*A-a-ah!*'

Joe fondled his four old friends once more, and went off with a lighter heart than he had had for a very long time. He jumped the first dyke as though it were a puddle, so exuberant of spirit did he feel. He now had something to look forward to! And nothing, or more significantly, nobody should prevent him from making this journey again and again. He stood still in the open landscape, dominated by the great cathedral, and rejoiced. He fixed his eyes on the beauty of the magnificent building's silhouette, and what it communicated to him was the sense of purpose in the face of difficulty. How on earth had the men who built it surmounted the difficulties they must have had? How on earth had he got himself into the present pass as far as Ivy was concerned? He saw clearly that the answer lay in his own weakness, not in her strength. He had simply allowed himself to be the simpleton she thought him; well, the worm had discovered that there was a way of turning, and turn it would.

She was at her most vitriolic when he reached home, his dinner being spoilt and the theft of the sugar discovered. She berated him and questioned him, yelled and swore and even held up her fists at him. He remained calm and silent, pushed away the dried-up dinner and helped himself to bread and cheese. After about an hour of termagant fury, she retired defeated to her armchair. Joe sat in his, and dreamed dreams. At first they were day-dreams, but his walk had made him tired, and he slipped into sleep in which real dreams centred round an object that had often been the cause of just such a row as they had had.

On his mother's old chest of drawers that stood in the living-room where they now sat was a brass-bound mahogany box, on the top of which lay his mother's big family Bible. Ivy had been curious about it, and he had shown her the secret drawer in the box, which was discovered by withdrawing a brass-headed pin about two inches long, thus allowing a false bottom to be removed. It was beautifully camouflaged by the fact that on the opposite side of the box an identical brass head which was nothing but decoration fooled any casual observer. Ivy knew that such boxes were valuable, nowadays, and made up her mind that one day she would sell it, and the old Bible, too; but her avaricious mind had informed her that the longer she kept them before selling, the more she would get for them. Joe had never suspected such depth of cruelty in her, and had never been worried. They were there, part of the cottage; he would no more have suspected her of removing them than he would have suspected her of removing the door or the window.

That afternoon, she had decided that the time had come. Maybe the very virulence of her intention had penetrated his dreams, for it was of that Bible he had dreamed. He roused with a sense of unease.

Ivy was asleep. Joe got up and crossed the room on tiptoe, opening the Bible at the fly-leaf where family births, deaths and marriages were recorded. His three brothers; his sister, Joyce Amelia, born 19 November 1900 (below this, in a very shaky hand, was added 'Gone to Australia 12 January 1918). His own birth, the last in his father's hand; his father's death, recorded in his mother's spider-scrawl; then his mother's death, and his own marriage, in the infant script that was all anybody had ever bothered to teach him.

He stood staring down at the names, aware of their significance to him for the first time. The thought that rose to the surface unbidden was that there should have been other entries by now. What if he had died when he had had bronchitis recently? His land – that precious patch of good English fenland earth – would have been lost to the Dunnetts. It would have passed to a woman who had no feeling for it at all, and no roots anywhere in the fens. She would have sold it for as much 'brass' as she could make, and have gone without a backward glance.

It was his fault. He should have thought about the land. It was too late now, but perhaps if he hadn't married Ivy there might have been some fenland girl born to the land who would have had him in spite of his face, so that there could have been 'a couple o' little ol' bors' running up the Cut-Dyke Bank to school now. He could have taught them how to care for animals, and how to fish . . . the dream faded. Short of killing Ivy, it was an impossible one.

He sighed. He had not the will to hurt any living thing, not even to crush a fly. Ivy was safe enough. Her strident voice cut through his musing like a chainsaw.

'What does thee want pokin' abaht theer for? Theer's nothing theer as concern's thee!'

Since his encounter with the mares and Mr Welch this morning had renewed hope, his normal keen sensitivity had been somewhat restored. It was a long time since he had taken much notice of Ivy; but his heightened awareness now detected at once a sharp edge of anxiety in her tone. He did not turn to obey her, as had become his habit, but stood silently turning the pages of the Bible – and thinking. Why should she care that he was looking at the Bible, so undeniably his, and for which she had no use? She shrieked at him again to come away, and 'leave bloody thing alone'. She was infuriated that he did not obey her – as he had grown so used to doing. He heard the passion rising in her voice but it fell on deaf ears. What could she do to him now that she had not already done, except leave him – which happy consummation he realized at once as being out of the question. So what had he to fear? *Nothing!* He knew in that second that he hated Ivy as he had never hated anything before, and that he was no longer afraid of her. Hate acknowledged had wiped out fear.

He took the Bible with him to his chair, and spent the rest of the evening reading it. Her continued ravings and rantings were as water off a duck's back. She advanced on him in physical rage, but the look in his eye when it met hers was something she had never seen before. She knew afresh, as she had not done for many a year, what it felt like to be helpless in the face of obstinate indifference. In the end, it was she who was reduced to tears of anger before leaving him to go, still raging, to her bed. He spent the night in his chair, much to her chagrin, because it meant that she had no chance of deceiving him by getting up early. He kept his eye upon her from the moment she emerged from the bedroom.

She gave him a spate of orders that would take him outside, and which, until yesterday, he would have obeyed in sullen resignation. This morning, he sat and watched her every move till, defeated, she set out for work and left him alone. He had done a lot of thinking in the night. Common sense said that her anxiety to keep him away from the chest of drawers had little to

CAVAN COUNTY LIBRARY

do with the Bible, and everything to do with the secret drawer of the box. What was she hiding there?

Once she had left, he went straight to find out. Money, of course. A roll of treasury notes – thirty pounds in all; what Ivy had put by since her last visit to pay into her private account at the Co-op. Joe hesitated. Whose was it? Ivy had worked for it, but so had he; it was his land on which the produce had been grown. He had never stolen as much as a potato from anybody in his whole life – but taking some of what was partly his own surely couldn't be counted as stealing? He helped himself to ten pounds of it, and set out. By the time Ivy came home from work, the cabbage patch was once again a rose bed, filled with a selection of carefully chosen new rose bushes. She was so anxious to get inside the house to keep an eye on the box that she neither suspected nor saw what he had done.

Emboldened, next day he raided the cache again to buy wood and netting and nails, and she came home to reconstructed hutches for a pair of pure-bred angora rabbits.

Her anger was as the wrath of Jove, though far less effectual. Joe listened with complete impassivity to the shrieking virago belting out her string of curses. When she grabbed up the carving knife, he reached for the poker – if only to defend himself with. She didn't know. She was now as helpless before him as he had been previously in her hands. She planned revenge on his roses and his rabbits, but he watched her all the time. Well, she could wait till Sunday, when he would set off to Ely; but this week he didn't go. With the rest of her savings, he enlarged his little farmyard, coming home with some bantam chickens and a nanny-goat kid. She guessed that he would not be able resist a trip to the mares soon, and bided her time. But she never had been a fool, and the time for reflection he allowed her before leaving her to go to Ely made her see her position more clearly. However much married she might be, neither the land nor the cottage was hers by right. Her tongue was her only weapon against Joe, and for that he no longer cared a jot. However many times she let his animals loose, or dug up his rose garden, he would replace them. She no longer handled all the cash. He had coped perfectly well on his own before her advent, with land, garden and cottage. He could do it again. She was becoming only a lodger who, perforce, had no choice but to share his bed because it was the only bed, and neither was prepared to relinquish a rightful claim to half of it. He prepared his own meals, and she hers – out of her own wages.

She bowed to the inevitable with very bad grace; he was happier than he had been for a long time. The knowledge that he had a friend in Mr Welch, who filled the gap left by Old Pope, gave him a sense of security again. It was that which had restored his self-sufficiency and given him the courage to stand up to Ivy. She fretted and raged, not only at her own impotence after such a long period of power, but also because she could not work out what it was that had caused her worm of a husband to turn so aggressively. He bought a puppy, and trained it both as a house dog and as a constant companion. At his command, it would have torn her throat out. It never took food from anyone's hand but his. Gradually, as it dawned upon her that she was more or less powerless against him, she realized that her mistake had been to accept other people's estimate of his intelligence. He forestalled her every move, as if he could read her thoughts. He was proving himself to be more than a match for her. It was the first time ever that she had been bested by a man – and by an 'idiot' of her own choosing. In inverse proportion to Joe's content, the burden of her frustration grew.

She lost control of herself on the evening that she found that the last of the banknotes had been used. In her fury, she picked up the box and hurled it with all her strength at Joe, screaming, 'Tha needna think tha'll be rid o' me, whatever tha does!' Joe dodged the box, and it fell heavily on to the floor. He heard the door slam behind her, which caused him no feeling other than relief; but one glance at the broken box almost overwhelmed him. At his feet, alongside the open box, lay a detached strip of polished mahogany. Joe picked up the box in distress, and turned it over and over to see where the strip had come from;

but look as he might, he could find no damage to the box itself. The strip must have been detached from the inside, so he turned his attention to that, his expression one of wonder and pleasure like a child with a Chinese puzzle. The mahogany slat had come from the back of the secret drawer, revealing a second secret within the first. Behind this detachable strip there were two tiny drawers side by side, each with a minuscule handle of brass lying flush with the wood, so as not to project when the covering slat was in place. His pocketknife's point was fine enough to insert under the small brass fitting so that it stood proud and allowed him to pull open the first miniature drawer.

It was empty, and he was disappointed; but in the second of the little drawers was an envelope, carefully folded to fit the tiny hiding place. Joe unfolded it, and smoothed it out. He read, 'To Whom it May Concern', written in a firm, beautiful, old-fashioned copperplate hand he did not recognize.

To his dismay, he heard Ivy opening the door. She should not know this last of his secrets! He shoved the envelope in his pocket, left the box as it was, and was at the door before she could get in.

He pushed her outside again, and turned the key on her. Her shoving and kicking was in vain, and eventually she strode off along the bank and out of his sight. At the moment, her welfare was the lowest of his priorities. He wanted to find out how the box's second secret worked. It was really very simple – the loose slat sat against two brass springs which were activated by pressure on the ends of the larger secret drawer. Having made sure he could open and close it at will, he sat down to think.

What could the envelope contain? If Ivy had not returned just when she did, he would have opened it to find out; but he hadn't, and now he did not know whether he ought. Did it concern him? Like most fenmen, he kept as far away from anything to do with the law as possible. The thought that it might contain some legal 'paper' made him anxious. It appeared to have been there, in his box, for a long time. Did that make whatever it was concern him? He had to find out before Ivy chanced upon it, or escaped his vigilance and sold the box out of spite. He kept the envelope on his person till Sunday came and he could take it to Mr Welch. He put box and Bible in the dog's kennel, and told the dog in his own way to 'keep'. She'd have to kill the dog to get at them. The thought made Joe smile – if only he had thought of putting things there before!

It took a lot of time and patience on both sides before Joe had made the farmer aware of the situation. When, with the help of his pocket diary and its pencil, as well as Joe's excited attempts at decipherable speech and a drawing of the box, the farmer at last understood (more or less), Joe produced the envelope, put it into Welch's hands, and made it clear that he wanted him to open it.

Welch was accustomed to the deep-seated distrust many rural people had of any written document – convinced as they were that 'the law' could never be on their side. Even his well-to-do farmer friends viewed all lawyers with dismay, and had to be persuaded to go even to make their very necessary wills. Any legal 'paper' – meaning any document – was as likely to be disadvantageous to them as the opposite. Let such sleeping dogs lie!

Joe seemed to be inviting him to open the envelope there and then – but even he was too cagey for that. God only knew what a hornet's nest it might contain – and in any case it had nothing to do with him.

'Read it,' pleaded Joe.

'Ought to have witnesses,' the farmer replied. 'Shall I take it to a lawyer?'

The agitation on Joe's face told its own tale.

'Will you leave it with me till next week? I'll think about it.'

Joe nodded. 'Tell me next Sunday,' he said, and went off to give his attention to the horses for a few minutes, though he was afraid of what Ivy might do if he stayed away too long. It was still only nine o'clock when he started his long walk back.

Welch found that the envelope in his pocket stuck to his thoughts and burned like a mustard-plaster.

Before Joe had got across the second dyke, Welch had taken the envelope out of his pocket and examined it again. It was more than he could do not to slit it open – and great was his consternation when he saw that what he held in his hands was indeed a legal 'paper' – a will, in fact. One sheet of cheap lined notepaper, in an unformed hand that bore no resemblance to the cultured copperplate on the outside of the envelope. He began to read the pathetic document:

> This paper is the last will of Hannah Mary Dunnett, writ now because the doctor as told me he can't give me no more hope as i shall ever get no better i shant live many more days, and mr pope come to see me and said as i must make a will to see as my poor boy joe is done proper by when i am gone but i can't forget my joycey what went to australie and was never heard on no more she is my only gel as i ever had and if she should ever come back i want her to have her share and i hope as all will be forgive and forgot. So i leave the land and the house and all there is to my joe and my joycey equal between them if she does ever come back and till she does i want my joe to have everything but if she comes i hope they will live together so as she can look after him when he hasnt got nobody else and i have gone to be with my dear husband and my three boys as was all killed in the war.

The shaky signature below was penned over a twopenny stamp, that scrap of coloured paper which all country people believed to be infallible in making any document legal. However, beneath this testimony of mother-love and duty in the face of impending separation was another signature, in an even more spidery hand, this time duly attested as the law requires by two witnesses each in the presence of the other, with names, addresses, professions and date appended. There was no doubt about the will being a legal one.

Hannah Mary Dunnett

Signed this 9th day of April 1933 in the presence of Albert Henry Pope, farmer, of this parish and [*so far all in the wonderful copperplate as on the outside*]

Richard Owen Groves, MB, General Practitioner of this parish. [*The second in a scrawl almost as illegible as Joe's speech was unintelligible*]

Welch was now in an unenviable quandary, and cursed himself for his curiosity. It seemed never to have been brought to light, but why?

He had known Old Pope, not well, but as farmers in the same region know about each other and recognize faces seen often at markets. He had been alive years after Joe's mother had died. Why hadn't he told Joe of the will's existence? If he knew Joe even as well as Welch did, he could not have doubted the man's perfectly normal intelligence and understanding. There must have been more to it than met the eye. Now he, Welch, had foolishly involved himself. What was he to do? It seemed that Joe had got the land safe enough, so wouldn't the best thing be for him to tear the thing up and scatter it in the Ouse?

But he had promised Joe that he would tell him what was in the envelope; besides, he was a magistrate with a healthy respect for the law. It was possible that without the will Joe might be in a better case than with it – he had been in possession of the land for a long time, and perhaps had thus by now acquired a perfectly valid title to it. With the will, he still had a perfect right to it – as long as his sister didn't turn up. He knew so very little about Joe – he had been led to this stupid position simply because of a shared passion for heavy horses. He did not want to land an already disadvantaged man with an unnecessary load of worry – so he had either to find out more of the background, or play some sort of deceitful trick on Joe. The thought of that went wholly against the grain. He looked at his watch; it was still only 10.30 a.m. He had time to visit Pope's Farm by car and still be home to lunch.

The pretext for this exploratory visit was that he happened to be passing and thought the previous owner might like to know how the Suffolks were faring. What he was really after was any sort of gleanings of village gossip concerning Joe and his background.

Young Pope was at home, and civil enough to ask a fellow farmer in for a drink. Welch took the conversation round to the four old mares, and Joe's visits to them; Pope had no interest in either, but had more sense than to brush off a man of Welch's wealth and standing.

'Bit queer in the head, Joe Dunnett,' he said. 'Worked for my old grandad as a casual labourer, and I kept him on in the same way till I got rid of the horses. I can't really say I know him, though his wife does work here. She's a better man than he is, if you know what I mean.'

'Is he? Not all there, I mean? I know he can't talk, but he seems normal enough to me in other respects.'

Pope shrugged. 'I really have no idea,' he said. 'I was away at school when he was growing up, I expect. I suppose I could ask his wife.'

Welch hastily disclaimed any interest that would warrant such an approach with more vehemence than he had intended. 'No, no, no!' he said. 'Don't bother. It's just idle curiosity on my part about a man who is as crazy about horses as I am myself. Crazy enough to walk fifteen miles most Sundays just to see them. If I could understand what he says, I could ask him.'

Pope refilled his visitor's glass. 'Well, most folk round here treat him as the village idiot, and from my own observation I would say that nobody but a complete loony would have ever married Ivy.'

He grinned, and pushed a falling log back on to the fire with his foot.

'Funny thing, actually. My old grandad had a sort of soft spot for Joe. When I was a teenager, I used to wonder if there had been a bit of dirty work at the crossroads, and whether the village idiot could be my half-cousin. But not after I had seen

Joe's mother for the first time! Grandad always had a keener eye for a horse than any woman – and Joe's mother wasn't the sort of rosy country wench the boss tumbles in the hay. So I came to the conclusion that Grandad's interest in Joe was the same as yours, I guess. A common love of horses. But that wouldn't apply to old Grove – the village doctor who was a friend of my grandad's. He's had one or two goes at me lately about Joe, sort of hinting that because Grandad wet-nursed Joe a bit, I ought to do the same. I refused to take his hints. It's time he gave up, anyway. The sort of old-fashioned GP who thinks he has to care for his patients' morals as well as their coughs and colds.'

Welch recognized the name. 'Still practising?' he asked, taking care to make it sound conversationally nonchalant.

'Ought to have given up years ago. A fen practice isn't an old man's job. Most farmers now have a private chap from Cambridge, but old Grove still suits those who want a bedside manner and a bottle of pink medicine.'

Welch had found what he had been after, and now had another line to follow, so he lost no time in making excuses that he would be late home for his Sunday dinner; but he drove slowly through the village till he found a public telephone kiosk.

Dr Grove was at home, and when Welch said that his call concerned Joe Dunnett, the Sunday chill in the doctor's voice melted.

'Come round here straight away,' he said. 'Sorry if I sounded a bit short. I thought it was another one of Luke Iseley's tribe with a mosquito bite they wanted me to spit on.'

Welch thought he was going to like the doctor a lot better than he had liked Young Pope.

In five minutes he had told the doctor his tale. It took him less time than that to register the growing consternation on Dr Grove's face. 'You witnessed that will,' Welch said. 'What happened when the old lady died?'

The doctor got out of his chair and went to the window, where he stood looking out with his hands deep in his trouser pockets, absent-mindedly stretching his old-fashioned braces to their very limit before letting them lift his trousers to their proper place again. He jingled keys in his pocket, and gazed out at the flying clouds for a long time in silence before at last turning to face his visitor again. He looked him over from top to toe, and then straight in the eye, for all the world like a judge at a dog show trying to assess an animal's temperament from its outward appearance. He obviously liked what he saw.

'We were in one hell of a jam,' he said, sitting down. 'Look at it from our point of view. Joe was only sixteen. His mother lasted only two or three weeks after making that will, and was barely conscious – though clear enough in her head to beg me to let her die at home. When she did, Joe was not clear about anything. We questioned him pretty thoroughly about any "papers" his mother might have left, but she had either forgotten she had ever done it, or hadn't thought to tell Joe. All Joe would say was that his mother had told him Mr Pope would see to everything for him. She probably believed she had done what she had obviously intended to. Anyway, we looked everywhere for the will, but it wasn't to be found. We could only suppose she had changed her mind.

'Nobody was questioning Joe's right to the property – but there were problems. The land ought to be registered in Joe's name – but if we started any legal processes it would most certainly reveal the existence of his sister. With the will, she would get half; without the will she would still get half – if she claimed it. If we kept quiet, she probably never would. If Joe went on farming the land, it could possibly work out that by the time she did turn up – if she ever did – he would have a sort of agricultural squatter's right to it anyway. We decided to keep our heads down. Nobody but us knew about the will having ever been made. In such out-of-the-way places, custom meant a great deal more than law, and we trusted to that. If Joe had looked as intelligent as we knew him to be, no questions would ever have been asked. We trusted to that – well, partly. But my old friend and I were both behind the times. Things had already begun to change. By 1934, farming was beginning to look up again, and some long-headed farmers had begun to read the signs – after Hitler's rise to power in 1933. If war clouds were gathering, farmers were going to be needed again, so they were after every scrap of land while it could still be bought cheap. Joe's three acres weren't to be sneezed at – but until it was put up for sale, they couldn't buy it. All we could do was to watch out that some clever dick didn't try to bribe Joe while our backs were turned. As I say, he was only sixteen.

'Then just at the same time, a bunch of fat-headed do-gooders in the village, led by a new schoolteacher who hadn't a clue what she was interfering in, and the new vicar's wife who wouldn't have known Joe from Adam if it hadn't been for his hare-lip, began a sort of welfare campaign on Joe's behalf. They'd sucked up the tale of him being a half-wit who couldn't look after himself, let alone three acres of very fertile land. I wonder which of the farmers was behind that one! They wanted Joe committed to "a safe asylum" – for his own good.' The doctor paused, and made a noise in his throat like a bull-dog snarling.

'Bloody, silly, interfering bastards! No conception at all of what they were doing! I suppose it made them feel better; but luckily for Joe they had to get their cranky scheme by me – and it would have been over my dead body! They didn't give in easily, I can tell you! God, how I do hate do-gooders! And the bloody world is full of them, nowadays. Do far more harm than they ever do good – except to themselves.' He caught Welch's eye, and broke off.

'Sorry! That's my private hobby-horse. I'll get back to my tale. We had got to make Joe safe, somehow. Pope decided to call in his solicitor, who was also a mutual friend. We told him everything, and his opinion was that before we tried to get the land registered in Joe's name, the sister must be advertised for. If she didn't respond within a certain time, he would take steps to see Joe's title safe.'

'And she never did turn up?' Welch's relief sounded in his voice. He, too, was now absolutely behind Joe.

'Not so fast, man,' said the doctor. He offered a drink which was courteously declined, and then took up his story again.

'You are jumping the gun. If that had been the case, there would be nothing to be upset about now. We were worried enough then. Joe's sister Joycey – damned silly name for a fen girl – had been gone for fifteen years. She wasn't a fen girl any more. Was it likely that if she did arrive one day from the Antipodes she was going to be running over with loving-kindness for a disfigured brother she didn't know? She would probably be as hard as nails – claim what was hers, which would have meant selling Joe up – and clear off again, leaving behind a homeless waif who couldn't articulate. Just the sort of situation to let the bloody do-gooders in again. If we could have found the will then, we should have burnt it without a qualm. We begged Bryce-Jones to get on and see Joe safe before some crafty farmer tried to prove he was not able to farm the land properly or keep it clean of weeds that would spread – you know the tricks folks will get up to when they think they can get something for nothing! But he wouldn't. He was on Joe's side all right, but he was an old-fashioned lawyer – one of the last few honest ones, I'd say. He insisted on obeying the letter of the law, and advertising for Joycey.'

'So you said. Where's the twist in the end of the tail?'

Dr Grove's eyes twinkled. 'Bryce-Jones was a Welshman through and through, and crafty as they come. He advertised in every national paper in Australia – but apart from her name the rest was all couched in Welsh. As she had presumably changed her surname, the chances of anybody drawing her attention to it were small.'

'So what happened?'

'The very devil was in it. Before the legally specified period was up, Bryce-Jones dropped dead in his office. Pope and I were stumped. We just let things drift. Then the war started. Pope took care to see that Joe's land was well enough farmed for the

War Ag not to poke their noses in. My guess is that it would now be easy enough to get it into Joe's name – but to be quite honest with you, my instinct is to keep my head down. For reasons that I can't disclose to you. However, as you are well aware, the matter is in your hands now. You know there was a will. I can't deny it.'

'Joe doesn't know it is a will. He wouldn't open it. Is it any threat to him, now?'

'No. My hunch is that while he lives, possession is nine-tenths of the law.'

'So what? Who would inherit?'

'His wife.'

Welch was silent. The doctor's flat tone warned Welch that Grove was not a very willing ally, for some reason that was none of his business.

'Look,' said Dr Grove. 'You have never met me till this morning. I'm only an old-fashioned GP on the verge of retirement. I should have done it long ago if it hadn't been for people like Joe. To old folk and such people as the Dunnetts, the medical man is still the shaman. Beveridge's Welfare Scheme is a splendid idea in theory, but it can't and won't replace that side of a doctor's work, especially in remote areas like this. I think I have been subconsciously hanging on till the last few of my pre-war oldies had stopped needing me. Joe's still a young man – I can't wait for him; but all the same I feel a sort of responsibility for him. I have my own reasons. All I can do is to throw myself on your mercy, and beg you to give me time to think this whole thing through properly. It would kill Joe to lose his land now – I don't want that on my conscience. Besides, that poor old woman would have trusted Pope and me to the bitter end. I need time to think things through. Would you be willing to leave the will with me till I make up my mind? I will, of course, let you know.'

'Except for one thing. What do I tell Joe next Sunday? However unimportant it could have been, it was still in his envelope from his box. I've got to tell him – or show him – something.'

'Wait,' said the doctor. He went out, and returned after a few minutes with some old scrapbooks.

'When my old friend Pope died, his grandson threw out everything that couldn't be turned into money. A typical post-war attitude, I fear. I asked for these as a memento. They contain all the records of his lifelong love affair with Suffolks. Yes, I thought so! Here it is. Take a look at that.'

It was a newspaper cutting, yellow with age. At the top was a photograph of a magnificent Suffolk stallion wearing a first-prize rosette, being led round a show-ring by a bowler-hatted and gaitered groom.

'Fenland Prince, with Fred Dunnett as groom,' read the caption.

'Will that do? What more natural than that Joe's father should have been given a copy to keep? Fred's widow would have treasured it like an icon – and Joe will understand that. In fact, I'd say he'll be as pleased as punch with it. That will would only cause him needless worry and a lot of trouble.'

'I'm glad to have met you,' said Welch, standing up and holding out his hand.

'And I you. Joe needs friends.' They parted, each feeling he had gained something from the encounter.

As Grove had predicted, Joe was overjoyed at the photograph, and returned it to its secret hiding place without further question. Welch put the matter out of his mind. He met Joe on Sunday mornings whenever it was convenient, and was glad to note that the man looked fatter, healthier and less miserable. If he had any qualms about suppressing the will, Joe's appearance soothed it. As Joe couldn't talk, and Dr Grove wouldn't, there wasn't much fear of his part in it ever coming to light. The summer passed into a mild autumn, and so to a cold, bleak winter.

The frost outside was no colder than the atmosphere inside the bungalow on the Cut-Dyke Bank. The spouses communicated only when absolutely necessary; Ivy's voice when she issued orders he no longer obeyed was like the jagged edge of the ice round the hole out of which they lifted the water they needed from the dyke. Joe suffered more than he had done in the long summer days, because he couldn't stay outside so long. She accepted her situation with a good deal of equanimity. She had married Joe to get herself a home and a living. She had got it; moreover, now that they lived lives that were parallel rather than joined, she was free to put by as much as she could. Her only real concern was to make her savings grow. If her husband was the price she had to pay for what she wanted, so be it. He endured her green-glass stare and her whiplash tongue in silence. If there was any difference between them, it was that Joe often caught himself regretting the might-have-been. Ivy had no such thoughts.

Joe lived for the weekends, when he visited the horses, whatever the weather, and more often than not had a few minutes with Welch.

On the last Sunday in November, he set out as usual. Joe noted the heavy grey skies, and pulled his cap lower to meet the scarf wound round and round his long neck.

'There's a lot o' downfall uppards,' he said to himself.

'More fool thee if tha catches thi death,' she said, and slammed the door after him.

Jumping a dyke that he had jumped every Sunday for a long time, he missed his landing and slid backwards into the dyke. His fall broke the ice, and he went in. It had happened to him many a time before, in spite of his mother's constant warnings about the ol' Hooky Man that dragged so many children to their deaths. He simply climbed out, wet as he was, and went on. His natural energy kept him warm enough until it began to snow when he was on his way home. Then the cold seeped through to his bones, and when he got home, to use his own words, he felt 'too lither and lawless' to bother with food. He had a hot drink, and went to bed to get warm. Next morning, he lacked the will to get up. His coughing kept Ivy awake, and he felt the lash of her bitter tongue, but she made no move to do anything for him.

'Serves thee right,' she said. 'Ah'm not sendin' for yon old woman of a doctor to thee! Tha'll be reet enough wi'out such stoof as he hands out. Keep t'fire made up.'

Joe lay in bed, and coughed. He didn't want food, and he got none. It was only another of his 'poorly turns', Ivy said. All it needed was for him to pull himself together.

When Joe had missed two Sundays, Welch began to get worried. He phoned Dr Grove to ask if he had seen Joe about.

Dr Grove was feeling his age badly, and the last thing he wanted was an unnecessary trudge down the Cut-Dyke Bank in the snow.

'You should see where he lives,' he told Welch. 'I can't go today, because his wife will be at home, and if he is all right I should never hear the last of it for going without being sent for. But I don't like the sound of it. If I can get down the bank through the snow tomorrow, I'll go.'

He kept his word, wondering as he slithered and slipped on the frozen snow and battled for breath against the 'black frost wind' what he would say if Ivy opened the door to him. She didn't, having left Joe to go to her work. The doctor let himself in, drawn by the terrible coughing from the bedroom. A shake-down bed made up in the living-room told him a great deal.

Within five minutes he knew the worst. Joe was not yet beyond all aid, but there was little time to spare. The new magic sulphonamides that were Joe's only hope were not carried in any doctor's black bag. Since the coming of the Welfare State, he was able to carry only the bare essentials. Somebody had to get to the nearest dispensing chemist, five miles away – without the loss of one precious minute. There was nothing for it but to go himself. He held Joe through another paroxysm, gave him a sip of water, arranged the sweaty pillows and left. By the time he had hurried the mile along the bank back to his car, he was very nearly as breathless as Joe himself. He drove to the chemist and obtained the wonder-drug, but he quailed at the thought of another trip down the bank. He went instead to find Ivy at Pope's Farm. He learned from a boy in the yard that she was on a tractor fetching some feed in.

The doctor's blood was up. 'Find her,' he said, 'and be quick!' It was not a request, but a command. The boy went, but the doctor sat with the brown bottle in his hands for what seemed to him an unnecessarily long time. Well, it would take more than a termagant wife to rob him of a patient. She should go home and do her duty – or else!

He was ready for her when she appeared at last, though not for her undisguised belligerence. It was in her walk, in her face, in her whole attitude of contempt for him and all he stood for. Her mood was plain.

He called her to his open window, and reluctantly she came. He was determined to get his blow in first. He told her in a few brusque sentences that she must go home at once and start to administer the pills that were Joe's only chance of life.

She protested. She was at work. He cut her short, telling her that he would take all responsibility. 'Get off home with those pills. He ought to have had them a week ago. Why didn't you send for me then?'

Her face turned even blacker. 'I didn't send for thee now,' she flashed. 'And I'd like t'know t'booger as did! Joe's reet enough. It's only another of his poorly turns.'

'It's double pneumonia,' he said grimly. 'He may stand a chance with the pills, but it isn't very likely. Now do you understand?'

'I want t'know booger as sent for thee! Interfering bastard! What's it got to do with thee, or any other interfering booger, what goes on in our house? I shan't go till thi tells me who sent fo' thee.'

'Let's say it was the proverbial little bird,' he answered. His temper was nearly choking him, and it was only with great effort that he kept his voice calm.

'Ah'll wring its bloody neck if ever I finds it,' she said.

'Somebody will have good cause to stretch yours if you don't go home with those pills this instant,' he said – and this time his voice was anything but calm. She heard the threat, and turned to her old bike, on which she rode to and from the top of the bank.

He followed her, driving slowly behind her till she got off her bike. He got out and went to speak to her. 'Now listen to me. Joe is to have those pills exactly as it states on the bottle. He is too ill to dose himself. His life is in your hands. He may get worse before they start to work. Keep him warm and give him a lot of drink. But you must send for me if he doesn't start to respond very soon.' She nodded, and left him.

When he had heard nothing for two days, he struggled through fresh snow down to the cottage again.

Joe was breathing more easily, but was thinner and weaker than ever. He was not a pretty sight to look at. The doctor looked down on a week's growth of beard, tangled hair matted with sweat, and a bed as tousled, frowsty and dirty as he had ever seen before in this poor bleak practice.

No sign of Yorkshire's reputation for spotlessness here, he thought. He had to go and find her to report – she had not bothered to accompany him into the sick room.

'He's better,' he said, briefly. 'I think he'll make it now. Keep him on the tablets. And freshen him up a bit – it'll do him good now to have a wash and a clean bed.'

It was another two days before the call he had been expecting came: a peremptory request for him to make that long and exhausting journey through the snow again.

She had been watching for him, and opened the door before he knocked.

He got his own breath back before attempting to speak.

'How is he?' he asked. 'Are the pills working?'

'Naw,' she said, 'tha's too late. E's gone. There's nowt for thee t'do but sign t' death certificate.'

He was defeated. He had lost his battle. It made no difference whether or not he ever heard the truth about Joe's last hours.

He was dead, and nothing in a doctor's power could bring him back to life. He sighed deeply, and told her he would have to see the corpse in order to fill out the death certificate.

She led the way to the bedroom, this time. The bed was covered with a pair of new, crisply white sheets, one of which lay over the still figure. He turned it back, and saw that Joe had been laid out in clinical perfection. He had been washed and shaved, brushed and combed for his wedding with eternity. His workworn hands, skeletal already, had been trimmed of their long nails, and now rested, crossed, on his best Sunday shirt.

'A pleasant corpse.' That's what these country folks always said about anybody who had lived too long to suit his heirs. The attention Ivy had paid to her late husband's earthly remains gave the old saying new meaning to him.

Well, it was over. Poor Joe had made his bed when he had married this alien woman, and now he was lying on it in tranquil peace. Used as he was to such scenes, there was something so unnaturally cold-blooded about it all that in spite of himself he was disturbed. No need here for the comforting word, the soothing pat, the sleeping draught. All that was needed from him was a piece of paper.

He turned to the little bedside table to find a hard surface to write on. In that instant he knew why Joe had died. There stood the brown pill bottle, which should have been empty, but was still half-full. A wave of helpless despair swept through him as he turned back to the waiting woman.

'These pills,' he said. 'Why hasn't he been taking them?'

'Nay, he has!' she retorted

'He can't have done. They're still here – at least half of them.'

'Oh aye. There's still some left. It's such a jaunt from here to t' chemist, Ah thowt I'd better keep a few put by for next turn he had.'

'You only gave him half the dose?'

'Ah! Ah knaws thee doctors, allus loading folks wi' expensive stoof like yon. He'd ha' done just as well wi'out any, if you ask me.'

He would indeed. Undoubtedly. Just as well.

The doctor put the bottle down, and drew up the sheet over the still, disfigured face. His task was over.

'Wilt tha send undertaker, t' save me t' walk i' this weather?'

As he struggled back in the dark along the bank, he thought he had never before been so disturbed by the loss of a patient. He recognized his own anger at Ivy's victory, and understood the warning it sent to him. He had been trained never to get emotionally involved with a patient – but he was an anachronism. How could a man live and work among such people as these for a lifetime, and not care about them? He did. It was time he gave up. Asking for a coroner's inquest on Joe would do no good at all. Nobody else would care why Joe had died. Why should he? He had done his best, and it had not been good enough. It was time for him to retire. A younger man would have dealt with Joe's case differently, and maybe better. He felt that it was his professional self that had died. He wanted no more – not even a single day.

His wife reported him unwell next morning, and said she was taking him to London to see a specialist. They set off to London the very next morning – mainly because the doctor did not want to be about when a double team of bearers slipped and staggered with Joe's coffin up the bank to the waiting hearse. Besides, as his wife had truly said, he was on his way to consult a specialist – though not a medical one. Apart from his plans for retirement, he had other matters on his mind.

In the Turfcutters Joe's unlooked-for death had been as good a topic of conversation as previously his equally unlooked-for marriage had been. In the years between the two events the habitués of the pub had seen so little of Joe that their concept of him had been, as it were, arrested. They still thought of him as he had been when his mother had left him – a gangling orphan, in their eyes no more than half-witted, at the age of sixteen. They had difficulty in believing him dead – and to cover the unease of guilty conscience that they had not bothered more about him while a bit of neighbourly kindness might have helped, they chose to make his demise as much a subject for ribaldry as his marriage. His death reminded them too much of their own mortality; besides, they had heard that he had been Dr Grove's last patient, and that the doctor was no longer at their beck and call. What would they do now without that familiar fatherly figure at their bedside?

Them young ones ain't the same, they all agreed.

The funeral was over, but the topic lingered on. Bill, George and Tom recalled, over and over and over again, what they had said when they had first heard the news of Joe's impending marriage. They sat in the same places, holding the same mugs – a little older, perhaps, in the leathern way of men exposed every day to the worst the elements can do, but unchanged in any other way. It might have been a scene from a pantomime of *The Sleeping Beauty* – except for one detail. It was almost unthinkable, so early in the war, for a woman to be sitting at the bar, getting herself a drink. Fenland women still shunned public bars, even with a male escort. But tonight there was a lone woman, sitting on a high stool near the bar. Well, even in places as remote as this, travellers sometimes broke down, and landlords served them while they waited for the AA to rescue them. That must have been about the size of it, George opined in a whisper, and they returned to the matter of their own talk, and took no further notice of her.

'Ah, poor old Joe. That were a bad job for 'im and no mistake,' said Tom. 'Still, they allus say that where there's no sense there's no feeling, but I am 'eard as 'ow pewmonia's a nasty ol' way to goo, like.'

'Were it pewmonia though?' asked Bill. 'My missus reckons that what he died on were nothink nor less than that 'e couldn't abide that land gal 'e married no longer. Jest give up, like, and died. Well, tha's what she says, and it ain't often as my missus is wrong about such things.'

'Perhaps she wore 'im out, like, a-nights!' put in George. 'He never were no match for 'er in nothink, accordi'ly to what folks

is saying. Never satisfied, Ivy weren't, so they reckon. Not wi'
nothink nor nobody. Pre'aps 'e just couldn't satisfy 'er that
way.'

'I thought you said as she were a moffradite,' Tom reminded
him.

'Ah, so I did, well then, pre'aps it were disappointment as
wore 'im down at last.'

'Moffradite or not, she'll be worth a pretty penny now, as
Joe's widder. I mean, she'll come in for everything, won't
she? Don't seem right to me, that don't – for a stranger like 'er
to come 'ere from some forrin part and come by three acre o'
beautiful fenland when the likes of us can't get a bit of
small'olding to work for ourselves, be it ever so. Besides, it's
Dunnett's land.'

'There ain't no Dunnetts left now,' George reminded them.
'If she were a moffradite, that would account for 'em never
'aving no children.'

'Ivy's a Dunnett. She's Joe's widder.'

'Can a moffradite be a widder? That don't seem right to me
no 'ow,' said Bill. 'I shall hev to ask my missus about that.
She'll know for sure.'

'We shall soon find out,' Tom said, wise as ever. 'As Bill says,
if she is a widder, she'll be a sight better off now than when she
fust come this way. She ha'n't got a rag to cover her arse with
then, only 'er Land Army garb. There y'are, George – there's a
chance for you to come by that small'olding you're so keen on.
Seein' as you are a widder-man yerself now. You'll hev to goo
along the Cut-Dyke Bank to keep a eye open for Ivy a-standing
a broom outside the door. Wouldn't do to let nobody else get in
fust.'

George spluttered his indignation. 'You wouldn't catch me a-
trampling down the bank looking for no brooms,' he said. 'It
'ould take a sight more'n a tumbledown place an' three acres o'
land ter get me within spittin' distance o' that there bloody Ivy.
Not if the land was to be worth a thousand pound an acre.'

'Tha's just about the size on it, George,' said Bill. 'My missus 'eard in the shop today as Young Pope 'as offered her a thousand a hacre a'ready.'

The woman at the bar slid off her stool, came towards them, and pulled up a chair, uninvited.

'Good on yer, sport,' she said. 'That's the bit as I'm been waiting to hear.' She picked up her glass and drained it, nodding at Bill. 'Good on yer. Thanks, Bill.'

They looked at her with gaping mouths. She laughed, a loud, high-pitched strident laugh. 'You are Bill, ain't you? And you're Tom and you're George. See, sports, I ain't forgot you, if you've forgot me.'

'Struth,' said Tom, 'as I go to school! If it ain't Joycey Dunnett, I'm a Dutchman.'

'That's just who it is, my old mates, Joe's sister as ever was.'

They eyed her in a mixture of disbelief allied to inner certainty. It was as if their conversation had conjured her out of thin air, and they couldn't quite believe their own eyes – though she looked solid enough. That was one of the difficulties. None of them would have recognized in this shabby, dumpy woman with the careworn face the precociously slim and pretty girl who had so often tempted them with what they were too scared to accept down along a lonely dykeside in time gone by.

'Well, I'll be bu – I'll be sugared!' said George at last. 'I thought as I had seen 'er somewheer before, when we fust come in tonight. I can see why now. She's the spit image o' poor ol' Joe.'

'Except as Joe 'ad an 'are-lip,' said Tom, kicking George under the table.

She laughed. 'Joe warn't no beauty, ever,' she said. 'But then, more ain't I now. Don't worrit, me ol' duck. You wou'n't hurt my feelings none. Fen born and bred I am, just like you.' She smiled at George. She was speaking in their own fen 'twang' just to prove it.

'Ah, that you are,' said Bill. 'There ain't no doubt about that. I can't wait to tell my missus about this 'ere.' He got up to go. There'd be hell to pay at home if anybody came by this bit of news before his wife did. But he had better get it right, and Joycey was speaking again, so he waited.

'Got to London by plane this morning,' she said. 'Then I come straight here. I come to the Turfcutters in the hope somebody as knowed me would be here to identify me. Now I'm off down the Cut-Dyke Bank to let Joe's widder know I'm here.'

'What, tonight, now? By yourself? In this weather?' Tom's anxiety was lest any of them should be asked to accompany her.

'I shall be safe enough, sport,' she said. 'I've done that walk in the dark many a time when it was as bad as it is now – and had to climb out o' the window and in again without waking Mam and Dad into the bargain.'

'Yew wou'n't get much of a welcome, I don't reckon,' warned Tom. 'Joe's wife don't come from these parts, you know. Kept 'erself to 'erself allus Ivy has.'

'Kep' everthing to 'erself, by all accounts,' added George.

'So I've been told,' said Joycey grimly. 'Don't you worry about me not being able to take care o' myself, me ol' ducks. I've had plenty o' practice at that since you see me last. I shall be a match for her – a lot more than Joe ever was. Besides, it'll be a bad job if a good ol' fen tiger as 'as been done out of its rights can't get the better of a nasty snapping Yorkshire tyke like her – which she is, from what I hear about her.'

'What do you mean – been done out of your rights?' This was Tom again. 'We all know as it were Joe's land, and he were married proper to Ivy. So by law, it'll all come to 'er – must do.'

She fished into her shabby handbag and from it took an envelope which in turn yielded a letter on dazzlingly white paper with an equally impressive black letterhead. To the letter was attached a newspaper cutting.

'From a solicitor in London,' she said. 'It says as I ought to have had half of everything when Mam died, only they couldn't find me then. Mam left a will to say so. She wanted me to come home and go and live with Joe. Well, he ain't here no more. So I shall go and live with his widder, if she'll have me, seeing as I ain't got no home nowhere else. If she won't have me in, I shall claim my half, to the last penny, 'cos you see the land never was made over to Joe properly in his name. This same solicitor as writ to me is willing to take the case on, and says it won't cost me nothing. So here I go to show her this letter, and hear what she's got to say about it. See you again soon, me ol' mates.'

She went out into the wintry night, leaving three men gawping after her.

'I reckon the fur'll be flyin' down the bank afore very long,' said Tom, at last. 'I can't see that there Ivy bein' one to go half shares wi' nobody once she's got her claws in it. She ain't one for no half measures, Ivy ain't.'

Bill nodded in agreement. 'Joycey said summat about a will as her mother made,' he said. 'My missus didn't know nothing about no will, and she knows most o' what goes on. That I'll swear on my Bible oath.'

'What I wonder is how in damnation that solicitor chap in London come to know Joe was dying, or about him ever having a sister out in Australia? I mean do those folks up in London know everything as 'appens to us, like? I didn't know that. I don't like the sound on it much either.'

'Them as lives longest'll see most,' said Tom, sententiously.

'I know what my missus'll say,' said Bill. 'She's allus ready with a bit o' the Bible as'll explain everythink. She'll say as God moves in a mysterious way, 'is wonders to perform, and that he set it all up so as Ivy didn't get no good by 'ticing Joe to marry 'er in the fust place, and then not taking no better care of 'im than she did. She knowed as he warn't only half a man, and she ought to ha' took more care of 'im than she did – according to all accounts.'

'And if you was to arst me,' said Tom solemnly, 'your missus wouldn't be far wrong this time.'

Bill looked pleased at this compliment to his wife's sagacity, but was reminded that he had better be getting off home with his budget of news before the others did. He looked back from the door. ''Night, Tom, 'night, George.' He was gone.

The other two made their preparations to leave in a more leisurely fashion. George settled his old cap very firmly on his head, and turned up his coat collar. Tom struggled into a very worn mackintosh that had never been quite big enough for him. They went slowly to the door.

With his hand on the latch, George paused, looking thoughtful. 'I dunno as I shan't be a-gooing down the Cut-Dyke Bank looking for a broom outside the door arter all, if Joycey gets her share,' he said.

Tom nodded. It was no use trying to speak. The icy wind from the Urals would have whipped his words away just as the blackness of the moonless night swallowed them up and the soft snow smothered the sound of their footfalls. Darkness and silence are partners in the fenland landscape. Only those not born to it find anything strange about that.

The Nightingale Ode

The dog in the perambulator was an Airedale, grey-whiskered and with old eyes clouded by glaucoma. Alys saw so much in the split second it took her to pass, because she was already slowing the car as she approached the pedestrian crossing area. With the sixth sense most experienced drivers acquire after years at the wheel, she knew instinctively that the woman pushing the pram intended to cross when she reached it, but Alys would be over long before she got there.

It was lunchtime, and Alys was hungry. The little country town with its long main street looked just the sort of place to offer a pleasant pub with substantial bar snacks, and she had already noted, just the other side of the crossing, a board standing on the pavement with the legend 'Hot meals now being served'. As she drove by the board, a strong gust of wind lifted it, and she automatically applied her brake. There was a scream of other brakes, and the unmistakeable sound of heavy tyres skidding to a halt. Her first thought was that she had failed to notice a heavy vehicle close behind her, and glanced apprehensively into her driving mirror.

The woman with the pram had turned on to the crossing, just as Alys had predicted, and presumably without giving the lorry driver warning or a chance to avoid her. She lay sprawled on the black and white lines with her head on the kerb, and the pram with a very dead dog inside it was squashed and crumpled under the lorry's huge nearside wheels.

Shaking, Alys drew her car into the kerb and reached for her handbrake. She would have to go back and offer assistance; but even as she began to open her car door, she was aware of other feet running, voices raised and still more people appearing from every side. She was not needed, and not being the sort of person to take a morbid interest in an accident for the sake of seeing the horrid details, she sat back in the car, trying not to look into her mirror again. She had not seen the accident happen, so she could hardly be called as a witness to it, but on the other hand there was very little other traffic in the street, and hers had been the nearest car. Perhaps she had better not go away. When a police car and an ambulance drove up, Alys decided that her best course was to go into the Waggoner and get herself a stiff drink, then order a meal and eat it while she waited to see if the police wanted to speak to her. A few yards farther on she found a two-hour parking space vacant. She got out of the car and walked back to the pub, determinedly keeping her head down so as not to see what was happening in the street ahead of her.

The pub was neat, clean, cosy and welcoming, but absolutely empty. She surmised that the landlord had heard the commotion, and together with his staff had rushed out to the accident. She was relieved at the unexpected solitude, and sat down at a table away from the window, making a conscious effort to calm herself. She tried to think of the journey that still lay ahead of her, but it gave her no pleasure to contemplate the end of it. Her mother would only look up at her coldly and ask why she was later than expected. There was never a word of greeting, or of gratitude that she had been driving for hours and hours just to get there. Alys continued to visit only out of a sense of duty. Her mother in turn accepted these regular visits resentfully, as a regrettable necessity brought about by the selfish demands of her paid attendants for time off duty. Alys sighed, and tried to think of something else, but all she could manage to revert to was that sickening squeal of brakes and the woman lying on the road.

She lit a cigarette, and allowed herself to think. It was the woman's feet she remembered, cursory as her passing glance had been, though she was surprised to realize how much she could recall of the victim's appearance, because naturally her attention had really been focused on the dog sitting up in the pram. A figure of middle height, she thought, probably stooping and shrunken from a once tall and upright stance. It was clad in a dirty old mackintosh belted at the waist, but hanging down in points at the front as if no buttons were left in use. Wrinkled stockings ended in a pair of brown walking shoes that had once probably been expensive, but were now down-at-heel and broken-backed. Alys had noted them particularly because of the curious way the woman had of picking her feet up higher than is usual, and setting each down again as if every time she stepped she was crushing something obnoxious under her sole. Alys had not seen the face, and was glad of it. She recalled straggling grey hair beneath a green woollen cap, and a scarf muffled round the neck of the old mackintosh. Perhaps the silly woman wasn't very badly hurt, though the dog had taken the full impact, and was undoubtedly dead. Poor old soul, what would she now do without the dog? It must have been dear to her, for her to actually push it about in a pram when it had got too old to walk. Funny how some women shower affection on dogs when they have no love to spare for people, even their own children – like her mother, and like Miss Barfield. She'd always had an Airedale, too, though her mother had favoured smelly spaniels. Still did. Alys sighed. She would have to take the present pampered creature to the vet, get its claws clipped or something, as usual. Alys didn't mind dogs, but she resented having to leave her own children for four days every third week to attend to the wants of an ungrateful, cold, old woman and a pampered, slavering dog. The worst thing was that in spite of everything, Alys still loved her mother, still longed for a sign of affection, just as she had done when she was a child. She knew, officially, so to speak, why she had been rejected by her mother, and not wanted by her father, though she never had been able to understand how anybody could treat a child as she had been treated all her young life. She remembered only too well the evening that dear old Louie in the kitchen had tried to explain it to her.

Alys sat back in her chair, slowly puffing a cigarette, while memory flowed through her mind like water from a mountain spring, directly from the source of thirty years ago. It was from that day that the vague unease of not feeling wanted had turned to the misery of knowing. She had got home late, that afternoon, and was sneaking into the kitchen to ask Louie for something to eat, having missed her official teatime, when her father had opened the door of the sitting-room and commanded her presence there. She went just as she was, dragging her satchel on its long leather strap behind her, and stood uneasily just inside the room. Her father was standing by the fire, her mother (as always) reclining in a chair with a dog by her side. She didn't bother to look up at Alys, but did glance pointedly at the clock.

'No need to ask where you've been,' her father said. 'So don't lie. There's no point. I know you haven't been to school this afternoon. Miss Fenton rang.'

'I didn't miss any lessons. Truly I didn't,' said Alys. 'It was only needlework and then PE. Not Latin, or maths or anything.' She spoke eagerly, saying anything, doing something, to avert that stern, accusing look.

'I'm surprised you even know what Latin or maths is,' he said, 'and that you understand anything at all that is not connected with horses. But it seems you do. Miss Fenton rang to tell me that you have been granted a place at Abbey Street Grammar School.'

There was no hint of pride or pleasure in his tone, and Alys heard the news with feelings decidedly mixed. She was gratified that she had been proved not to be the dim-wit she was so often called at home, but at the same time she had no burning desire to be a pupil at Abbey Street Grammar. For one thing, she knew it would be impossible to play truant from there, and go and put Mirage over the jumps at Bottomdale Farm.

'I shall never understand how you came to achieve this honour,' her father was saying, sarcastically. 'As I just said, it surprises me that you can read any other word than "horse".'

'Or "food",' said her mother. 'Her greediness is disgusting. They are always stuffing her, down at that farm. I think she goes there for the fruit cake they give her, not for the horses at all.' It was a long speech for her mother to make – well, about her, at least. She usually ignored Alys as if she simply didn't exist, or had never been born.

'In that case, she can be punished today by going straight to bed without her tea, and not coming down to supper.'

'Oh, no!' said Alys, looking up and pleading with huge blue-grey eyes, twiddling the end of her long blonde plait with agitated fingers. 'Oh Father, please! I promise I won't do it again! And I'm so hungry.' She actually moved a step nearer to him, dragging her satchel over the rich carpet.

'Pick that thing up!' he said sharply. 'And don't whine! Go to bed at once – but have a bath first. I can't bear the reek of horses in the house.'

Alys turned, trying not to cry. She knew she couldn't go till breakfast time without food. Would it be wise to sneak into the kitchen now, and grab something, or wait till later and then creep down? She guessed, fairly confidently, that Louie would sum up the situation and smuggle something from supper for her. It had happened before. She hesitated outside the door of the sitting-room, and the voices of her parents came through to her.

'Of course she won't go to Abbey Street,' he was saying. 'Whatever she is, she's my child I suppose, and I can hardly have her sitting next to a miner's child, or the son of the local dustman. I'll put Miss Bellairs on to finding a boarding school for her.'

Her mother made no reply. Alys could imagine exactly the look on her face, because any mention of Miss Bellairs always produced it. When her mother did speak at last, it was merely to say, 'Will you be in to dinner?'

'No,' he replied, shortly.

'Where are you going?'

'Out.'

Now there was cold, brittle tension in both voices. Alys could not bear it. She fled upstairs to bath and bed, and tried to drug herself to sleep by thinking about Mirage and the marvellous way he had jumped this afternoon. She was going to be allowed by the farmer to ride him at the local agricultural show, and enter the junior show-jumping competition. It was worth getting into trouble for, if only she were not so hungry. She heard her father go out, and his car wheels crunch over the gravel. She heard her mother, and the dog, cross listlessly from the dining-room to the sitting-room, and Louie clearing the table. In a few minutes, Louie would be having her own supper. That was when to go down. If her mother's dog didn't hear her and give her away, she would have no difficulty at all.

Louie, it seems, was expecting her, and had saved her a good supper. She had also had enough forethought to put Alys's tea into a paper bag that could be secreted somewhere about the child's person, in case she should be caught in the kitchen before she had satisfied her hunger.

'Hide it quick, love,' said Louie.

'Where?' said Alys, despairingly, for her plain nightie had no sleeves or belt, and her dressing-gown pockets were too obvious.

'Sh! Eat your supper, quick, and I'll take it up and put it under your pillow. You can have a midnight feast, like they do in boarding school, in them tales on t'wireless.'

When Louie came back, Alys had gobbled half her supper.

'They're going to send me away to boarding school,' she said, and her throat suddenly closed up with the desire to cry.

'Shame on them!' said Louie. 'Poor love!'

'Why don't they want me at home, Lou? I've got a scholarship to Abbey Street Grammar, but I'm not to go there. Why? Why can't I stay at home with you, where I can still ride Mirage when Mr Whiteley will let me? Why don't they want me?' She was crying now, and pushed her plate away.

Louie growled, as if she would burst if she didn't give some vent to her feelings. She was a big, raw-boned Derbyshire woman with a heart that in no way matched her millstone-grit outward appearance. Alys got up from the kitchen table, and stumbled towards her. Louis pulled the child down on her knee, comforting her with such words as she could find. But Alys would not be put off. 'Why?' she kept asking. 'Why?'

So Louie had done her best to explain. When Alys had been born, nearly twelve years ago, her mother had been young, and healthy, and very beautiful. But she had had all sorts of complications, 'what such women as me 'ave never heered on' (said Louie), and as a result had been more or less an invalid ever since. 'An' then she couldn't never 'ave no more than you, you see.'

Alys was sorry – for her mother, and for the lost brothers and sisters she might have had; but it didn't explain anything.

'That ought to make her love me more,' she said. 'But she doesn't love me at all.'

'She blames you for being as she is,' said Louie. 'It was you as caused it all, see. And she couldn't 'ave no more, like I said.'

'Did she want some more, then?' Alys was really puzzled, and looked at Louie for enlightenment, but poor Louie was struggling in waters deeper than she had intended to get into.

'She wasn't pretty no more, y'see, love – or so she thought. Not 'ticing enough to your father, like. And she daren't risk 'aving another, 'cos the doctor said it would be the death of her, if she did, see?'

Alys did see, suddenly and with the vivid clarity of her own adolescent feelings to help her. All that had so far lain in her mind somewhere between fairy-tale and day-dream suddenly became hard-edged reality. She saw where Miss Bellairs fitted into the picture. Her mother didn't simply not love her: she positively hated her. And her father didn't simply not want her. He didn't want her mother, either, or his life with them at all. He wanted his secretary.

'Hark!' said Louie urgently. 'Your mother's coming! Get up them stairs.'

Alys knew quite well that her mother never moved, once she had sat down after dinner; but she understood now why Louie wanted to stop the conversation. She would certainly not talk to Alys about her father's affair with Miss Bellairs. But Alys had become a woman in the last ten minutes. She didn't argue, and went back to bed to think it out for herself. She ate her tea from its paper bag before she went to sleep, and dreamed that Miss Bellairs broke her neck riding Mirage over a six-foot parallel.

Term ended, and Alys left her prep school for ever. She won the junior show-jumping class on Mirage, and the farmer let her keep half the prize money. As the holidays wore on, she kept expecting to be told that she was to go off to a boarding school, but it didn't happen. Then one day, Louie unexpectedly announced that she had been told to take Alys into town, and fit her up with uniform for Abbey Street Grammar School. No explanation was offered, and Alys did not know whether to rejoice or to mourn. She accepted her lot as if she were a bit of waste paper blown willy-nilly by a capricious wind, and went to Abbey Street Grammar School expecting neither good nor harm, joy nor sorrow to come from it. Since nobody anywhere loved or wanted her, what difference did it make?

It came upon her, therefore, with a sort of heartwarming shock to find herself being praised, day after day, by Miss Allen, the English teacher. Her essays were always marked 'Good'; Miss Allen sometimes read bits of them out to the other children. She talked to Alys as one adult might to another. If Alys met her on the way to school, she let the girl carry her bag, and chatted as easily to her as if Alys had been her younger sister. Try as she might when in bed alone at night to find the flaw she felt (from past experience) there must be, she couldn't detect it. Miss Allen liked her. Not for any particular reason, but just for her own sake. As for Alys, she put into her love for Miss Allen all the frustrated longings both of childhood and of adolescence. For the first time in her life, she was happy in a deep, inner, satisfied way. She grew prettier, and developed in body and mind. Her spirits soared, and even the unhappiness of home could not depress her. It was in this frame of mind that she first encountered the 'Ode to a Nightingale', introduced to the class by Miss Allen. It made little impact on most of the stolid children, but to Alys it was magic. She knew exactly how Keats felt when he wrote it, and committed it overnight to her memory, so as to be able to savour it during the long hours of darkness that separated her from the next day, and school, and Miss Allen.

She would lie awake and say it softly to herself, luxuriating in its sensuousness.

> 'Already with thee! Tender is the night,
> And haply the Queen-Moon is on her throne,
> Cluster'd around by all her starry Fays.'

But she stopped before she reached the last stanza. As she understood Keats's ecstasy, so she sensed his despair. As he felt about the nightingale, she felt about herself; she was afraid of being too happy in her happiness, and when her bird of ecstasy flew away suddenly, she was not surprised, though utterly forlorn. She had been vaguely conscious that her parents had noticed the change in her, and were seeking vainly for the explanation. She had heard them discussing her once, in that terrible, cold and distant way they had of communicating with each other, as if they were on opposite sides of a sheet of ice that was standing between them.

'She seems to be quite happy at that sixth-rate school,' her father had said. 'I wonder what goes on there?'

'She's getting too fat,' her mother had replied. 'She'll soon look like the char's daughter she probably sits next to. Why don't you do something about it? You're always going to, but never do.'

He refused the bait. She knew quite well why he procrastinated with all affairs connected with his household.

'It can't be good for her to like school so much,' he said. 'It just isn't natural.'

Alys had hugged her happiness to her, glad that they had no idea of the secret well of her Keatsian paradise. It never occurred to her innocence that her happiness was a thorn in their pillow, that to see the child they disliked and despised so contented would serve to accentuate their own domestic misery. To keep her where she was, being a constant irritant, was beyond either of them. She must go. So after a blissful year at Abbey Street Grammar, she was brusquely informed that from September she would be going to boarding school, to an independent establishment called Cedary Hall in a large industrial town just too far away for her to come home often. She made no outward protest, though parting with Louie proved to be more of an ordeal than she had expected. Her father was to deliver her to Cedary Hall on the appointed day, 'because he had business there'. (It did not surprise Alys that Miss Bellairs was to accompany them; she was always going places with father 'on business'.)

But exactly a week before she was to go, the Second World War broke out, and when they arrived at Cedary Hall, things were far from normal as the school strove to cope with ARP regulations and all the rest of the new situation. It was unfortunate, therefore, that they arrived about four hours sooner than they had been told to do. Alys's father turned what charm he had on the distracted assistant matron, who said bluntly that he would have to take her away again until the afternoon. He looked despairingly for Miss Bellairs, who had got out of the car to stretch her legs. She came, listened, and declared in a cold, detached, businesslike voice that she, personally, had informed the principal's secretary that Alys would be arriving before lunch, and had been assured that it would be perfectly acceptable as long as they expected her. This was quite true. The conversation had taken place in mid-vacation time, and before the international crisis had reached its peak. The school secretary had failed to note it down, and thereafter had been far too occupied with more important things to remember it. So it was that Alys was foisted into the assistant matron's unwelcoming care, and her father, barely raising his hat to the matron, pecked Alys on the cheek and drove off without looking back.

'Well!' said the assistant matron, who was used to tearful scenes as crying new girls clung to weeping mothers. 'Well! I don't know!' Alys did. As usual, she had been sent off on the wrong foot, unwanted again, even by these total strangers. She was taken to see Matron, but that good lady was much occupied with blackouts for dormitory windows, and told her junior to find the child something to eat, and send her into the garden.

She had been there for what seemed like eternity when a dog appeared and cocked its leg against the tree Alys was sitting under. She had a natural rapport with all animals, and felt a rush of affection for the Airedale out of all proportion to the situation. It was like oxygen to a suffocating man for her to see the friendly wag of his tail as he came in response to her call. He jumped up on her, and licked her face, while she put her arms round his neck and rubbed her cheek against his crisp and crinkly coat. In doing so, she pushed the ribbon from the end of her long blonde plait of hair, which then escaped and hung loose. She had rubbed green dust from the bark of the tree all over her new uniform, and the few tears she had shed in her loneliness had not improved her face. It was at this moment that she heard the peculiar tread that she was to grow to hate so much, as Miss Barfield sternly called her dog to heel.

Alys guessed at once who the tall, tweedy woman with the deep voice was, and scrambled to her feet, shy and embarrassed, but smiling timidly at what she had hoped would be a substitute for Miss Allen. There was no smile in response.

'You must be that new girl who arrived too early. I am Miss Barfield. How do you do? Come here!'

Alys went. Miss Barfield had secured the dog, and put him on a lead. She looked Alys coldly up and down, and then said, 'You must learn two strict rules that apply here at once, I can see. The first is that no one, no one, is allowed to pet Dominic. He is my dog, not the school's pet. Feeding him or playing with him is absolutely forbidden. And we expect every girl who is privileged to come here to care for her own appearance. Yours is disgraceful. I do not care for my girls to have long hair. If you cannot keep yours under control, it will have to be cut. Now go at once to your dormitory and get yourself made clean and tidy, before the other girls' parents see you.'

'Yes, Miss Barfield,' said Alys meekly, belying her feelings, because she felt anything but meek. Resentment and rebellion were flowing through her as if she had drunk a cup of vintage that was anything but cool and tasting of sun-burnt mirth. Hemlock all right, but fiery, bitter poison had Miss Barfield's welcoming words been to her. She was certainly not going to exchange any love with Miss Barfield, and was already forbidden to love her dog. Miss Barfield turned and strode away, every step squashing underfoot any last glimmer of hope Alys had entertained. She determined not to cry and to try not to care. As she tore the hope of love from her heart, hate rushed into the vacuum. She would henceforth do as she was done by.

She was older by a year than most of the other newcomers, and was put into a dormitory among girls who were by no means new, but were already well known to each other. But for her brush with Miss Barfield, she could have made friends there, but as it was she didn't really try. She had no one to rely on but herself, no comfort but her resolve not to conform or to try to please anybody. She was wary and distrustful of any overtures of friendship, and the girls soon began to leave her alone and take up their old relationships with each other.

Once in her strange bed, the memory of her loss hit her again, and Keats was no help to her. She was forlorn, and knew only too well the meaning of the word that 'like a bell' was tolling her back from everything she had loved to her 'sole self'. But with the new agony came new resolve. Somehow or other she would get her own back – on the school, on the girls, on her parents. If they didn't want her, they should at least notice her; and she would find some way of escaping from Cedary Hall, and getting back to Abbey Street Grammar and Miss Allen. To be obliged to have her back would be about the worst punishment she could inflict on her parents, especially if she could go back in disgrace. The warm thought of rebellion and revenge soothed her till she fell asleep.

It was only a matter of a few days before the next upheaval, and in that time nothing of consequence happened except that she found in her beautiful hair the thin end of a wedge with which to irritate everybody. She seized upon it as a symbol of her revolt. (It was, after all, the only thing about her that had ever given a moment of pride or satisfaction to her mother.)

She contrived that it should be as untidy as possible whenever Miss Barfield was anywhere near, and succeeded in eliciting rebuke after rebuke, each more acrimonious than the last. Matron was told to see that she kept it tidier, and that good lady dragged it back till it nearly lifted Alys's scalp; but it was springily rebellious of its own accord, and at the sound of Miss Barfield's footfall it took only a second and a headshake to release it and get the blonde tips into the ink. After about a month of such tactics, she had her first real success, reducing the dignified Miss Barfield to shouting at her.

'If you do not keep that hair under control, Mitchell, it will have to be cut off. I will *not* be disobeyed. Do you hear me?'

'Yes, Miss Barfield,' said Alys, pertly. Mitchell, indeed! As if she were a convict, or a slave. Even the boys at Abbey Street had been called by their Christian names, unless they were in disgrace.

But she had, for the moment, no further chance of carrying out any of her vague plans. The industrial town on the outskirts of which Cedary Hall was situated made steel, and was a very likely target for German bombers. Efforts had been made to find a suitable place to evacuate the school to for the duration of the war, and a decision had been taken. They were packed up, lock, stock and barrel, and moved to a run-down stately home called Viney Chase, in the middle of woodland somewhere in East Anglia. The main part of the old building had not been lived in for years, and lacked warmth, comfort and modern amenities of any kind. The staff took over the rooms formerly occupied by 'the family' (who had skedaddled to Canada at the outbreak of war). The girls endured primitive conditions that till then none of them had even heard of in stories. Some of them were removed at once by loving, worried parents. Alys knew that that would not be her lot, and suffered less than most at the physical discomforts that ensued. If she was cold and hungry and cut off in the middle of nowhere, so was the hated Miss Barfield. She was astute enough to observe that lady being very British, very stiff-upper-lipped, and very irritated nevertheless at the change in her comfortable lifestyle. She was short-tempered with everybody – her staff, her pupils and the workmen who were everywhere, trying to seal the worst leaks in the roof or make antiquated water-closets work. They were mostly young, seemingly stolid East Anglian types who had not yet been called up, a species that Miss Barfield had hitherto never been called upon to deal with. She took them at face value, quite misjudging their native ability and their innate gift of wry, sly, humorous wit that often left her stinging from getting the worst of a verbal encounter.

Try as the staff might, it was no easy matter to maintain discipline and exercise the strict supervision that had been the rule at Cedary Hall. Supplies were short, and though the war was still in its early stages, a vigorous campaign of 'make-do-and-mend' was instigated as a counterbalance to rising costs and falling profits. One result of this was a plethora of gum-pots everywhere. It was one of these that led Alys to hit upon a momentous plan for carrying out her escape from Miss Barfield and getting sent home in disgrace.

She had been set to mend the broken backs of some worn-out dictionaries as a punishment for being found speaking to one of the workmen. She had an open pot of runny gum in front of her, with a brush sticking through its lid. Her ears warned her of Miss Barfield's approach, and quick as thought she whipped the rubber-band from the end of her plait, pulled her hair loose and knocked the brush sideways, neatly timing the tip-over of the pot to the moment the headmistress paused beside her. The gum splashed on to the desk and ran over, dripping stickily around the lady's beautiful brown brogues.

'You stupid girl!' said Miss Barfield, withdrawing with much self-control and discipline the hand she had raised to slap Alys. 'You did that on purpose!'

'I didn't, Miss Barfield. You made me jump.'

'I will make you jump, if you do not pull yourself together at once. No, Dominic! No!'

Her command was too late. The dog had pattered through the gum that was oozily spreading out over the floor. Unfortunately for herself, Alys had seen the dog first, and not wanting him to be distressed, had leaned forward to try to prevent his approach. Her loosened hair trailed over the gum-covered desk and books, and in trying to rescue the straggling ends, she took hold of the mass of it with gum-covered hands. It was all too much for Miss Barfield's self-control. She slapped Alys hard, and shouted, raising her voice in a most unladylike fashion.

'Get this mess cleared up, and then go to your room and stay there till I tell you you may come down! You are not fit to mix with decent girls! I cannot and will not endure that hair of yours any longer. Get it cut off at the very first opportunity! If you don't, I will cut it myself.' She went, crushing the dishevelled gum-covered girl under every step, or so it seemed. Alys giggled, from tension mixed with some apprehension; but Miss Barfield did not turn again, and Alys bent to her task of clearing up the mess she had made. By the time she reached her cold and comfortless dormitory that night, the gum had set on her hair, and there was no hot water anywhere to help her get it off.

'Whatever did you do it for?' asked Kate, the prefect who was in charge of the 'dorm', and who was kind to Alys on the whole, when Alys would give her a chance to be.

'To aggravate Miss Barfield, I suppose,' said Alys, who was nearer to tears than she would admit. 'She's always on at me about my hair. She ordered me to get it cut off, today. She says if I don't get it cut, she'll cut it off herself.'

'She won't do that, you know,' said Susan. 'She'd be scared of what your mother would say, or that your father would take you away. She wouldn't want to lose the fees they pay.'

Alys's throat ached. As if her mother or father would notice if Miss Barfield shaved her head bare! And her father would be willing to double the fees he paid, rather than have her home again.

'Has anybody got a pair of big scissors?' she asked, rummaging in her locker.

'What for?'

'I'm going to cut if off – short. Now!'

There was a gasp. 'Oh Alys, you couldn't!' said Kate. 'You mustn't!'

'I must, and I can,' said Alys. 'Only it will take a long time, with these.' She held up a small pair of curved nail scissors, the only ones she had.

The group of girls gathered round her as she began to naggle the long strands off, bit by bit, as close to her head as possible.

'Fetch Matron, Sue,' said Kate, afraid of the consequences.

Alys sprang to the door. 'Don't you dare!' she said. 'If anybody tries to, I'll stab her!'

Julia, a mousey girl at the spotty stage, pulled on Kate's sleeve. 'She's mad,' said Julia. 'My mum said she looked as mad as a hatter, when she saw her the first day of term.'

'Oh did she?' said Alys. 'Well, she was right. I'm mad all right!' She glared menacingly at Julia.

'I'm frightened,' Julia whimpered, clinging to Kate, and Alys (who had only meant to convey that she was 'mad' with anger) saw that she had been taken quite literally. Julia's fear had begun to infect the others, too.

'Let's shout, altogether,' suggested Kate.

'Better not, till I've finished this,' said Alys, gesturing with her scissors.

Kate sprang back, as if Alys had meant it as a threat.

Alys's spirits were rising every second, and in fact she was beginning to enjoy herself. She saw that if she could hold her own for the next five minutes, she would never be an insignificant nobody in the dormitory again. They might not like her any better than they had done, but they wouldn't ignore her, either.

The last bits of hair yielded to the blunt little scissors, leaving her with rat's-tails of jagged ends round a little shorn poll. The blonde locks lay on the floor at her feet.

'Gosh! Maggie Tulliver!' said Kate, and distressed as she was, there was a note of reluctant admiration in her voice.

Alys responded with a surprised grin. She hadn't expected anybody present to guess the source of her inspiration, not giving them the credit for ever having met Maggie, to whom Miss Allen had introduced her along with Keats. Alys was, for a moment, in danger of forgetting her new role as a madwoman, more akin to Mr Rochester's wife than the heroine of *The Mill on the Floss*. There was an instant when it might all have ended quite differently, had not mousey Julia intervened. She was hiding behind Kate, from where she took courage to jeer at Alys's appearance.

'She won't half catch it when Matron sees her! And Miss Barfield. Look at her! She *is* mad, like my mum said. Mad Maggie! Mad Maggie!'

'Shut up, Julia,' said Kate, clapping her hand over Julia's mouth. 'Somebody's coming!'

The girls melted into their beds, suddenly aware that they were quaking with cold and quivering with apprehension. Alys kicked the sawn-off plaits under the nearest bed and made a dive for her own, but the heavy footsteps continued past the door. It would not have been so at Cedary House. Kate didn't know whether she was relieved or not.

'They'll see you in the morning, anyway. You can't get away with it,' she whispered to Alys. Alys knew that of all of them, Kate was the one who didn't mean to be unkind to her.

'She said I had to get it cut,' Alys whispered back. 'She doesn't have to know that you all watched me do it.'

'I shall tell my mother,' said Julia. 'I'm not going to be left in here with somebody mad.'

'Will you shut up, Julia?' said Kate. 'Maybe they'll be too busy to notice, Alys.'

Alys fingered the ragged ends of her hair, and thought that was too much to hope for; but Julia's outburst had given her an idea so splendid that she forgot how cold and miserable she was. She would convince them all that she was genuinely mad. She didn't know quite where it would get her, but anywhere, even an asylum, would be better than Viney Chase with Miss Barfield in it. And just imagine the effect on her parents of having her sent home, declared insane!

There was less fuss than there might have been, next morning, for a variety of reasons. The ragged ends had curled in a way not even Alys might have expected, and the worst of the visual aspect of her deed was reduced. Matron was at her wits' end with general problems, and Miss Barfield lay low and said nothing. She didn't want to lose either another pupil, or her precious dignity, and wisely decided on discretion as the better part of valour. Alys felt let down by the lack of fuss, and made up her mind to think of other ways of convincing everybody that she was indeed 'potty'. Though Julia's nickname for her stuck, Julia herself didn't. She failed to return after the Christmas vacation, her mother having needed only the mousey girl's story of 'Mad Maggie' to tip the balance already slightly weighted towards removing her darling child from the discomforts of Viney Chase to a pampered home again. So Christmas came and went, with little relief and no pleasure to Alys other than that of being made much of by Louie. By the time term began again, one of the worst winters for decades had set in, and everybody's mind and energy at the school was turned to personal survival in the intense cold. The war was in its 'cold' phase, too, and bothered them less than the weather. Everyone at Viney Chase was so numbed with cold as to reach a point of apathy akin to lethargic amnesia, even Alys.

But spring came at last. The woods budded and the birds nested; squirrels mated and primroses and bluebells bloomed; and Hitler began his onslaught on the Low Countries, which ended in the evacuation of the BEF from Dunkirk. Food was scarcer than it had been, and the girls at Viney Chase began to be really hungry, as distinct from always wanting more than they were given, which was usually the case.

Alys had almost given up her design to become insane, partly through the general apathy, and partly because her relationship with the rest of the girls in her dormitory had improved after Julia had left.

The surrounding woodlands were out of bounds to the girls, but there were no physical obstacles to keep them out. Alys found consolation and solace – even the beginnings of joy – in the silken primrose-scented greenness of the early summer. She slipped away for long walks by herself, watched baby rabbits play, counted the eggs in a thrush's nest day by day, gathered bluebells by the armful, and read her favourite books sitting on the moss under an old oak tree. It wasn't always warm, or always dry, but it was always solitary. She began to think, somewhat ruefully, that she was acting much more sanely than she had been for a long time, and that it might be a great deal more difficult now to convince all and sundry that she was mad than it would have been in the previous autumn. The truth was that she was becoming reconciled a bit to Viney Chase, as the pain of being torn away from Abbey Street lessened with the passing of time.

Then, while the world rocked at the speed of the German advance across Europe, Alys caught a chill and became feverish. Matron decided that she must be moved from the dormitory at once, not for her own welfare, but in case it should prove to be the beginning of an infectious illness. There was a floor above Alys's dormitory which was not in general use. She was moved into a room there, put to bed, and told on no account to get up till Matron herself should visit her and give the word.

She wasn't hungry, and for the first twenty-four hours barely noticed that nobody came near her. On the second day, hunger began to reassert itself, and she looked forward to lunchtime, but nobody came. She drank the stale water from her carafe, and resigned herself to wait for supper. By breakfast time next morning, she was starving and a bit scared. She got dressed and decided to go down, only to find the door at the end of the corridor leading to the back staircase bolted against her, as it would have been in days gone by when only the servants used rooms on the top floor. She regarded her situation without much panic, so used to relying on her 'sole self' that she accepted the truth of what had happened without much surprise. She guessed that Matron had forgotten to report that she had been put up there; the girls had thought she was in the ordinary sick bay; and somebody (probably Miss Barfield on the prowl) had found the door unlocked, and promptly dealt with it.

Alys looked out of the window, and to her relief, saw some workmen on the ground directly below her. So she could shout, and beg them to go and find somebody. But caution advised against such a commonplace course of action. It could be risky. They might not believe her and simply ignore her, thinking she had been locked up as a punishment, or something. Then it might be days before anybody came within hailing distance again. Next, if the men succeeded in getting somebody up to her, whoever came would put her back to bed, and the most important thing of all to her now was to get at food. It was almost lunchtime, and the thought of food, even such as was provided at Viney Chase in wartime, pulled at her like a powerful magnet. She had to go towards it, fearing that it would not come her way if she were put back into bed.

She gathered up her dressing-gown, nightdress and toilet things, and made them into a bundle. Then she opened the window wide, and looked down. An ancient drainpipe was within reach of the stone sill. Next moment, Alys was on the sill, her bundle beside her. But she needed both hands on the pipe, so she took the bundle in her teeth, and began her descent. By the time she got as far as the floor below, she knew she couldn't do the rest with the bundle, and would have to let it drop on or near to the workmen below, who so far hadn't noticed her. Of course they would raise a hue and cry when they did, but it would be too late to stop her by the time anybody got there. She would be down by then, one way or another. She rested on the sill of a window directly below the one she had started from. When ready to continue, she shouted, 'Hi! Catch!'

A workman looked up – in fact all three did; but for all the reaction they showed at seeing a long-legged schoolgirl balanced precariously on a window-ledge forty feet from the ground above them, they might as well have been watching a rather tame circus act. They simply stood stolidly below her, gawping; so Alys dropped her bundle. The youngest of them caught it neatly, and set it on the ground. Then they watched, without comment, as Alys grasped the drainpipe again, and clambered safely to the ground.

'Well, as I go to school!' said one, by way of exclamation. They returned to their work.

She now had the embarrassment of her bundle, because the bell had rung for lunch, and she daren't risk trying to get it back to her dorm. So she hid it under an old stone seat in another part of the overgrown garden, and like a homing pigeon made for the dining hall. She joined the end of the queue with some trepidation, fearing that the sight of her might jog the memory of somebody, teacher or domestic staff, as to where she was supposed to be. But she collected her meal, and sat down with it unnoticed. She was ravenous, and gobbled it down, feeling that it was no more than a tit-bit thrown to a dog. When the first sitting rose and left, she obeyed her hungry instinct and went back to join the queue again, for the second sitting. In doing so, she met both the under-matron and Miss Barfield face to face. Neither registered the least interest in her. Nor did the servers who had filled her first plate half an hour before. It seemed that as far as her physical presence went, she might as well have been invisible, even climbing down a drainpipe from the top storey of a pseudo castle. When the rest of the girls returned to their classrooms, she was in a dilemma. Safety lay in the herd, as at lunchtime; but she had to pick up her bundle, somehow, and get it back to the dormitory. She went to the lavatory, and locked herself in to think out the next moves, and there she reached a staggering sort of conclusion. It wasn't just herself that was 'invisible'. Everybody was invisible to everybody else, except where absolute routine was concerned. The adult staff were so preoccupied with the news from the front; so apprehensive of the air-raids just beginning; so worried or grieved about husbands, sons and brothers in the forces; so wretched physically in the conditions Viney Chase had to offer; so miserable to be cut off in East Anglia from their north Midland roots – in fact, so generally unhappy all round that all feelings were turned selfishly inward, and other people, especially the pupils at the school, simply did not matter. Rules and regulations were carried out by habit, not by conscious thought, and anything that was not in the tramline of routine was either not noticed, or dismissed as too much trouble to be bothered with 'for the time being'.

While Alys did not exactly work all this out in detail as she sat cogitating on the toilet, she did sense vaguely the general gist of it. Moreover, she saw that the girls were in no better case than the adults. The reason why everything had so far gone along at Viney Chase fairly smoothly and without major catastrophes was that the girls in their wretchedness were also obeying the force of habit. They conformed because it was the habit to conform and in their apathetic discomfort couldn't even bother to be naughty, or exploit the adults' mental preoccupation with other things.

Having worked out that if she could climb down a drainpipe in full view and get away with it, get two good dinners even though food was scarce without comment, and absent herself – albeit unwillingly – from classes and meals for three days, she decided that she could boldly cross the garden and go for a walk in the woods. If she were challenged, she would say she had been sent out for a walk because she had been ill. Then she would pick up her bundle on the way back, and appear in the dormitory as usual before suppertime, as if she had merely returned there from sick bay.

She spent a delightful afternoon in the woods, and went further afield than she had ever been before. And in a little clearing, she had first a scare, and then a wonderful find. Under the trees stood an old gypsy caravan, its colours faded and its carvings broken, but apparently whole. She thought at first that somebody must be camping there, but a few minutes' observation from behind a tree convinced her that it was derelict. So she explored it to her heart's content, which didn't take much doing, because it was quite empty. A wooden bench ran down one side of it – seat or couch as required. Nothing else. But it was perfect. She had a place of her own, to go to whenever she liked.

Her heart rose as she went back out of the door of it and sat on the front driving board, imagining a horse in the shafts. Then above her, to crown the magic moment, a bird began to sing, and she knew instinctively that it was a nightingale, broad afternoon though it was. The tears trickled down her face unheeded as she recited the ode through to herself, responding both to the poetry and to its associations. Courage and determination returned to her in full strength. It occurred to her as she walked back to school that she was probably the sanest person in the whole establishment. At least she knew what she was trying to do, which was more than most of them did.

She sauntered into the dorm, carrying her rolled-up bundle, and threw it nonchalantly on to her bed. Leaves stuck to her shoes, and she had the casual air of untidiness and relaxation of someone just returned from a weekend's camping.

'Mad Maggie's back,' said Susan to Kate, and Kate turned to look at her. Kate was sixteen, and some inklings of adult responsibility were beginning to dawn on her. She flushed guiltily as she looked at Alys, because it was quite evident that this girl she was looking at had not come back from sick bay, and Kate realized that she ought to have enquired about Alys's whereabouts and welfare from somebody long before now.

Guilt always puts people on the defensive, and Kate used attack as her own best defence against negligence of prefectorial duty.

'Gosh, Maggie, you do look a mess! Where on earth have you been?'

'In the woods,' said Alys, shortly but truthfully.

Kate looked at the bundle. 'In your nightie and dressing-gown?' she asked sarcastically.

'Yes,' said Alys, lying happily at the fuss she was causing.

'In the middle of the day?' Incredulity was beginning to turn to apprehension. The other girls gathered round to hear the rest of the exchange. 'You really *are* mad!' said Kate, wondering whom she could tell, and how much anybody would believe her.

'Don't be daft,' said Alys. 'Of course I haven't been wearing my nightie in the middle of the day.' She spoke without thinking, and saw, not her mistake, but her opportunity, immediately.

'You didn't sleep in the woods! You couldn't! You wouldn't dare! All by yourself?' That was Susan. Poor Kate was crushed under the awful thoughts that were forming themselves willy-nilly in her mind. Alys had been in disgrace once before for chatting to a young workman. She surely hadn't been going out to 'sleep' with him in the woods? Kate saw expulsion looming for herself as well as Alys, if that were the case, and Miss Barfield ever found out. Somehow, she had to cope with Alys by herself, and that, in effect, meant shielding her, and saying nothing of her escapade, if that were possible.

Alys, having re-established herself as the centre of the dormitory's attention, was prepared to exploit the situation to its fullest advantage.

'I was hungry,' she said, guilefully simple. 'I've come back for some food and a bath. Then I'm going back to my caravan to sleep. Not tonight. But I will tomorrow.'

'Your *what*?' gasped Kate. 'Did you say your *caravan*?'

'Don't talk to her, Kate,' said Sue, urgently. 'You can tell she's bonkers!'

'What caravan?' persisted Kate, suspiciously, adding significantly, following her own suspicion, 'Whose caravan?'

'Mine,' said Alys. 'I found it, in the wood. It doesn't belong to anybody else, so it's mine now. And I'm going to sleep there always.'

'You wouldn't dare!' said Diana. 'All night by yourself, in a caravan? What if the Germans come?'

'What if the gypsy who owns it comes back?' That was Chrissie.

'What if you see a ghost?' asked Penny, shuddering.

'She's just showing off,' said Susan. 'Or else it's because she really is mad. Nobody would dare to!' Then she turned on Alys. 'You're just making it all up. You won't dare even to go out when it's dark, let alone sleep out! And how would you *get* out? Don't talk rot, Mad Maggie.'

Alys was nettled by Susan. 'Yes I dare, then. And I will. Only you'll all have to swear not to tell on me!' She grabbed a Bible, which by Miss Barfield's rule lay on every girl's locker, from the nearest one. The bell rang for supper. Alys went to the door with the Bible in her hand, much as she had once stood there with her nail scissors.

'Touch the Bible as you go out,' she said. 'That means you won't tell anybody about my caravan, ever!'

Kate saw immediately the advantage to herself of keeping all the others quiet, especially as to where Alys might have been last night. So she nodded to the others, and herself touched the Bible, saying, 'I swear.' The rest followed her like sheep through a gap. It was exciting for the dorm to have a secret, just as in a school story, and not one of them really expected Alys to go through with her dare. They filed out to supper less dully than they had done since coming to Viney Chase.

Alys washed herself hastily and followed them. She was still hungry after her three days of involuntary fasting, and for the moment thought of nothing but the food in prospect.

Later, as they lay in bed in the summer twilight, she began to have doubts as to whether she might not have bitten off more than she could chew, but she had to go through with it now, come what might. She comforted herself by remembering the nightingale. She sat up on her elbow, and said, in the hoarse whisper they habitually used at night, 'Do you know why I like to sleep in the wood? It's because of the nightingales. I bet you didn't even know there were nightingales there. Did you?'

'Nor do you,' said Susan, crossly, because she would hardly have known a nightingale's song from a jackass braying. 'So shut up! We'll believe you when we see you go.'

'That'll be the day!' scoffed Diana.

'You mean the night,' giggled Chrissie.

'You'll have to wait till after lock-up, or we shan't believe you,' said Penny. 'So how will you get out, Maggie?'

'Down the drainpipe,' said Alys.

'Oh, be quiet and go to sleep,' ordered Kate. She felt less worried, all of a sudden. Of course Alys wouldn't be able to get out. She might be mad, but she was neither witch nor fairy, and couldn't fly. How stupid she had been to believe Mad Maggie's wild tales. She had probably been in the sick bay all the time.

As the next day wore on, Alys's courage waned a bit, but her resolution never wavered at all. She had to get away from Viney Chase, and even more so from Miss Barfield, in whose person was summed up the total of Alys's unhappiness. It was not that she wanted to go home, because she was as unwanted there as here (in spite of which she yearned for what it meant to other girls). She had no real hope of getting back to Abbey Street Grammar, especially if she could only escape from here by proving herself mad. If she had been able to reason it out at all, she would have understood that what was motivating her was a desire to do something positive to counterbalance all the hopeless negatives that had beset her short existence so far.

To be hauled back ignominiously before she got away tonight would be worse than not making the attempt at all. That meant she would have to wait until after bedtime, and get out via the drainpipe after dark. The weather was warm, the nights had been fine. All the same, it would be necessary to wrap up, and carry an extra covering of some sort. Food would be a great problem. She'd just have to be hungry, and trust to luck to getting back in before breakfast next day.

She rolled an extra cardigan into her dressing-gown, and tied it with the cord, making a loop to go over her shoulders like a rucksack. Then she got into bed fully clothed, and waited for the moon to come up.

'She's just waiting for us to go to sleep. Then she'll undress and get into bed, and in the morning pretend she's been and come back.'

It was the coming back that had begun to worry Alys. If

anything did happen to prevent her from spending the night safely, how was she to get in again? She didn't doubt her ability to climb up the drainpipe as well as down it – but would they open the window? Better not ask. Better not show the least sign of dependence or weakness. Better go now, before further doubts set in.

She scrambled out of bed, put on her warmest jumper, and opened the window as gently as she could. (If the workmen had progressed as they should have done, it would have been barred by regulation. As it was, egress was still free and, to as she found, easy.)

Kate, terrified, watched her climb on to the sill. She knew she ought to rush out and report – but what might be the consequences of that, now? She should have done it yesterday. The other girls were timidly shocked, and guiltily, tensely apprehensive. It wasn't half such a lark as it had promised to be, now that they saw Alys meant what she had said.

She went down the pipe like a monkey, and keeping to the shadows, made away from the house. At the boundary of garden and woodland, she turned to look back. Kate was leaning out of the dorm window, straining to catch a glimpse of which direction Alys was taking. The fugitive saw Kate's strained face in a shaft of moonlight, and felt more affection for the older girl at that moment than she had ever done before for any other of her own generation. Kate would have a far worse time tonight than she would.

Now that she was out, though, she was happy, and not in the least afraid of anything. She found the caravan with ease, and lay down on the bench, wrapped in her dressing-gown, with her head on her spare cardigan. She hoped that the nightingale would oblige, but it failed her. Instead, she heard the snortings and snufflings of a pair of hedgehogs, which did not disturb her because she knew what the noise was. So she lay very still, and sleep came almost at once.

She was roused a couple of hours later by the barking of a dog at no great distance away. Alarmed, she strained her ears for information, and to her horror soon distinguished heavy footsteps. The voices of her dormmates rang in her head as her heart began to race and the blood to fill her head. She dared hardly to breathe.

Suppose the Germans come! Suppose the gypsy comes back! Suppose you see a ghost?

She shut her eyes tight and lay tense and rigid as the footsteps – human and canine – drew nearer.

Stifled with fear and petrified with the terror of not knowing what to expect, she listened to the sniffings and fumblings at the caravan's broken door. Next minute, a stabbing beam of light probed her refuge and in its glow she recognized the blunt snout of Dominic. The panic she had felt before receded, leaving a different kind of fear in its place. She was, after all, only a thirteen-year-old schoolgirl, and in spite of herself and her determination to rebel, still in awe of authority in the shape of Miss Barfield. And the shape of Miss Barfield it certainly was, standing in the doorway.

'Alys?' said the hated voice. 'Alys, are you in there?'

Alys cursed her dormitory companions with all the strength of her tormented young heart. They must have chickened out, and told on her, after all. If not, how did Miss Barfield know where to come? She lay still, and did not answer the voice. The woman and the dog climbed into the van, and the merciless torch was directed full into Alys's face.

'Alys!' said Miss Barfield sharply.

Alys sat up, dragging her dressing-gown round her. 'Where am I?' she said, putting on as lost an expression as she could. 'Where am I?' She sprang off the bench, and looked wildly around her. 'Who brought me here? I want to go home!'

Miss Barfield shone the torch on to her own face, and then on to Dominic. Alys let out a little scream, and drew away, jumping back on to the bench, as far as she could get.

'Come along now, there's a good girl. I've come to take you back to school.'

'Who are you? Go away! Take your dog off me!'

Dominic had always liked Alys, and was trying frantically to lick her face.

'I'm Miss Barfield, Alys. Dominic won't hurt you. You know him well, don't you? He likes you, that's all.'

Alys heard the change in the woman's voice, and knew she had got the self-assured headmistress considerably perplexed and rattled.

The teacher took hold of the girl, prepared to use force to remove her, if necessary. She pulled with some vigour, and nearly lost her equilibrium altogether when Alys came suddenly, without resistance. At that moment a bird began to trill.

'Hark, hark, the lark,' said Alys wildly, uttering the first words that came into her head. She nearly giggled at the effect it had on Miss Barfield. Her act was really going well now. She knew perfectly well that the singer was a nightingale, and that knowledge sent ideas racing through her brain. She held up one finger in Miss Barfield's face, as if to command silence. Miss Barfield recoiled.

'It is the nightingale, and not the lark,' Alys proclaimed in a hoarse whisper. Miss Barfield was fast losing her grip, consumed now with anxiety and the problem of getting her mad pupil into custody, with no aid but that of her dog.

'Away! Away! for I will fly with thee!' said Alys, giving the woman a beaming smile and making for the door of the van. She picked up her cardigan, and plonked it in the teacher's hands, as a Roman matron might have handed a garment to an attendant slave. Miss Barfield meekly took it, and arranged it neatly over her arm.

Alys deliberately set off in the wrong direction, and had the pleasure of seeing Miss Barfield skipping about in the moonlight with Dominic at the full stretch of his lead, for all the world like an inexperienced shepherd trying to shed a recalcitrant sheep from a flock.

'Come along, dear, there's a good girl. We'll soon have you back in your nice cosy bed in school.' This motherly rôle sat very uncomfortably on the lady who had always deputed any caring for her pupils to a paid assistant trained in such matters.

'In school?' repeated Alys, crinkling her brow and turning a perplexed face towards Miss Barfield in the moonlight. 'What school?' She was striding freely along beside the principal now, much to that lady's relief. She had to humour Alys at all costs, till she could get her charge within reach of other assistance. She spoke to the girl as one might to a backward toddler who had to be coaxed to put his coat on.

'Our nice school at Viney Chase. Don't you remember? We all came here because of the war.'

Alys put on a look of dawning recollection, cocking her head on one side as if trying to remember. Then she began to whimper, and made as if to turn away, or even to bolt.

'No,' she whimpered. 'Don't take me back there!' She looked wildly round her, and then quoted in a dismal whisper:

'Here, where men sit and hear each other groan;
Where youth grows pale, and spectre-thin, and dies.'

She was aware of the shock her words caused Miss Barfield, and was about to continue with the next line when she hit on the notion of making it more personally apt. She skipped in front of her teacher, thus bringing the woman to a sudden halt, and peered searchingly into her face. Her voice quavered (she was struggling with an hysterical desire to laugh) as she delivered her verbal blow, and made the words sound positively sepulchral:

'Where palsy shakes a few, sad, last, grey hairs.'

Miss Barfield gasped at the insult, comforting herself that the child was indubitably deranged beyond hope of recovery.

'Come! Come!' she said, over and over again, as a farmer's wife might apostrophize a sick cow.

Alys, in a dazed, pathetic fashion, held out her hand and Miss Barfield took it. Alys trotted along like a weary toddler, with her head hanging down.

'I cannot see what flowers are at my feet,
 Nor what soft incense hangs upon the boughs,'

she said. She stopped, and gazed upwards.

'Oh Alys, please come with me.' There was a distinct quiver in the firm tones now. Alys decided to let well alone and, clinging to her guide's hand, walked obediently along on the opposite side to Dominic. She had remembered Miss Allen explaining the meaning of the next stanza that declares fancy to be a deceiving elf that cannot cheat as well as she is famed to do. She'd pushed fancy rather far already, she thought, and the bleak stones of the school were now in sight anyway.

As they approached the heavy doors, Alys sighed ostentatiously and shook her head.

'Was it a vision, or a waking dream?
 . . . Do I wake or sleep?'

she queried, earnestly.

'You are not well, Alys. Matron will put you into bed, and in the morning we will get a doctor to you.'

'Thank you, Miss Barfield,' said Alys, in a perfectly normal voice. 'Wasn't Dominic a clever dog to find me?'

The sudden return to apparent normality utterly demoralized Miss Barfield. She left Alys standing, and went to find Matron, who had been alerted before she set out and was standing by with cups of hot cocoa. Matron said little as she tucked Alys into the bed in the room on the top storey, the one from which she had escaped down the drainpipe less than seventy-two hours before. But this time the bed was warm with hot-water bottles, and there were sandwiches and steaming cocoa by its side. Alys was neither disturbed nor surprised to hear the bolt on the door click as Matron went out. She demolished her extra supper with relish, and cuddling the hot-water bottle drifted blissfully off to sleep, giggling as she remembered Miss Barfield's face when she had quoted the line about the last grey hairs.

Breakfast was brought to her in bed, and she began to

wonder what line she was going to take when the doctor arrived; but at breaktime Matron came again, and sat down by her side. She had the air of one whose difficult task it was to break bad news.

'There has been a phone call from your father's office,' she said. 'A bomb fell close to your home last night.'

Alys shot up in bed, terror flooding through her. If her parents were dead and she had last night convinced Miss Barfield that she was genuinely mad, what *would* happen to her?

'No, no,' Matron was saying, pushing her down on the pillows and stroking her forehead. 'No one was hurt, at all. But it has made your father decide to move your mother away to safety, to a cottage in the West Country. You are to join her there as soon as ever we can pack your things. Miss Barfield's own car will take you as far as Cambridge, and your father has arranged to meet you there.'

Alys was limp. No sort of reaction shook her at all. She saw no one else at all before the assistant matron came to see her off. She had hoped for a kind word with Kate, but she was dispatched quickly while all the girls were still at lunch, and her last glimpse of Viney Chase was of Dominic cocking his leg up against a tree.

So had begun a new phase of her life with her mother, but without Louie, who had gone into munition works, or her father, who of course could not leave either his business or his secretary.

It was not until twenty years later, when her father had died and she was going through his personal effects, that she was able to satisfy her curiosity as to whether her removal from Viney Chase had been demanded by Miss Barfield or whether her escapade had gratuitously coincided with a heaven-sent bomb, from her father's point of view. No doubt he had long had in his mind a plan of action to get rid of her mother. The letter to her father had been in Miss Barfield's own hand.

Your telephone message of this morning, instructing me to

arrange for Alys to join her mother at once, came as a great relief to me and my staff, as I was just about to request you to remove her from our care. I regret to have to inform you that we have found Alys rude, disobedient and a disruptive influence on the other girls. Indeed, I am afraid I must say quite bluntly that I consider her deranged and in need of urgent psychiatric treatment if there is to be any hope of her becoming a normal, sane adult.

I note that you are willing to pay a term's fees in lieu of the required notice. I am happy to accept that arrangement.

Alys had been hurt and shocked to read that letter, though by that time she was a university don in her own right and the mother of three lovely children. Her parents had never once asked her anything about her life at Viney Chase, or given her the least chance to explain. They had simply accepted and believed Miss Barfield's assertion, and selfishly hushed everything up. How absolutely typical – especially her father's willingness to buy his freedom to enjoy life with Miss Bellairs at the cost of a term's school fees. And how ironically true it was of Miss Barfield that she would be 'happy' to accept the cheque, while ostentatiously washing her hands of a child so much in need as Alys had been then.

Alys's mouth was quivering, and her eyes stinging as tears gathered under the lids at the memory of that letter. She pulled herself together, and looked at her watch. The reverie in which she had relived that bit of her childhood had lasted less than ten minutes. She lit another cigarette, noting that the last had smouldered into a strip of ash in the hotel ashtray at her elbow.

Then the door clicked, and several people came in, all talking at once. The proprietor let himself through the bar flap and began to dispense drinks.

'Oh yes – dead as mutton, by the time I got there,' he was saying. 'The dog as well.'

'Did you know her?' asked someone at the bar.

'Well, I'd seen her going by here, often enough, pushing that dog in a pram. I asked a policeman down there about her. They all knew her. Seems she was an educated sort, name of Barfield, who used to be a teacher once. Came here to retire, about twelve years ago – well, when that old dog that got killed just now was a tiny puppy. But she went clean off her head – not violent like, but potty, absolutely cracked in a harmless sort of way. So they couldn't do anything about it, only take her home when they found her wandering about. She used to walk the streets all night sometimes, especially if it was moonlight, pushing that old dog in a pram, talking to herself out loud. Well, spouting poetry is what the copper said. Poor old soul. Nasty end to come to, all the same.'

He turned towards Alys as she reached the bar. 'Yes, madam? What can I get you?'

Alys, for the first time in her life, ordered a double whisky.

Death by Misadventure

'Get in!' he ordered, growling oaths under his breath, though just loud enough for her father to hear the gist, if not the actual words. 'I thought you said you wanted to get home.'

She paused to wave once more to her mother, who was hovering in the door of the house. Jerry slammed the door of the car so hard that she only moved her hand away just in time. She could see that her father was saying something, so she wound down the window while her husband went round to the driver's side. She had to do all she possibly could to reassure her parents that everything was fine, now that Jerry had come at last to pick her up.

He started the engine, revving it unnecessarily so as to drown her father's parting injunction to him to drive carefully.

'There's a lot of fog about tonight,' the old man said. 'I just heard it on the ten o'clock news. Be careful going along the Pringle Bank.'

Jerry ground his teeth and let in the clutch so suddenly that the car leapt forward and stalled. Then it roared down the narrow drive and swept into the side street before Anne had time to wind up the window or grope for her safety belt.

'Bloody old fool,' Jerry said. 'Does he think I can't drive? Or does he think I'm drunk?'

Anne played with the clasp of her seat belt, fighting for composure, before replying. Answer him she must, because she knew of old that nothing would poke the smouldering fire of his anger so much as silence on her part. She didn't think he was drunk – she knew he was, as she had known for the past two hours that he would be when at last he came. The moment she had seen his face as he opened the door of her mother's sitting-room, she feared the worst. A little less drink, and he would have been pleasant and witty, courteously soothing her parents' irritation with the cultured charm he could always exercise over them when he tried. A few drinks more, and he would have accepted black coffee, and then let her drive home. As it was, he had just had enough to make him nasty, impossible to reach either by reasoned argument or by loving, submissive acceptance. In any case, things between them had been so bad just lately that she knew that whatever she said or did would be wrong, and she sensed that he was in the mood for the sort of quarrel that so often led to violence.

She had to say something, but her mind refused to function, and her throat was so tight that it hurt. She went on fumbling with her belt, and fear began to set in. One thing she knew, which comforted her a little, was that he was an excellent driver, and never more so than when he had had a little too much alcohol. It was as if he had some sort of in-built adjuster, that made him able to measure for himself the exact level of his clouded judgement. She had often wondered about this, because it was in some strange way alien to the rest of him. He acted at such times like a child who has been made to learn a lesson, like writing with the right hand when every instinct urged him to use the left. Whatever the cause, it served her in good stead, so she didn't question it. It belonged, like the other women in his life, to the past, and didn't concern her. On the other hand, the mess he had made of getting away, just now, with her father watching, had infuriated him beyond bearing. She'd have to be extra patient, that's all.

She'd been waiting for him for four hours and more. He had been supposed to pick her up at six o'clock, on his way home from work. She had left home for her work, with him, at eight o'clock that morning, and all she had had to sustain her was two crispbread biscuits and an apple – and endless cups of coffee and cigarettes. She had declined the invitation to share the evening meal at her parents' house, partly out of expectation that he would come at any minute, though mostly because of his predictable anger if she didn't cook for and eat with him when they reached home. She was tired, strained, hungry and un-happy, tense through and through with the effort of pretend-ing to her parents that all was well. They had never quite approved of her marrying Jerry. They liked him, but were not at ease with him, and though they had never actually said so, he was not the sort of man they had hoped Anne would marry. But then, nobody really fitted that category. She had been aware that in that respect she would probably never please them, from the time they had taken her away from the local technical school, where she was doing a secretarial course, because of her friend-ship with a plumber's apprentice she had met there. She had always treasured the memory of Mac, her first, and she some-times thought, her only real love. Her parents hadn't any idea what Mac was like. They had reacted to the word 'plumber' and she had been forbidden ever to see or write to him again. She had had no option, at seventeen, and he had understood, and didn't try to fight the decree. But he had said, 'Whatever happens, I shall always love you. And if you ever really need me . . .' but the sentence was never finished, because he turned and walked away. She had never seen him since.

If only she could reach Jerry, as she had reached Mac, down into the depths that were really him, but she couldn't. Most of the time they were reasonably happy, but situations like this one tonight were getting more and more frequent.

There had been a moment of real difficulty about an hour ago, after the nine o'clock news on television was over, and her father began looking at the clock every two minutes, and making irascible remarks about wanting to be in bed by ten. He wondered sarcastically what could be keeping Jerry.

Anne was quite helpless to do anything but sit and hope. There was no public transport on that day of the week to the remote village ten miles away where they lived, or she wouldn't have been there in the first place. She dared not ask her father to drive her home, or get a taxi (even if she could have found the money to pay for it), because of the consequences when Jerry did eventually turn up. So she squirmed inwardly in frustration and anger, both at her errant husband and her well-meaning but heavy-footed father, who was always trampling on the tender and lacerated spots of her life.

She had lit yet another cigarette, her last, and apologized for the tenth time or so for giving them the trouble and anxiety; but, she explained, she wasn't really surprised at Jerry being so late. He had told her that he had to meet a man late in the afternoon – a chap who was coming down after a conference in Leicester – and he, Jerry, had promised to wait for him till he turned up.

'I should think he was so late that Jerry had to take him for a bar snack, or something,' she said. 'He'll be here soon.'

'As soon as the pubs turn out' might just as well have been spoken aloud by both her parents. All her father said, however, was, 'I shall have to teach that young man how to use a telephone. Might come in very useful to him, some time.'

It was the memory of that remark that suddenly unlocked Anne's lips, and the words tumbled out before she could catch them back.

'Why didn't you phone?' she said.

He trod on the accelerator and the powerful car surged in response. The orange light in front of them turned to red, and the squeal of brakes brought them to a shuddering halt just beyond the stop line. The street lamps showed her his white knuckles as he gripped the wheel, and she waited for the outburst.

'God damn and blast you, you bloody shit-bag! Why the bloody hell should I phone? I'm not your fucking house-boy, at your beck and call day and night! Slavery went out in the last century. Perhaps you and your fucking parents haven't heard the news yet! I'm a free man. Get that into your thick skull. Being married to a bloody tart like you does nothing to alter that! God-all-bloody-mighty, can't I go out for a drink now without having to phone to ask you and your fucking clod-hoppers of a family if I may? Where I am and what I'm doing is no concern of theirs, or of yours. I'll go where I like when I like, and do what I like, and to hell with the whole fucking lot of you!'

'The lights have changed,' she said, in a small, controlled voice. 'Let's get home, Jerry. I really am hungry.'

'OK. If that's what you want, you silly bitch. I'll get you home! What's my record? Eight minutes? All right, we'll do it in seven, tonight.'

The car roared forward. She knew better than to try to dissuade him. All she could do was to sit small and quiet and not do anything to distract his miraculous hairbreadth judgement. In spite of her quivering stomach muscles and the taut fingers gripping her seat belt, she could not but admire the skill with which he took the car at top speed round the roundabout at the end of the town. Then the streetlights petered out, and they were on the lonely 'B' road, full of twists and turns, that would lead them home. He knew every bend in the road, though, and she had often driven it with him before when he had had a few drinks too many. And yet tonight she began to be nervous. She had trained herself not to look at the speedometer when he was in this mood, but she could feel the car gathering speed all the time, and at last glanced at it in spite of herself. It registered 75 m.p.h. and was still pushing upwards.

'I'll get you home, you bloody, fucking, good-for-nothing bitch!' he muttered. 'Seven minutes? I'll do it in six. That'll teach you. So look out – here we go.'

'Jerry! Don't! Jerry!' She couldn't help it.

He laughed, taking his eyes off the road ahead to look down at her as she cringed in her seat, afraid now to look ahead for herself; but of course she had to, treading hard on imaginary brakes as panic mounted. They had turned now into the long, straight, dangerous stretch her father had mentioned, along the river bank. The river itself lay the other side of the high wall that kept its slow-moving waters from spilling out over the flat, low-lying land in flood times. There was a wooden fence halfway up the grassy bank, made of chestnut paling and wire. Anne knew perfectly well that the fence would be no barrier at all against any car, let alone one being driven at speed. All the same, it gave her a psychological feeling of some comfort. At least it marked the road ahead, because the headlamp beam fell on it and picked it out a long way in front of them. It would, at any rate, tell Jerry where the bottom of the bank was, so that he didn't misjudge it on that, the near side. The real danger lay on the other side, where only two feet of bumpy roadside verge lay between the road and a canal, only ten feet or so wide but deep, dark and dank as fenland main drains in winter always are. There was no friendly fence on that side. Only the long bents of dead grass catching the beam of light showed them where the road stopped, and death waited – the Hooky Man Death who pulled unwary fenland travellers into his watery gullet. She had known about him from her early childhood.

The speedometer registered over 80 m.p.h. now. Anne wanted to scream, but she clung to her reason, and tried not to look forward. A line of poetry shot into her head:

> I could not look on Death, which being known,
> Men led me to Him, blindfold and alone.

She was being executed as surely as the cowardly soldier in the poem, and she was just as helpless to prevent the execution being carried to its ghastly conclusion as he was. She raised her eyes, and saw in front a bank of the mist her father had mentioned. A momentary hope that it would slow Jerry down turned to icy fear as he pressed the accelerator down still more and they swept, blinded utterly, into the fog. She thought of her children, her parents, her brothers and sisters, and then she prayed. She really could not have said to whom the prayer went; but before it was properly formed, let alone silently uttered, they were out of the mist and travelling faster than ever, with Jerry's eyes on the fascia-board's clock as much as on the road ahead.

The next bank of fog was thicker and denser, and went on and on. The terror of being trapped in it set off a panic worse than Anne had felt so far. She was trapped, utterly and hope-lessly, in every way. Trapped in the fog, trapped in the car, trapped by her seat belt; trapped by her situation, married to the maniac at her side who loved her only when that love did not interfere with his own desires. The catalogue of her bonds having been gone through, clockwise, she went through it again in reverse, desperately seeking escape. She could not escape from the marriage; she couldn't face divorce again. The fog all round her was metaphorical, as well as real. There was no escape from the car; her seat belt was choking her. That, she had control over, and yet in that alone lay any hope of safety if they did hit the bank. She must not undo it. But what if they went off the road the other side, and down into the drain? She kept her finger on the release button, as thankfully she noted the thinning of the mist, and a clear stretch of road ahead again.

'Right!' said Jerry. 'Now we'll really move.'

She uttered a tiny scream, cutting it off almost before it sounded. But he had heard, and laughed in triumph, exulting that he had conquered her self-control. He told her so, pouring out strings of obscenities such as she had never heard before, even from him at his worst.

Disgust calmed her panic, but her sudden calm was only one of realization that she was doomed. For once Jerry's safety mechanism was going to fail him at a crucial moment, of that she was sure. She sat crouched and silent, waiting for the crash, while thoughts raced through her head. Better dead than crippled, or blinded. Surely, at this speed, death would be instantaneous? Not if they went into the drain. She prayed again, not for rescue, but for instant death. And she thought about those who had truly loved her – her teenage children, her mother and father, her brother and sister; and Mac, who had loved her enough to erase himself from her life rather than create difficulties they couldn't solve. She wondered, longingly, what sort of a life she might have been having now if she had followed her heart then.

'Oh Mac,' she said aloud. 'Oh Mac! Where are you?'

'What did you say?' He broke into his spate of oaths at her voice.

She had forgotten Jerry, shutting her ears to his ravings as her mind sought refuge from danger. She had no idea that she had spoken her thoughts aloud, anyway, and he hadn't heard them. But his question roused her, as she glanced ahead.

'Something in front, Jerry. In the fog. It's the police!' She had caught sight of four pinpoints of light a long way ahead – two white, one blue, one red.

'Fucking bastards! They'd better not try to stop me,' he replied, and drove straight on.

The policeman swinging his torch stood on the edge of the fog, at the bottom of the bank on the near side. The powerful main beam picked him out in the distance as a tall, handsome figure in a police officer's uniform. Anne relaxed. Jerry would have to slow down, now.

Then came the sickening realization that he was not going to stop; that he was behaving just as if the policeman with his torch was not there. He went on bawling oaths, now mainly directed at the police. Twenty yards from the figure with its red torch his voice changed, and rose suddenly to a high-pitched screech – a screech of utter terror, it seemed to Anne. Then he braked at last, and pulled on the wheel, turning the car not away from, but directly and deliberately towards the bank and the man standing on it.

With her last conscious thought, Anne pressed the release button on her safety belt, as if in response to an order she could not disobey.

There were policemen at her side in the hospital. Drifting in and out of a fog of pain and delirium, she knew that the two figures, one each side of the bed, were policemen. It was only after many days that one of them resolved itself into an oxygen apparatus, and the other into a locker. But when memory at last returned unsullied, they told her. She had had a miraculous escape. Jerry was dead.

'The police are waiting to interview you,' the brisk sister said. 'We'll let them know as soon as you feel well enough.'

Of course they would want to know what had happened. She wanted to know, too. They hadn't mentioned the police officer, no doubt out of kindness, but he must have been killed. What should she tell them? That Jerry was under the influence of drink they would have established; but should she tell them that he had driven deliberately straight at the man? Wait a minute, though. Had Jerry done that? Was she certain? Could it not have been that his safety mechanism had functioned again under the stress, forcing a split-second decision that to hit or mount the bank was preferable to going into the drain? But why hadn't he gone straight on? Perhaps because he had deduced that the police were trying to warn him of an obstruction hidden by the fog? She didn't *know*. She would say nothing. The policeman was undoubtedly dead, or very seriously injured, and what she said could make no difference now. And she certainly didn't want to relive that terrible journey, for any reason, if she could possibly get out of doing so.

There were two of them, when they came: a sergeant about her own age, calm and solid, and a young whippersnapper – a whizz-kid who wouldn't be long in uniform, she guessed. They were very kind, and expressed condolences. Like a practised hostess, she found herself trying to put them at ease. The older man began. 'We hate to have to bother you, Mrs Temple, but there are aspects of this case that we don't understand at all – lines to be followed up before the inquest, you understand.' She nodded. 'Could you just tell us in your own words what happened?'

'I don't remember much. We were travelling fast – my husband wanted to get home. I saw a patch of thick fog ahead, and then suddenly there was this policeman, waving his torch to stop us. My husband shouted, and braked. I woke up here.'

She saw the look of surprise on the face of the younger man, and caught the glance he shot at his phlegmatic superior. She'd said something they weren't prepared for, or at least something of significance. It was like playing blind-man's buff in the dark.

She decided to take the initiative, and find out what they knew – or thought they did.

'I haven't been able to talk to anyone, you know, till today. I don't know any details. Please tell me.'

The sergeant nodded and the youngster produced his notebook. 'The RTA was reported by telephone: caller gave no name or address – just reported the accident and then rang off. One of our cars was standing by at the main road end of Pringle Bank, and proceeded at once to investigate. There were two other cars already at the scene when they arrived. One driver had caught sight of you lying on the bank, and had waved the other down to help. They had approached from opposite directions, and the fog was quite thick just there. They both believed that you had been walking along the road, and had been hit by a passing vehicle. Our men radioed for an ambulance, and while rendering first aid, noticed heavy skid marks on the bank, and on the road. Following the marks, they found a car upside-down in the drain on the opposite side of the road. There was nothing they could do.'

Anne broke in. 'In the drain?' she said, incredulously. 'But we hit the bank. I know we did!'

The young policeman agreed. 'Yes, the markings prove that.'

The sergeant coughed, and silenced the other. His tone was far less official as he took up the questioning. 'We can only assume that you were travelling at such speed that the car mounted the bank, somersaulted and rolled back across the road and into the drain. The force of impact must have burst the door on your side open, and you were not wearing your safety belt. That saved your life.'

She remembered. 'I undid it. I felt trapped.'

He looked grim. 'It was the million-to-one exception that proves the rule,' he said. 'Seat belts aren't much good if you undo them at the crucial moment.'

'Tell me – about Jerry,' she said. He did, as gently as he could. The car wasn't lifted till the next day. Jerry was still strapped into the driver's seat.

'You say you heard your husband shout?' asked the young one. The room began to spin around Anne, and waves of terrible nausea suddenly overwhelmed her. Her retchings brought a nurse to hold her head, and she groped with her hand for something to hold on to, while the world rotated. It was taken in a strong, firm, manly grip, and she clung till the spasm passed. But through it all, she had resolved that she could not tell them of Jerry's shriek of terror when face to face with Death.

'What was it your husband said?' pursued the younger questioner. The sergeant patted her hand, and let go; but Anne closed her fingers round his again, feeling comfort and strength from the contact. The nurse was looking dubious, but Anne gave her a weak smile.

'I'm OK,' she said. 'The doctor says I'm bound to get attacks of vertigo for a time. It's gone now.'

'You hang on to me if you want to,' said the big man.

'It does help,' said Anne. 'I honestly can't remember. He'd been swearing at the fog. It was probably an oath – "Christ-all-bloody-mighty" or something like that. Does it really matter?'

'I'm afraid it does,' said the sergeant. 'Are you sure you want to go on?'

Anne was weary of it, suddenly. She wanted it over and finished for good. 'Yes,' she said, firmly. 'So why does it matter what Jerry said?'

'There had to be an autopsy, of course. It established that your husband had had a great deal to drink – but you knew that, of course.' (Anne suddenly realized that the contact of their hands would offer unspoken information both ways.) 'His seat belt had saved him from all but superficial injury on impact.'

'He was drowned,' she said, in a small voice.

The fingers round hers tightened. 'No. That is why what he said is important. He was dead before he reached the water. There was no evidence at all that he had made any effort to release himself.'

She tried to take it in. 'Heart failure?' she said. He shook his head again. 'No – nothing. So far, the cause of death has not been established. He just died at the wheel, but what caused his death is a mystery.'

Anne pulled herself up on to her elbow, in spite of the restraining hand.

'But that's absolutely absurd!' she said. 'Look! There we were, Jerry as drunk as a lord, and driving like a madman, straight towards a patch of thick fog. I warned him that there was a police car ahead – I could see its blue lamp. Then there was a torch waving us down, and the policeman standing on the bank. I could see him as clearly as I can see you, but Jerry shouted and braked. And we hit him!' She closed her eyes and opened them again with an effort.

'I suppose he was quite dead, too?'

There was silence. Then the sergeant gently disengaged his fingers from hers, and stood up. The youngster, disappointed, put away his notebook.

'You've had enough for one day. We'll come back again tomorrow,' he said.

'No – let's get it over! I'm sorry if he was a friend of yours. But he's dead now, anyway, like Jerry.'

The big policeman stood looking down on her. 'I suggest you try to get some sleep, Mrs Temple,' he said. 'I'm afraid that bump on the head you got is still giving trouble. You see, what you've just said is the first we've heard about a policeman being involved, alive or dead. You probably imagined him in your delirium, and he now seems real to you.'

She was angry, now, furiously so. 'No! No!' she shouted. 'He *was* there! He caused it all. If he hadn't tried to stop us, we should have got home safe. It was only another mile or so.'

She suddenly began to cry. Sister and a nurse bustled up, and the men left. She knew they would be back. To be told that she was hallucinating seemed to break the composure she had so far retained. It just made no sense at all, and she was suddenly overwhelmed with a feeling of utter helplessness. She cried and cried, until the nurse brought her something to swallow, and she slipped into sleep.

It was two days before the policemen were allowed to see her again. The big man, gentle and solid as ever, told her that they had not been wasting time in the interval. Exhaustive enquiries had failed to reveal anything of the mysterious policeman with the torch. The only officers on duty in the area had been those standing by at the junction of Pringle Bank and the main road. Moreover, every man in the force was alive and well, and able to account for his movements on the night in question. Nor had any neighbouring force lost an officer.

'But I *saw* him!' expostulated Anne. 'And what about his car? I saw its lights, and the blue lamp – through the fog, it's true, but quite clearly.' The young officer smiled in a superior sort of way that exasperated her almost to tears again.

'Mrs Temple,' he said, enunciating as though she was deaf, as well as a bit feeble-minded. 'There were two cars at the scene of the accident when our men got there. They had approached from different directions. There are no turnings off Pringle Bank, as you know – not even into a field at that point. Neither of the witnesses, nor their passengers, saw a car at all, let alone a police car. And neither of them had met one. Now, how do you account for that?'

'I don't!' said Anne desperately. 'That's your business! I only know that I saw him.' Her voice rose. She was very near to tears again.

'Look, sonny,' said the older man. 'Leave this to me. You go and chat up that pretty little nurse. I'll call you if I want you.' The boy left, a bit sulkily, and the sergeant sat down. He reached for Anne's hand, and held it close in both his own.

> 'There are more things in heaven and earth, Horatio,
> Than are dreamt of in your philosophy.'

he said.

Anne was astounded. She didn't often meet people who knew that poetry existed. She didn't expect it from a police sergeant.

'You're surprised because I can quote Shakespeare,' he said. 'You ought not to be, really – because we studied *Hamlet* together, twenty-odd years ago. At the Tech. I thought I recognized you when we came the other day, and when I learned your maiden name, I knew I was right. I don't really expect you to remember me, though. You only had eyes for young Mac Neill.'

She was silent, trying not to cry. She suddenly felt at ease with the big man, as with an old friend, and smiled.

'Can I go on with the business now?' he asked.

'Of course,' she said. 'Your quote from *Hamlet* means that you believe me, even if you can't prove I'm telling the truth. But haven't you missed something? What about the man who reported the accident? He must have seen everything. Where did he telephone from?'

He shook his head. 'That's just another mystery. There are no roadside telephones. We've checked every private phone in a radius of two miles. The informant couldn't possibly have got further than that. From you leaving your parents' house to the call being received was less than ten minutes.'

There was a long silence.

'The easiest explanation is that you imagined it all *after* the accident,' he said. 'It will be brought in as "Death by misadventure". Isn't that the best way?'

She nodded. Of course he was right.

'That's a good girl. I'll get sonny-boy out there to prepare a statement and read it to you. Then if you'll sign it we probably shan't have to bother you again.'

He got up and went to give the boy his instructions. When he came back, she said, in a small rather shy voice, 'Do you know what happened to Mac? Did he become a plumber?'

He looked hard at her, searching her face with serious, troubled eyes. 'No,' he said. 'Didn't you know? His father had a big business as a heating engineer, and wanted Mac to take it over. But Mac left the Tech when you did, so his father sold up and the whole family moved away, down to the south coast. I kept in touch with Mac, and when I joined the force, so did he, down in the south.'

'So he's a policeman, too!'

The one at her side stood up and went to the window, with his back towards her. 'Not any longer. He was doing well – climbing the promotion ladder just as you would expect old Mac to. He was picked up dead on a lonely road with his torch still in his hand, ten years ago or more. No witnesses. It was surmised that he'd tried to stop some bloody DD and failed. Oh – sorry! I forgot!'

He had seen her stricken face grow suddenly deathly white. He sat down and took her hand.

'I beg your pardon,' he said. 'But old Mac was my best friend. I'd give my right arm to get the bastard who ran him down.'

She looked straight at him. 'I think you have got him,' she said in a whisper. 'Try the mortuary.'

The Helmet of Salvation

Cora staged her one and only rebellion against the injustice of life on a glorious June morning a few days before her eighteenth birthday. She was on her way home from teaching Sunday School, and she was both hot and bothered when she encountered her cousin Debbie.

Cora was hot because she was unsuitably dressed for a summer morning. Her second-best grey flannel 'costume' was too heavy for comfort, and her lisle stockings too thick. She did not need the white cotton gloves she wore on the hands clutching the *Methodist Hymnal*, but like the grey felt hat that came low on to her forehead and almost rested on her spectacles, they were dictated by propriety. She was bothered because she knew that there would be trouble at home when she got there. It was her duty to make the batter for the 'bake-pudden' which was the inevitable first course at Sunday dinner in every house and cottage in the wide, flat fenland scene. If she was late, dinner was late: then the whole family was late for afternoon service at chapel, where she was the official organist, as she was at Sunday School. But how was she to know in advance that Old Harry Timms, who usually played for morning service, was going to fail that day? What could she do but 'oblige' when asked? All the same, she had run almost all the way home – or, to put it more accurately, she had more than walked fast. To have run in her second-best clothes on a Sabbath morning would have shocked her, as well as everybody else.

By the time she reached her uncle's farmyard, she was sweating and panting, and had paused for a moment's respite when down the path from the farmhouse came Debbie. Debbie was nearly eighteen, too – but there the resemblance between them ended.

She came swinging along, clad in a low-necked, sleeveless, white silk dress. Her dark, sleek, Eton-cropped head was bare, and her bare legs, long and smooth and tanned, ended in feet encased in pretty, open sandals. She carried a tennis racquet in one hand, and a bag of balls and a pair of tennis shoes in the other. She called a greeting to the stocky, grey-flannelled figure panting in the road, and held up the tennis racquet in salute. Before Cora had had time to do more than take the vision of her cousin in, a brand-new, shining, powerful motorcycle combination drew up beside the two girls, and while Cora gawped in incredulous dismay, Debbie climbed into the sidecar, and was driven away. Gone – there was no getting round it, gone to play tennis, alone with Frank Redhead, on a Sunday! The shock hit Cora somewhere in the region of her solar plexus, and made her gasp even more.

She had been having curious, disturbing sensations in that part of her anatomy for some weeks now, a sort of unease that upset her usual placid routine. She was not given much to introspection or self-analysis, belonging to the category of the meek who accept what happens to them without question as a rule; but she had wondered enough about these new feelings to reach the conclusion that they were somehow connected with her approaching eighteenth birthday. Though true majority did not come till twenty-one, eighteen signalled the end of real childhood – and being grown-up brought in its wake things that until very recently Cora had not allowed herself even to think about. But she was three months nearer to these adult pleasures than Debbie, and yet here was Debbie . . . off with the rich butcher's son to goodness knows what!

Then, as the combination roared and curved away with a clatter of dust and exhaust fumes, the wave hit her – or perhaps it was more like the vacuum following a bomb blast, sucking everything out of her except the pain itself. Envy – griping, paralysing, unendurable envy, making her sob, and writhe, and sweat. The shimmering fields with their criss-crossing ribbon of dykes blurred as the scalding tears rushed to her eyes, and her muddy complexion, already flushed with exertion, turned to a dull purple, like mould-covered beetroot. It wasn't fair! It wasn't fair! It wasn't fair!

It hadn't been fair for the last eighteen years, since the babies were born, three of them within the space of twelve weeks, though Cora was not aware of that. Cora's mother, Emily, was the youngest of a family of four. The oldest, Jane, though married young, was childless; the second, John, had married late, to a girl his sisters thought both unsuited and unsuitable; the third, Minnie, had disgraced herself by marrying her cousin and leaving her native fenland for the industrial north, where she proceeded to produce offspring at a rate that offended her sisters' sense of propriety and gave them such a source of grievance against her that they sought gradually to disown her, except for an annual letter at Christmas. Emily had been married for several years when John committed his indiscretion of marrying Bessie Palmer, but she had so far remained barren. Then it happened, and she was soon whispering to Jane – her constant companion, mentor and protector – that she had hopes that she might be 'in the fam'ly way' at last. They hugged the secret smugly to their tight, corset-uplifted bosoms, until it was too late for the earth-shattering surprise they had planned. Bessie was joyfully, unashamedly (vulgarly, they thought) letting it be known that she was already 'expecting'. And from Doncaster came the usual Christmas letter containing the usual Christmas news that Minnie was 'like to have another child', which she did hope would be a girl, because she'd already got three boys.

Jane and Emily hoped for a girl, too, while John and Bessie declared stoutly that as long as the child was healthy and whole, its sex was quite immaterial. John's sisters Jane and Emily regarded this attitude as scandalous as Bessie's flaunting of her condition. He had inherited the family farm, a cause of enduring jealous bitterness, in spite of the fact that they had had their fair share in money, leaving him struggling for want of cash to run the farm on. They considered that the least he could do to compensate them for loss of their birthright was to keep the family name going by producing sons.

Emily had been the first to give birth. There had been much consultation with Jane over the choice of a name. Jane had taken it for granted that, if a girl, it would be 'named for her', and was put out when Emily suggested timidly that her husband, George, would like the baby to be called Beatrice after his mother. When the baby turned out to be female, poor Emily scented a family feud, and being of a somewhat appeasing disposition, at least where Jane was concerned, was inclined to give in; but George wouldn't budge. So in the end, the baby was named Beatrice Jane – but even that left the question open of what she should actually be called. Emily took a great and unprecedentedly bold decision. 'You've both had your way,' she said, 'and now I shall 'ev mine. He name'll be Cora Beatrice Jane, and she'll be called Cora.'

'Whatever for?' asked Jane, bristling. 'Who after? There's never been a Cora in our family afore.'

'Never you mind,' said Emily. 'Cora she shall be.' (She had found the name in a story in *Peg's Paper*, but dared not admit to reading such loose literature, so the origin of it had remained for ever obscure.)

Then Bessie's baby bounced into the world, and was called Deborah Elizabeth. Once again the fat was in the fire. Deborah (pronounced Deb-*or*-ah) was the name of John's (and therefore of Jane's and Emily's) departed mother, and her mother's before that, back to the time when somebody searching for a given name had slipped a knife into the Bible. Totally ignoring the fact that they had had first chance to use it, Emily and Jane let it be known that they were bitterly hurt, offended, insulted, and robbed of their inalienable right by this usurpation of their mother's name by someone as unworthy of it as Bessie Palmer. They told their brother so, but he only laughed. He was too happy to let the 'maunderings' of his sisters upset him. 'Only Bess says as it shoul'n't be pronounced Deb-*or*-ah,' he told them. 'She says that it's got to be *Deb*-orah.'

'Well, of all things!' exclaimed Jane to Emily. 'That shame-faced 'ussy 'ould say anything. As if we di'n't know 'ow to say our own dear mother's name!'

To John she merely said grimly, 'That's as maybe. If I call her anything, I shall call her Deb-*or*-ah.'

'Suit yourself,' said John amiably. 'I shall call her Debbie. That'll suit her. Born on a Sunday – you know what the old rhyme says:

> The child that is born on the Sabbath day
> Is blithe and bonny and good and gay.'

Jane growled, and Emily suppressed a whimper. Cora had been born on a Wednesday, and was therefore doomed to be 'full of woe'.

The letter announcing Minnie's latest disclosed that she at last had the daughter she wanted, born between Cora and Deborah. She had been christened already, being a somewhat weakly child, and had been burdened with the name of Flora Victoria Wilhelmina.

'Lawks!' was all that Jane could find to comment, and Emily said nothing, being secretly impressed and a bit jealous, especially of the Wilhelmina. In all this anxiety about names, it had been only John who had considered the fact that to the given name a patronym would also be added. By the time the three grandiosely named infants appeared on the register of their elementary schools, they had, in hard reality, become Cora Potts, Flo Tibbles and Debbie Nightingale. There is no justice in luck: fate lays its icy hand even on innocent unborn babies.

Of Flo, nothing was known. Of Cora and Debbie, everything. Cora was a stumpy, dun-coloured child; Debbie was dark, rosy, lithe and sparkling. At eight, John bought Debbie a piano, which she simply sat down and played. Jane and Emily countered with an organ, which Cora eventually conquered, after years of unhappy lessons and miserable practice. At thirteen, Debbie got a scholarship to the local grammar school and entered a different social sphere. At fourteen, Cora left school to 'be at home with her mother', who had bad legs. Cora was smug about it – most of her peers were condemned to crawling on hands and knees up and down the black fields, winter and summer alike, or to the drudgery of 'service'. She did not argue about the decision, thinking, as her mother told her she must, how lucky she was in comparison with others. She acquiesced with her accustomed meekness, thereby selling herself into eternal bondage. She was thereafter monitored, day and night, not only by Emily but by Aunt Jane too. She passed her organ exams, and graduated, with pride, to the organ stool at chapel when Old Harry began to fail occasionally. Emily and Jane could hardly contain their pride in her. Compare that achievement to Deborah's gift of playing jazz! (And/or anything else that was put before her, but this the sisters ignored. Jazz smacked of the Devil as much as hymns smacked of God.)

Though John refused resolutely to be put out by his sisters' overt disapproval of everything his family was, had, or did, there was no love lost between the two camps. Debbie and Cora, living less than half a mile from each other, simply inhabited different worlds. Debbie's friends were all girls (so far) that she met at her grammar school. Cora had no friends. Debbie was set to go on to 'college', whatever that was, and had exams to pass, but she still seemed to have time for everything else, and did her bit in the secular life of the village when asked. She played the piano with gusto for village dances or concerts, when her special crony from school would come and play duets with her, or sing solos in her fine, well-trained soprano – very different from the tremulous croaking efforts Cora was used to accompanying in chapel. The only place the two cousins met socially was at the monthly meeting of the Women's Institute, but even that came to a nasty end. At Debbie's suggestion, they were going to enter a play for the county drama festival. She badgered the president (the village schoolteacher, of course) to give Cora a part. Emily and Jane were very dubious about the morality of 'play-acting', but as the cast were all women, they couldn't fix on anything concrete to object to. Then it transpired that Cora had been allotted the role of an inebriated Irish washerwoman. She was withdrawn on the excuse of a bad chest that prevented her going out at nights in winter. Half-grateful for the release from the ordeal of appearing on the stage, she developed a wheeze to prove the truth of her mother's assertion, and never thereafter lost it. To the end of her long life she wheezed and gasped and coughed at will, deeming herself asthmatic.

She was wheezing and gasping more than usual as she watched Frank Redhead's combination disappear down the road. When the dust cleared, she remembered the time, and the bake-pudden, and panicked. She set off again for home, but the envy inside went with her, burning and scalding, singeing and searing, till she could hardly bear it at all.

Aunt Jane and Uncle Ted had already arrived for Sunday dinner when she reached home. The men were in the garden, the women in the 'house-place'. Emily barely paused in the tale she was telling Jane, but looked balefully and meaningfully at the old wall-clock. Cora caught the look, fair and square, and noticed how it was magnified, in intent as well as in actual size, by the thick lenses of her mother's pebble spectacles.

'I had to play for chapel,' Cora said, with more spirit and resentment than it was her wont to display. The two sisters looked at each other, and then at the girl, noting her flushed and excited condition.

'Where have you been since then?' asked Emily. 'That bake-pudden'll never be done if it ent in the oven in ten minutes.' (She always said 'ent', having gathered that 'ain't' was vulgar, and regarding 'isn't' as stuck-up.)

'Bother the dratted ol' bake-pudden,' said Cora, banging the *Methodist Hymnal* down on top of the organ. Then she followed that unprecedented outrage by sitting down on the organ-stool and bursting into tears. To her mother's sharp enquiry as to what the matter was, Cora answered, plain and full with complete honesty. The two sisters were stunned, shocked, and righteously affronted. Aunt Jane, endeavouring to pour oil on waters she perceived were becoming even more turbulent, asked, 'What has Deb-*or*-ah got that you haven't?' A foolish question, to which there was only one answer, which Cora gave in an anguished wail.

'Everything!'

'Hold yer row,' her mother commanded in a hoarse whisper. She had no desire for the men to hear. 'I'll tell you what you've got that she ent,' Emily said, low and meaningful in tone. 'An' that's a good gel's name! That's something she'll never 'ave no more, try as that mother of hers may! Like mother like daughter!'

'She'll come to no good,' opined Aunt Jane. 'I'm surprised that a brother o' mine should bring disgrace on us all like this! All them boys, and them shocking clothes, and that muck all over her face! And that there Eaten Crop! Is that what you want, you bad gel?'

Cora sensed that the truth would get her nowhere, so she shook her head miserably, and sobbed afresh.

'Well, what then? Answer me – what then?'

The momentary surge of common sense forsook her again, and she blubbered, 'She'll get engaged and be married and have babies, and I shan't!'

She should have had more sense than to mention the word 'babies', or imply that such impure thoughts as those of the process of human procreation ever entered her mind. Her mother brought a large flat hand stingingly on the girl's cheek, and commanded, 'Get upstairs and take them Sunday clothes off, and then go and make that batter. I'll deal with you later, but your father shan't go without his dinner to please you!'

Cora crept away, and the two women indulged in a few private tears of dismay and vexation. The Sunday lunch was a hurried, miserable meal, but before setting out again for afternoon chapel, they found time to indulge in a session of 'forgiveness' in Cora's bedroom as she took off her overall and re-donned her flannel suit.

'Never you mind, my gel,' Aunt Jane said, in a mollifying

tone of voice, having accepted Cora's apology and bestowed a kiss on the still weeping girl. 'Your turn will come. One of these days Mr Right'll come knocking at the door. You'll see. There's no need to make yourself cheap like that little 'ussy up the road.'

'And when he does,' added her mother, seeing that Jane had taken the right line, and in spite of herself experiencing a wrench of compassion at the sight of Cora's red eyes and woebegone expression, 'when he does come, he'll find as good a gel as God ever made in this fen, that 'e will.'

'And one who knows the way to a man's heart,' added Aunt Jane. 'Everybody knows the old sayin' about the way to a man's 'eart being through his stomach. There ain't many gals about who can turn out a bake-pudden like you can, so there. 'Er up there (indicated with a sideways jerk of the head) 'Er up there couldn't make a cup o' tea properly!'

Such criticism of Debbie was joy to Cora's ears, particularly as she had no evidence to disprove the truth of it. She was worn out, and utterly subdued by the events of the forenoon. Her short-lived spell of rebellion had left her dejected and more dun-coloured than ever. She clung to her mother and sobbed out that she was sorry, receiving half-hearted shoulder pats and a muttered, 'There, there, that'll do!' as consolation.

On the way to chapel, she put behind her all wicked thoughts both of envy and of yearning for the wrong things, and made a resolution to keep her good name at all costs, and to trust her aunt's assertion that Mr Right would one day appear, though she did allow herself the tiny privilege of hope that he wouldn't be too long in making his entrance into her uneventful life.

It happened that Cora's rebellion occurred on the special Sunday of the quarter, when their village had the privilege of the services of the ordained minister for the circuit for the whole day. Cora had been very proud that she would be at the organ that afternoon, but her passion had caught her out, making her forget for the moment what was afoot. Once inside the chapel, however, the atmosphere took her into its control and intensified the feelings of guilt, as well as all the good resolutions she had made on the way there. When the minister mounted the pulpit and said, 'Friends, let us pray,' those in the body of the chapel swayed forward and with one accord hid their faces in the hands they had rested on the ledge (designed for hymnbooks) attached to the seat in front. Cora, on her organ stool, could only rest her hot, flushed face against the music stand, but she could, and did, pray. As she had been taught, she prayed, not for the material things that made Debbie's life so pleasurable, but for the spiritual gifts of meekness, obedience, goodness, helpfulness and faith. She did not follow the minister's prayers for the general welfare of mankind, feeling that the heathen (especially the Japanese, who, for some reason, appeared to be taking pride of place among them this afternoon) could for once be left to their own wicked devices. She had a much more personal plea to the Almighty which she put with fervour. She decided that He would not take it amiss that she should add to her list of requests the great gift of continued hope in the existence of Mr Right, and of faith in her mother's assertion that all she had to do was to be good, and wait.

When she sat up to fumble for the chords of the first hymn, she felt better, heartened and calm. All would be well, with time and patience. It seemed almost a miracle to her that when the minister began on his sermon, he announced, 'My text for this afternoon is taken from the first epistle of Paul to the Thessalonians, chapter five, verse eight. "Hope is the helmet of salvation." God had spoken to her, it seemed, almost directly. In hope only lay her salvation.

Summer slipped by, with the Potts household restored to its normality. News (gossip, rather) reached them all occasionally about young Debbie's continued 'goings-on'. The butcher's son had been superseded by a wealthy young farmer who had a car – some even went so far as to say this attachment was 'serious'. Emily and Jane were of the opinion that it would soon be made plain to everybody how serious it really was, when Debbie (and her mother) 'got their combs cut' by the inevitable result of such loose behaviour. The person apparently least affected by all this was Debbie herself.

She appeared in public, openly and happily, with the farmer's son, who was handsome, rich, well-educated and 'posh'. He was so far out of Cora's reach that common sense came to her aid, and she wasted no emotion or envy of him or his like. In fact, she had to admit, though only secretly and to herself, of course, that he seemed absolutely right for her cousin, of whom, in spite of herself and her mother and aunt, she was both fond and proud. In casting Debbie as first class, she relegated herself to second class, and once she openly acknowledged the distinction (again, only to herself) she accepted it, and struggled no longer to deny it or change it. So she did not envy Debbie her Raymond, but she did envy the other girl her freedom. If something didn't soon change the unvarying pattern of her life, how would she ever meet Mr Right? The only real difference being eighteen had made was that she could now be enrolled as a full member of the newly formed WI instead of the 'associate' she had so far been – a category invented on the spot by the president to catch some extra members young.

The time wore away towards Christmas, and the annual WI social. It was at that function that Cora first became aware of Alf Townsend, though she had known him all her life. She found herself as Alf's partner in a game that required of them only that they should not be standing on a mat when Debbie stopped the music. In their effort to synchronize their steps, they involuntarily held hands, and as luck would have it, won the tiny prizes. They were still standing together when Debbie struck up a one-step, and Alf asked Cora to dance. For the first time in her life she felt a male arm round her waist, and forgot her mother and her aunt, sitting watchful at the end of the room. Cora danced as she walked, without rhythm, in short truncated staccato steps that jolted her through and through. Alf did not seem to notice, and when the dance was ended, led her back to a seat at the opposite end of the room from that her mother occupied. Cora sat down, but glanced nervously towards her chaperones. She caught again, even at that distance, the spectacle-magnified glare of warning from her mother's eyes, and her aunt's sideways

headjerk that indicated she was to join them at once. Too
late – Miss Downes was already announcing that they were now
to be favoured by some songs by Miss Evelyn Oldfield (Debbie's
friend). Debbie was already playing the introduction. Cora had
to stay where she was, by Alf's side. It was sweet, it was
dangerous. She felt the eyes of her protectors focused on her,
making her wriggle as if their spectacles acted like a burning-
glass. To avoid any accusation from them later, she concentrated
on the singer, and her song.

> 'O who will o'er the downs so free,
> O who will with me ride?
> O who will up and follow me
> To win a blooming bride?
> Her father he has locked the door,
> Her mother keeps the key,
> But neither bolt nor door shall part
> My own true love and me.'

There were more verses, more songs, more encores, but the end
had to come, and Cora crossed the room with an aching dia-
phragm and a tightly tearful throat to sit out the rest of the
evening between Emily and Jane. However, two days later,
when Cora came out of afternoon chapel into the December
dusk, she found Alf waiting in the shadows. She set off for
home without a word or a glance at him, but he fell in behind
her, and caught her up before she had gone a quarter of a mile.
They both understood the ritual, and asked for nothing more,
parting discreetly before they reached the Potts' domicile; not,
however, before they had arranged that Alf would be there
again next Sunday – and the next, and the next.

The neighbours, of course, meant no malice. If anything, they
were relieved to observe 'poor Cora' being a natural and normal
girl at last. But gossip is as much a part of the village pattern of
life as the sun or the wind. The news of their association reached
Jane after three or four weeks, and she left off making her mince
pies to go straight to her sister with the news.

Cora had, it seems, been guilty of 'running after the first chap who'd looked at her' (her mother); 'being too-easy won' (her aunt); 'going the same way as that Deb-*or*-ah (her mother), Alf Townsend not being what they'd hoped for' (her aunt) and so on, till the singing that had been in her heart turned to moaning, and the blazing light that had been the approaching Christmas faded to a dull glow. There was no more rebellion. Training, obedience and lack of spirit held her in their grip, and hope still remained the helmet of her salvation. She was even mollified by Aunt Jane's slight softening of attitude and the dim hint of jam tomorrow to soothe today's gnawing hunger for Alf.

Aunt Jane said, 'They are all hardworking, God-fearing folk if they ain't reg'lar at chapel. If he is the one meant for you, he won't give in easy. When 'e comes knocking at the door to ask if you can go for a walk with him, that'll be time soon enough.'

'So no more walking about with him without permission, now,' her mother said severely. 'We'll see what sort of stuff he's made of when he comes.'

Alf was more than usually shy. Nobody ever knew what it had cost him to ask Cora to dance, or to be seen waiting for her after chapel. When she dodged him the next Sunday after being found out, he concluded he was unwanted. But he did not give in without doing all he could. It wasn't enough.

In spite of her misery, Cora's first little essay into romance fanned the flames of hope, and made the next few weeks bearable; but gradually, as the sharp winter advanced, Cora's spirit faded again, until even her gaolers noticed how pale and listless she had become. A hard frost had set in, and the flooded fens were frozen over. Tales reached them of Debbie skating in the moonlight with her Raymond 'till all hours of the night', but Cora stayed indoors, wheezing and coughing, gazing out of the frosted windows and hoping that Alf might come by.

'It's a pity you never 'ad no more child'en,' Jane said to Emily. 'What she needs is a bit o' company, another gal's company, I mean.'

'Pity you never 'ad none at all,' Sarah rejoined. 'It 'ud a bin nice for 'er to 'ave 'ad a cousin she could a-gone about with. Different from that dink-me-doll up the road.'

'The Lord di'n't see fit,' Jane said, thereby passing the blame for Cora's friendlessness on to shoulders broader than her own.

'He works in a mysterious way,' Sarah said. 'He's seen fit to give Minnie plenty.'

Jane snorted. She didn't blame the Almighty for Minnie's brood. It was, she said, all due to her youngest sister's lack of self-control. However, it was a very short time after this conversation that Fate gave the mixture another stir. Minnie's Christmas letter had not been a long one, and both Jane and Emily read between the few lines. They were not surprised when another letter arrived a few weeks later, but for once their assumptions were out of line. The letter was concerned, not with a new baby, but with her firstborn, Flora Victoria Wilhelmina.

Flo was now the oldest of six still at home and had gone to work in a shop when she left school; but Minnie now reported that the girl had 'outgrown her strength' according to the doctor, and was in danger of 'going into a decline'. She had had to leave her job, and Minnie was at her wits' end because she really couldn't do with her at home, what with little Violet having abscesses in her ear, and Bob having scalded himself by tipping over a pot of boiling potatoes, and the twins not yet left school. The doctor said what Flo needed was a change of air. There was no direct request that she should be invited to take a holiday in the fen, but the message was clear enough.

The two sisters discussed the matter fully, turning it inside out and back to front and upside down to discover any catch there might be in it. They could find none. It was an appeal for help, and as such it flattered them. To do them justice they had a very strong sense of kinship, and though they might disapprove or even quarrel with other members of the clan, when it came to the crunch they fought alongside with vigour and courage. Moreover, narrow and restricted as their religious code was, it did include the command to love their neighbour. It was, in the event, Jane who made the startling suggestion.

'I don't reckon a fortnight'll do the gal a lot of good,' she said. 'And from what I can read between the lines, Minnie would be glad not to have another mouth to feed at home. Seeing as the Lord has not seen fit to bless Ted and me with child'en, I reckon as we might take Flora and keep her altogether, as one of our own, like. She could help me in the house, like as not, and then go into the field when Ted's overbusy, at harvest time, or weeding onions, or picking potatoes. She'd earn her keep, that way, easy enough. What do you say?'

Emily was a bit flabbergasted, because much as she kow-towed to her sister, she was not blind to Jane's faults. Besides being domineering, Jane was decidedly mean, and was not given to large gestures of generosity. Emily had the softer heart of the two especially when Jane was not present to witness any weakness.

'It would be a good, Christian action,' she opined. 'Young Flora would have a good home where she was the only one, and be well fed as well as getting a change of air. Besides, she'd be a daughter to you and Ted, and you'd have somebody of your own to look after you in your old age.'

'And she'd be a companion for Cora,' Jane added. 'Two can do a lot more together than one can apart – going to socials and whist drives and suchlike.'

So the proposition was made, and accepted (though ruefully and reluctantly, as far as all those in Doncaster went – but they had no option. One does not look a gift horse in the mouth).

When Cora was informed, she was as ecstatic as anyone of her dun-coloured character could be. She had not seen cousin Flo more than twice in their lives, the last time being when they were seven. She proceeded to invest her unknown cousin with all the attributes of the dream-friend that she had long ago created, to balance Debbie's friendship with Evelyn, who could sing; but what these attributes were she could not exactly formulate. Suppose Flora turned out to be like Debbie? Common sense squashed that thought flat: Aunt Jane would not tolerate such a creature under her roof! Yet Cora wanted her to be lively and attractive – otherwise what benefit could accrue to her from Flora's advent? Not attractive to boys though – well, not too much so. Cora did not wish for a rival for the attention of Mr Right when he did come. It was all a bit difficult. How could cousin Flo be like Debbie and yet not like Debbie?

A year or two ago, Aunt Jane had given Cora an autograph album as a birthday present, and Cora had collected in it the gems of rural wit that went the rounds, year after year. Hilda Thompson, who had been away for a bit, had added one previously unknown to Cora. She had drawn a picture of an onion – at least, that is what Hilda said it was. Under the sketch, she printed the legend, 'The cause of many a silent tear'.

And then below that appeared the rhyme that now sprang to Cora's mind.

> O that some kind, inventive man
> Would patent, make, and sell
> An onion with an onion taste
> But with a violet smell.

That summed up exactly what Cora hoped and expected of her unknown cousin and destined friend-to-be. It had all been arranged. Flo would arrive in time for the Sunday School anniversary, the great day of Cora's year. Even the news that Debbie had given up ideas of going to college, and instead had got engaged to Raymond, failed to stir Cora to anything but mild interest. Her own future would be rosy, once Flo arrived. Doors would no longer be locked on her, and her mother would be forced to give up the key. Alf could, and no doubt would, come riding o'er the downs to her – or at least come across the fen on his old pushbike to ask her out. All would be well, when Flo came. Aunt Jane said so, and her mother concurred. Everything depended on Flo. She came, at last.

She came reluctant, miserable, rebellious. She saw her exile from the smuts of south Yorkshire to the bleak, windswept fens only as rejection by her family. She hated Aunt Jane on sight, and more upon acquaintance. She loathed the fens, and everybody in them, from the beginning. Such intelligence as she had was focused upon getting home again as soon as her 'holiday' was over. No one had told her that her exile was liable to prove permanent.

The disappointment was not one-sided. Flo had neither the all-embracing usefulness of the onion, nor the sweetly decorative qualities of the violet, let alone the combination of both that Cora had hoped for. Her disabilities were congenital, probably due to slight brain damage at birth, though in those days nothing not immediately visible was attributed to that cause. She had a tall, gangling frame, loose-jointed and clumsy, with over-sized hands and feet (in contrast to Cora, whose hands and feet, like her personality, seemed truncated). Flo took a size eight in shoes, and had to wear men's woollen gloves because those meant for women simply were not big enough. She dropped things, fell over things, and smashed Jane's best teapot by ramming it against the wall the very first time she cleared the table. Her hair, long and thick and shot with carroty highlights, was nevertheless of the kind that no pins or bands could constrain, and fell about her face in untidy wisps. As to her countenance, it has to be said outright that she was downright ugly, without a single redeeming feature to soften that harsh judgement. Her face was dominated by a Roman nose so long and so sharply angled that it appeared to have been broken and badly set. It was probably because of this that she sniffed constantly, being definitely adenoidal. Moreover, she also had a misshapen palate that caused her front teeth to protrude a little, so that she found it difficult to close her mouth, and consequently dribbled. Her voice, with its north-Midland accent was strident enough, even among the clarion-voiced fenlanders, to make them wince.

Aunt Jane seemed unmoved by Flo's appearance, one way or the other, but found plenty to complain of in her behaviour. The poor girl was miserably unhappy, longing for home. However poor the food there had been, there was enough of it and she had been welcome to her share. Aunt Jane was appalled at her appetite, and after the first week rationed her both in quality and quantity, so that she was continually hungry. She found the work expected of her beyond her strength, especially when it included work in the fields, which she had never done before. As she crawled beside the other hooded women up and down the black fields, her whole being ached, what with the protests of unaccustomed strain on every muscle, and with the lassitude and weariness that made it physically impossible for her to obey her aunt's commands 'just' to do this, or 'just' to do that; and her soul ached also with bitterness and hatred. This all-pervasive hate included the Almighty, towards whom her week-ends were perforce orientated. She hated Him and all His doings, but particularly His 'word'. She seethed with hate at suppertime every night, till she felt as if her bowels writhed with worms and maggots composed of It. There they sat, Uncle Ted consuming plates of home-cured ham and Aunt Jane eating toast plastered with homemade butter, while she struggled to swallow her basinful of bread and milk (salted and peppered, with a specified 'basseloney nut' of butter floating yellow on the top). In front of Aunt Jane was a well-worn Bible, and as she ate she droned in her butter-greased voice through the Sermon on the Mount, or St Paul's second epistle to the Corinthians. Now and again, though, the knife ritually inserted into the Bible before supper began resulted in Jane uncomfortably but nonetheless resolutely mumbling through one of the cursing Psalms. Then, and then only, did the Word find any response among the contusions and abrasions of Flo's battered spirit.

'Let them be as chaff before the wind: and let the angel of the Lord chase them. Let their way be dark and slippery, and let the angel of the Lord persecute them. For without cause have they hid for me their net in a pit, which without cause have they digged for my soul.'

Flo had no doubt at all who 'they' were. She scooped the last drop of her bread and milk noisily into her mouth, and said 'Amen' with such vehemence that Jane actually paused and looked up, which was unfortunate because she lost her place, for one thing, and for another, Flo was almost caught in the act of secreting a slice of Uncle Ted's bread and butter up her knicker-leg for a bit of midnight sustenance.

Chief among Flo's trials was Cora. When Jane got over the disappointment of not having a rival for Debbie, ready-made, under her roof, she saw the advantages of having the opposite to what she had imagined. If for nothing else, Flo was good for work – a providential slavery. But cooking was not among her accomplishments. After several attempts at making the inevitable Sunday 'bake-pudden', she was invited to watch her cousin accomplish the task. Cora obliged, a bit smugly, and turned out a pudding that Flo had to admit was as good a 'Yorkshire' as her mother had ever produced in its native land. If she hadn't been so hungry, she would have choked on it; but as it was, she swallowed each mouthful as if it were a gobbet of Cora's flesh. The two girls were forced upon each other at every opportunity, and both hated the association. Flo did her best to take Cora's 'goodness' down a peg or two; Cora was more than usually prim and proper, to show up Flo's vulgar gaucherie. Flo had been told to 'sit with Cora' in chapel. When Cora was on the organ stool, this resulted in Flo establishing herself on a bench at right angles to Cora, from which she did everything she could think of to put the organist off her stroke. She wriggled, giggled, whispered, dropped her hymn book and ejaculated 'Lawks!' instead of 'Amen'; and worst of all, she sang, too loud and off key, right into Cora's ear. This was bad enough when she sang the proper words. It reduced Cora to a quivering jelly of embarrassment when Flo let rip with such parodies as

> Hallelujah! Skin a donkey,
> Cut his tail off, amen!
> Hallelujah! Chop his ears off,
> Revive him again!

As Flo grew more bitter, more unhappy, more homesick, and less well, Cora grew more prim, more meek, and more satisfied with her lot. One day in chapel, when Flo had been more than usually tiresome, Cora leaned her flushed face on the music stand and prayed and prayed, desperately and intensely. She prayed that she might be relieved of the guilt of hating her cousin, and that something might happen soon to relieve the situation. And as always, she added a half-hearted, rather tentative and guilty little request to remind God that she was still pinning her faith on Mr Right. Sitting up to reach for the music for the next hymn, she caught sight of Flo's face. Flo had used her prayer time to repeat what she could remember of Jane's mumbled cursing Psalm. The effect on her visage did not exactly add to its charm. In that split second, Cora felt a great weight lifted from her heart. If she was, as she acknowledged, a second-class runner in the marriage stakes compared with one cousin, she stood in exactly the opposite relation to her other one. As Debbie to Cora, so Cora to Flo. She looked back again at Flo, and a lot of the dislike transformed itself to pity. One of her prayers, at least, had been answered. She was no longer guilty of hate towards Flo.

Being Cora, she put her new-found feelings into practice, and in the weeks that followed set out deliberately to 'be kind' to Flo. To the recipient, her attentions smacked of patronage, condescension, and the meek goody-goodyness that above all Flo detested in Cora. It was the last straw, the drop that overfilled Flo's cup of misery. On the next Sunday morning, Flo had an attack of diarrhoea that prevented her from going to chapel. When the family retired to bed that night, Flo was still in bed, though making frequent trips 'out the back'. On Monday morning, she had gone, together with Jane's housekeeping money, most of the portable food from the pantry and Uncle Ted's chapel seat-rent collections. Flo's plans had been carefully made. Every time she had retired to 'the back' on the previous day, she had secreted something more of her belongings outside. She had let herself out in the dark of the autumn morning, and by the time she was missed was on the train heading for Doncaster. Jane, Emily and Cora had no self-recriminations, and few mutual ones. They had all done their best for Flo. If she did not respond, it was not their fault. Their letters to Minnie were hurt and accusing – Flo, besides being ungrateful (etc), was a thief.

Minnie was devastated, but stood firm in her defence of Flo (having by this time heard her side of the tale). She appealed for a loan from John, to pay back what Flo had taken for her train fare. John, true to the maxim he always employed, declined to lend what he could not afford to give – so he gave. He paid every penny of Flo's debt to her aunt on condition that no word of the theft was ever breathed outside the family.

The only effect Jane's excursion into charity had, therefore, was to concentrate her affection and attention even more firmly on the niece who met all her conditions so unprotestingly. Her father had locked the door, her mother kept the key, and her Aunt Jane acted as the dragon guarding the golden hoard of her good name and her virginity. Not that Cora noticed it, immediately. She was aware that her second prayer had also been answered – she was free of the unwanted presence of Flo. She had now no doubt that all she had to do was wait, and Mr Right would turn up. Then – ah, then, she would know all the delights of physical contact with a man, such things as she sometimes dreamed of at night, and even allowed herself to imagine, secretly, when wide awake, even if they did make her sweat and tremble, and call for extra prayers for forgiveness.

So she waited. She waited while Debbie became engaged, then married, to her Raymond. She waited till the marriage was blessed with children. It was a bad day for her when she heard that Alf Townsend had also led his bride away from the altar (Alf had already left the district some time before, but she had survived, wearing hope as the helmet of her salvation). At thirty, she was more prim and proper than ever, but more forceful, having graduated to be the sole organist at the chapel (though congregations had dwindled almost to nothing) and a member of the (declining) WI committee. At forty, she found herself an orphan, though still with a protective aunt. She had inherited a house and a home, but no income. So she found herself a job in the local shop, and continued much as before.

To everybody else, she was now an 'old maid'. To herself, she was as she had always been, still waiting, except that she now had a lovely home to offer Mr Right when he came, and it had crossed her mind once or twice that he might have to be a widower.

Relations with Minnie and her family had been re-established on the death of Emily. (Death is a great healer of family quarrels.) Cora was invited north to visit Minnie, and on Aunt Jane's advice, she accepted. She came back with health and self-esteem replenished wholly. Flo, at forty, was even more queer than she had been at eighteen. The cousinly proportion sum still worked out right. It gave Cora deep satisfaction.

When Aunt Jane succumbed to passing years, Cora found herself with some capital – not much, but enough to make her feel 'comfortable', at least as far as security went, and to give up her job. She was not so well off as Debbie, true, but infinitely more so than Flo. She now had everything to offer, including her long-preserved virginity, but what had poor Flo? Cora suspected that the answer was nothing, not even virginity, and for a second or two harboured thoughts of envy, such as had once attacked her on the road home from Sunday School. She was now forty-five. Was time really beginning to run out for her? She agonized at the thought of being for ever *virgo intacta*, and of everybody else thinking of her as an 'old maid'. Her one consolation was that though Flo could not perhaps claim to be an old maid, she was still unmarried, and likely to remain so. Even Cora could see that. She looked in the mirror, and saw there a comely, well-preserved, neat, tidy, respectable spinster. (Others would have seen a dun-coloured middled-aged woman, with personality to match.)

Whatever had to be said of Flo at forty-five, she was certainly not colourless. Her face had become, if anything, more ugly, but it was not plain. Hardship and experience had given it character; and a character was what Flo had become in more ways than one. She was headstrong and impulsive, with a great gift for loving, and of serving where she loved. She was a thorn in the flesh of her brothers and sisters, who nevertheless made allowances for her and rallied round if, as often happened, she was homeless and penniless. Her few holidays were spent with Cora, who had the satisfaction of a chance to be charitable according to her lights and her training, and of being able to compare herself favourably against her ageing, eccentric relative. In spite of her still-unmarried status, Cora remained otherwise satisfied with her lot. It was never to be the same, after the dreadful blow fell on her. News came from Doncaster that cut the ground from under her happiness as effectively as the hangman's lever cuts off a murderer's life. Flo was married. A rough-and-ready widower had found a rough-and-ready way of providing himself with a permanent, if rough-and-ready, housekeeper.

The details of Flo's match did not interest Cora in her anguish. There was no one she could talk to. Her only living relative in the district was Debbie, whom she saw but rarely, since they now lived in quite different social circles. Not that she could have brought herself to admit to anybody her unmentionable feelings about the event of Flo's marriage. After days of self-imposed incarceration, when Cora sat before the grey ashes of a fire that had gone out for want of stoking, or lay in bed, weak and hungry for lack of effort to feed herself, and wheezing and coughing more than usual because of throat and nasal passages blocked with tears, she got up to face the world again, a different woman. Her neighbours told her that she did not look well, and left it at that.

In Cora, though, there had been a change. It was more a change of outlook and purpose than anything else. Till now, she had waited for Mr Right with all the longing of an adolescent girl daydreaming of the physical privileges of married life. Her dreams never took her very far, because her upbringing had brainwashed even her instincts, and she often had to pray for forgiveness when she had gone too far and given the man in her dreams Alf Townsend's face. She remembered the words of Jesus. If a man looking at a woman like that had already committed adultery with her, what was she doing thinking like that about Alf?

After the news of Flo's marriage, Cora faced the fact that she was now never likely to experience in the flesh the pleasures of sex such as the young know. 'The change' was already upon her. Her dun hair was greying, her dun skin sallowing, her already stubby figure thickening. Her mirror warned her that if Mr Right did come, now, he might not even notice her. She gave up the thought of marriage as a physical thing without too much anguish, never having been in any respect of a passionate nature – but that only made worse the misery of her unmarried social status. She felt now as if she wore a placard round her neck, announcing to the world that she was Cora Potts, 'spinster, of this parish'. She heard imaginary sniggers from the girls at Sunday School, and jibes from the boys, though in fact neither sex regarded her as anything more than a bit of the furniture that had always been there. She felt the pitying looks of all matrons, young and old, and the derision of all the men, though in reality they had long since ceased to give her even a passing thought. She was convinced that everybody pitied her for having been left on the shelf. In other words, she believed herself to be the only one unwanted, and she was ashamed. Her small, dun-coloured soul shrank, her plain personality dwindled. She still hoped – but hope now was upon any man who could, or would, take the stain of spinsterhood from her, and allow her to triumph in the married state at last.

The years went on passing. Hope never died – but Flo did. It was in the train, on the way to Flo's funeral, that she met him. They found themselves sitting opposite each other across the little table in a second-class non-smoking coach. Before the train left Peterborough, he had asked her politely if she would like the window closed. By the time they reached Doncaster, he had learned most of what there was to know about her, even to the fact that she had mice in her pantry. She had learned little, except that he had been recently widowed, and was lonely.

'I have some relatives in your area,' he said. 'I visit them now and then. Would you allow me to call on you, next time I'm that way?'

What harm could there possibly be? She was now sixty-five. Things had changed since the war. The neighbours could think what they liked. They weren't to know he was a stranger, picked up on a train, were they? Her heart leapt, and her skin flushed with satisfaction. She drew on her black nylon gloves and smoothed them on her short fingers, easing them over swollen knuckles showing a tendency to arthritis.

'I shall be pleased to see you, any time,' she said, primly.

'We had better exchange names and addresses, then,' he said. Cora wrote hers, neatly, in the schoolgirl hand that had never changed since she was ten. He tore out a page from his diary, and wrote boldly. She didn't even glance at the folded piece of paper as she put it safely into the zipped compartment of her black handbag. It was only as she searched for a handkerchief into which to shed the few obligatory tears for Flo as she waited with her other, more-or-less stranger cousins for the cortège, that her curiosity could no longer be suppressed. Under cover of the handkerchief she took a surreptitious glance at it, and read 'Arthur Wright', followed by an address in Doncaster. Her head swam, and her legs would scarcely hold her as she tried to stand for the entrance of Flo in her coffin. Exultantly, she saw the procession as herself advancing to meet Mr Wright at the altar. Her elation was tempered only by the thought that Flo would never be obliged to acknowledge her triumph, or to admit the truth of the adage that she laughs longest who laughs last. She left the chapel standing straight and firm. The placard, 'unwanted spinster', had fallen from her neck like Pilgrim's bundle at the sight of the Heavenly City.

She went home to wait for the news that Mr Wright was on his way to her. She was not unduly impatient; after all, she was used to waiting. But all the same, things had changed. She saw her little home through new eyes – his eyes, in fact. There was no doubt that it was shabby. She set about smartening it up, using all the housekeeping skills Emily and Aunt Jane had taught her as part of the way to a man's heart. She lashed out and bought new stretch covers for her old suite, and recovered the organ stool herself with a tapestry panel that she had worked forty years ago, and had put into her bottom drawer. She changed her old black and white telly for a secondhand colour set, bought from a neighbour. She sang as she went about her work, humming to herself the Sankey and Moody hymns that had delighted her dear mother and Aunt Jane. How pleased they would have been that she had followed their advice and kept herself inviolate for Mr Wright. She paused in the middle of the kitchen floor, to look upwards and send a message to them where they rested in their heavenly abode. Coming back to earth, her eye fell on the old electric cooker that had been her mother's, and she had never thought to replace. Perhaps he would come to lunch, and she would have to cook for him. Well, she could – but not on that old cooker! Why shouldn't she treat herself to a new one? She put on her hat, caught the bus, and went to the poshest electric showrooms in Peterborough. The salesman's spiel was double-Dutch to her, but she produced her cheque book and unflinchingly bought the latest and most expensive model. The salesman beamed his thanks, and informed her that their delivery man would see it installed and in working order before he left, next Wednesday afternoon.

She went home, and made a last cake and a batch of buns in her old, faithful cooker. She waited for the new one, on the day appointed, with unwonted excitement. It was a harbinger of joy, a herald of a new life to come.

The van drew up at last, and two men wheeled the great carton containing the new cooker right up to the back door, and knocked. Cora opened it in a daze of delight, and indicated where it was to go, her eyes on the present she had bought herself. Then she left them to it, under the impression that there was some danger attached to messing about with electricity. She sat in her refurbished sitting-room, and admired it, till a discreet knock on the door told her that the job in the kitchen was done.

'Come in,' she said, and in came Alf Townsend. Cora stared,

and Alf grinned – a lopsided, embarrassed boyish grin in an old man's face.

'There y'are, me ole duck, all ready fo' yer to use,' he said, the broad fenland dialect thickened by his shyness. 'Tha'ss a beauty, an' all, that is! Though why in the Lord's blessing you wanted one as you could cook a meal for a rigiment on, I dunno! Ay yer going to start takin' in lodgers, or somink?'

'Oh dear, oh dear!' said Cora faintly. 'Oh dear, oh dear! It's Alf, isn't it? Fancy it being you as brought it! Of all the queer things. However did that happen?'

'There ain't nothing very queer about that, far as I can see,' said Alf, holding his cap in his hands and turning it about, making feints now and then as if he were about to don it and leave, and thinking better of it. 'Arter all, I'm wukked for the firm as a storeman an' delivery man ever since I went that way to live – ever since I – well, that is, ever since you – Glenn bor!' (The last in a stentorian bellow to his young assistant in the kitchen.) 'Glenn! Do you goo an' git back into the van and wait fo' me.'

He waited till the boy went past the window. Cora still sat on the organ stool, too bemused to take anything in other than the fact that the man before her was indeed Alf. He advanced a little further into the room.

'So what about a cup o' tea, Cora me ole duck,' he said. 'For ole times' sake, like?'

Cora got up, and went to put the kettle on, acting like a zombie in a kind of hypnotic trance. She nodded to a chair as she passed it, a gesture Alf rightly interpreted as an invitation to sit down. As she made the tea and put together an offering of lemon cake and cherry buns, she felt no contact at all with reality, because there seemed to be none. In the sitting-room behind her was Alf, the only man whose arm had ever been passed round her waist, whose hand she had ever held, who had once sought her out of all the world. Before her stood the gleaming white cooker, symbol of the future, and of Mr Wright, who had come at last as a reward for patient waiting and hoping. The present moment did not exist. She was suspended wholly between past and future.

She took in the tea, and looked again at Alf, seeing in the grizzled man the boy with the cheery face and twinkling eyes whose image had haunted her dreams for well-nigh fifty years. She offered the plate of cakes, still unable to find words. Her silence did not distress Alf. In fact, to the contrary, he was thinking how little she had changed. That was how he had liked her, when she was eighteen, not all clack like some. He munched appreciatively. 'I allus thought as you'd be a good cook,' he said. 'Cor! When I think what I'm bin a-missin' all these year! 'Er at Peterborough — 'er as I went an' married, I mean — ain't never bin much of a cook. Can't even bile a hegg proper. Buys a lot o' that sweet sticky muck as they sell in the shops. 'Tain't like this 'ere, though.' He reached out and helped himself to another wedge of cake, and sighed deeply as he bit into it.

'But there y'are, tha'ss the way it goes. I never did 'ev much luck.'

He finished his cake without more ado, though now and again giving Cora a look that intimated he had more to say if only he knew how to say it.

When he set down his cup, he said, 'Ah, I never ought to 'ave married 'er. It weren't all 'er fault as we never got on together, b'rights, like. You was allus the on'y gel in the world for me, Cora me ole duck. But you didn't want me, so what were I to do? Can't be 'elped, now, anyways. I shall be sixty-five come next month, an' takin' me pension. Then I shan't be this way no more. We're a-gooin' to move, Cambridge way, to wheer she come from, like. Funny as one o' my last jobs should a-sent me to you. But there, life do play some funny tricks on yer, don't it?' Cora sat still, with her small hands in her lap, while inside her the atom bomb burst and the mushroom cloud of her love for him rose till it burst from her in a wail.

'But I did!' she said. 'I did!'

'Did what?' asked Alf, aware that somehow he had said something that was causing her distress.

'I did want you!'

She felt almost a physical pain as the admission, torn from her, robbed her of her moral maidenhead. She had declared to his face her love for another woman's husband. She did not add, 'And I still do', but the truth of it hung in the space between them like a spider swinging on the end of a thread. They both watched it, as if waiting for a sign from it as what to do next.

Alf stood up, and then sat down again. The twinkle had gone from his eyes, and his voice had lost its edge of badinage when he next found words. 'Then why di'n't you come – to meet me, I mean – that next Sunday? I were there, like I promised, but you never even looked at me. An' a good many Sundays arterwards.'

'They wouldn't let me,' she said.

'So I were right!' he said, jumping up and standing in front of her. 'I guessed as much! Sod 'em! Sod 'em! Sod the whull bloody lot on 'em!'

'They' were her beloved mother, and her dearly loved father, and her loved and loving aunt. Moreover, she had never heard a swear word used in that room since Flo's hurried departure so long ago.

'Alf!' she said, low and urgently. 'Alf! Don't go on so! They di'n't mean to part us.'

'Oh di'n't they, then?' he said. 'Oh yes they did, the sods! When you wou'n't speak to me no more, I plucked up courage to come an' ask you, at this 'ouse, to come for a walk wi' me, so as we could talk. Afore I got 'ere I met your aunt, ol' Mis' Toseland. She asked me wheer I were a-goin', an' said as 'ow I were a-wastin' my time if I was 'anging about arter you. She said a lot o' things as di'n't come out o' the Bible, an' hinted at a lot more. Like as you was fond o' the new minister's son, an' come another Christmas, there might be news of a grand hengagement. Ah, proper downed me, she did. And when we'd got nearly to your 'ouse, she said, "So you clear off, Alf Townsend. Cora's got 'er sights fixed on a long way above you." So I went 'ome, an' never tried no more. Then I met 'er – you know – an' afore I knowed what were 'appening she were telling me she were in the fam'ly way, an' we'd got to get married. I di'n't care. All I wanted were to get away so as I di'n't have to see you wi' somebody else.'

She heard, but did not take it in – partly because for sixty-five years she had regarded her parents as the acme of adult perfection, and had obeyed the fifth commandment to honour them to the letter, both in spirit and in truth; but mainly because Alf's belated declaration of his love for her had covered her with a carapace of gold, impervious to all other stings and darts.

'Oh, Alf!' she said, over and over again. 'Oh, Alf!'

He heard it as a *cri de coeur*, matching his own agony at the thought of all the wasted years, past and future. It was, in truth, more in the nature of a paean of joy. She had been wanted, had been desired – not as Flo had been, for a convenient drudge, but even as Debbie might have been by her Raymond. If nobody else ever knew about it, she did, and would, for ever. She glowed. Her sallow skin took on a pleasant flush, and her pale eyes deepened in colour. She stood up.

'I shall 'ev to goo,' Alf said, indicating with his head the van and the waiting boy. 'I shou'n't think we shall ever meet no more, but I'm glad as I'm told you. So give us a kiss, gel, an' we'll say goodbye.'

A huge sob rose in Cora's throat as he put his arms round her. She clung to him, lost, completely, in the glorious moment. He held her and kissed her, again and again, as if fifty years had somehow been stripped from them both. His hand felt for her breast, and she could not reprove him. She was almost swooning when it slipped lower, and she felt it fumbling between her legs. Her untried body leapt as if with an electric shock, and she knew that she could not, would not resist its further intrusion. She closed her eyes, and waited. He let go of her, snatched up his cap, and was gone.

In the hours that followed, Cora experienced such extremes of emotion that she was worn out, physically as well as spiritually. She relived the ecstasy of the few minutes in Alf's arms till she was as drained physically as if she had spent a hectic honeymoon with him. In its turn this brought such guilt that she spent a great deal of time down on her knees by the side of her bed, reaching out with real yearning for the God who had previously always seemed to be there to help, as her mother and aunt had assured her He was. But could she now believe anything her mother or her aunt had said? Did she believe what he had told her? Had she got to acknowledge that her whole life had been one great mistake?

> Her father, he has locked the door,
> Her mother keeps the key

Her anger turned against Alf. Why hadn't he been like the lover in the song, then, who said,

> But neither bar nor bolt shall part
> My own true love and me?

Why had he come back, just now – to take both her past and her future from her? She hated him. No she didn't. She loved him, and always had done, more than anything or anybody else in the world. More than Mother? Back came the guilt, and the tears. She ate nothing, and slept hardly at all, except for dropping off now and again in her chair out of sheer exhaustion.

She had not tried her new cooker. She remembered, as a sort of long-faded dream, why she had bought it. It was in case Mr Wright should announce that he would be paying her a visit. What should she do, now, if he did?

Another week went slowly past. By the end of it she had returned a little to normality, going as usual to chapel on Sunday and coping from sheer habit with the ritual, to a congregation of five old folks. All the same she felt queer, and unable to think straight or do things with the same unhurried deliberation as had characterized her in the past. Then came the letter that a fortnight ago she would have given almost anything for. Mr Wright was proposing to visit her, next Sunday morning. She didn't know what to do about it, partly because of her confused emotions, but mostly because something seemed wrong with her ability to think properly. She supposed he would want to have lunch with her – that was why she had bought her new cooker. She had never used it, yet, though. She'd better make a bake-pudden, to try it out before Sunday came.

She couldn't bear to dirty the cooker. It symbolized Alf; she wanted it left just as he had last touched it. But Mr Wright had come. God had answered her prayer. Surely He intended her now to respond? Reluctantly, she tried to read the instruction book. It appeared that she now had two ovens. Read it as many times as she might, she could not make head or tail of the print. There was only one thing to do. Make the batter, and switch the cooker on, and see what happened.

She broke the eggs into the flour, added the milk, and began to beat the mixture. 'Make it sound as if it's a hoss a-trottin',' her mother had said, week after week, as she first attempted the task fifty-odd years before. She could now produce that sound to perfection, and did. But her legs didn't want to hold her up while she did it. They felt numb, and a long way off. She looked round for something to sit on, and then, with Emily's voice still in her ears, took the bowl into the sitting-room and sat down on the organ stool. That was where she had sat sobbing, on the morning of her rebellion about Debbie. The memories flooded back, tripping each other up in their haste and insistence to reach her troubled mind. 'It wasn't fair,' she said aloud, re-echoing her cry so long ago. 'It wasn't fair,' she said, again, more in anger than sorrow. And as she said it, she felt again the weight of her mother's flat, heavy hand on her cheek, and the sound of the slap rang in her ears like the breaking of a staylace. With it, the tightly bound emotions burst through their corsetry of training and habit, and the inhibitions of years broke free.

She gazed down into the yellow mess in the bowl, her tears making little salt pools in its surface, just as they had done on that fateful Sunday so long ago, but through her tears she saw everything in a new perspective. She saw the long, wasted years stretched out behind her, like the black flat fields of the fens in a bleak winter. She saw her mother's warnings as myths, as insubstantial as the tales of the Hooky Man that inhabited fenland dykes, and prevented children from gathering flowers there while they bloomed. She saw her aunt's interference as ice she should have broken through, her father's weakness in the face of his womenfolk as blight on her youth. They hadn't loved her – not as Uncle John and Aunt Bessie had loved Debbie. They had only owned her. She saw, too, how in depriving her of her past, they had also reached out from beyond the grave to rob her of what future might have been left. She knew it, now. Mr Wright had come too late. 'Sod 'em,' Alf had said, and she had been shocked and hurt, knowing whom he meant by 'them'. The bowl in her hands seemed heavy. She wanted to set it down, and turned, to put it on top of the organ. There, standing where they had always stood, were photographs of 'them' – her mother and Aunt Jane, taken when young, in Edwardian high collars and 'Mizpah' brooches; her mother and father on their silver wedding day, Mother seated with a flower in her hand, and Father, stiff-collared, standing behind her; and herself, at twenty-one, in her best dress, seated on a stool as if at the organ. She had been pretty, in her own way. Not sparkling, like Debbie, but pretty enough, before hope had begun to dim and shrivel with every passing year.

A huge sob rose in her throat, but it was a sob of anger, abhorrence and contempt for them all and most of all for herself. With one swift swish of her aching arm, she sloshed the runny batter towards them. It rose in a yellow, distended arch, and then fell, thick and sticky, in blobs and splashes over everything. It slid down Emily's vacant countenance, and lodged at her throat, replacing the 'Mizpah' brooch; it landed fair and square on Jane's stolid bosom, and trickled towards her corseted abdomen. It obliterated her father's embarrassed countenance, and landed in her mother's ample lap. It covered Cora's own head, like a helmet without a vizor.

'*Sod you!*' said Cora, loudly and vehemently. 'Sod you all!' And she smashed the pudding bowl down on the carpet at her feet. She picked up the photo of Aunt Jane, and looked at it. 'You nasty, interfering old humbug,' she said. 'I hate you!' She flung the photo down, to join the broken bowl. Next went the silver wedding photograph. 'Kept me at home, didn't you? Locked the door, an' kept the key!' Down went the silver frame, the glass smashing as it landed on a jagged edge of earthenware. Cora snatched at her own likeness, and spat on it, before consigning it to the heap. There remained her mother. She took the photo into her hands, and gazed down at the batter-spattered image of all that had meant love, and trust, and faith, and hope to her for so long, but the magic had gone. Cora could not even bring herself to think, charitably as she had done so many times before, that 'she meant well'. She felt her own face stinging with the slap that hand holding the rose had delivered.

'Sod you!' she said, low and vehemently. She knew no other swear words, but in any case Alf's was enough.

'Sod you for a domineering old bitch!'

She flung the photo on to the batter-bespattered heap, and jumped-ed on it for good measure. Her legs felt better for her sit-down, but her head felt worse – she was dizzy and short of breath. Tears streamed down her face and her throat was clogged with sobs, though she didn't know she was crying. She didn't feel like crying – only like smashing things, as if by doing that she could do away with everything that ever had been or now could be.

'Sod 'em!' she kept saying, as she kicked the broken mess from side to side. 'Sod 'em all!'

Broken images from the past floated before her, odd snatches of old hurts never properly expurgated. Debbie at the piano, playing jazz; Flo bawling 'Hallelujah, skin a donkey' in chapel. Cora laughed. Good old Flo! She picked up the sides of her old tweed skirt, and danced among the débris, singing:

> 'Hallelujah! Sod the lot of you!
> Hallelujah! Amen!
> Hallelujah! Skin a donkey,
> And sod you again!'

She stopped, her hands to her throat, wanting air that didn't seem to be there. A voice from a long way off said, 'And what about Me, Cora? What about My Word? You know it well enough! "He who curseth his mother shall die."'

She paused, irresolute, fearful, looking over her shoulder as if she expected the speaker, in all His almighty wrath, to be standing behind her; but her anger and grief were greater than her fear. She looked upwards so as to direct her insult, and shouted. 'You? What did You ever do for me? Sod You! Sod You most of all!'

She took a great breath, to force the air down where it didn't want to go, as her head began to whirl and the room to spin round her. She crumpled like a marionette snapped from its control, and fell with her grey hair in the broken pudding basin.

The night nurse feeling the feeble pulse was slim and compact, her dark head with its short cropped hair framed in the glow of the shaded light. The tiny white cap perched saucily above the lively young face highlighted youth, beauty and vitality.

Opening her eyes, Cora struggled back through many memories to reach for recognition of the face she knew so well. Then suddenly she smiled, and pulled feebly on the hand the nurse still held. The nurse understood the signal, and leaned low to hear the confidential whisper.

'Debbie,' said Cora, I'm going to be married. Mr Wright has come. From Doncaster.' She shut her eyes, still smiling, and didn't bother to open them again.

'Queer, wasn't it?' said the little nurse to her boyfriend, later the same night. 'How she hit on my name, I mean?'

'Forget her,' he said. 'We can't get involved with patients. Come to bed.'

Twin Halves

Alien they seemed to be:
No mortal eye could see
The intimate welding of their later history,

Or sign that they were bent
By paths coincident
On being anon twin halves of one august event

A grey, overcast day, with little wind to agitate the sea, or to blow away the smoke, once the great battle was joined. Wednesday, 31 May 1916.

A grey day, too, in London's suburbia where smoke palled low over the featureless rows of chimneypots; and a day no less dull among the Derbyshire hills, where the trails of smoke hung heavy over little grey stone cottages amid endless miles of grey stone walls.

At three thirty in the afternoon, five ships of the Hochsee Flotte fired the first salvo, and those of the Battle Cruiser Forces lost no time in sending off a reply. Great events were toward, and those less great as well.

While the two biggest fleets the world had ever known stalked each other like a couple of strange tom cats over the North Sea, in Harrow-on-the-Hill Winifred Blake lay in labour. Things were not going easily, and the hired midwife sent hastily for the local doctor, who in turn dispatched his new, very nervous assistant. At four fifteen, just as a German shell landing on the *Indefatigable* blew her to pieces and sent two thousand souls to glory, the doctor and the midwife managed to get Winifred to launch her one and only child into the world.

Ten minutes later, at four twenty-five, a direct hit on the *Queen Mary* sent her and another two thousand men to the bottom. In compensation, as it were, up in Derbyshire, Gert Wood heaved through a wave of pain and deposited her seventh child and fifth son into the toil-roughened hands of her mother-in-law. In the cottage's only other room, Gert's husband, straight in from the fields, kept the old soot-blackened kettle boiling over the smoky fire, kept the other children from making too much row as they ate the bread and jam he had provided, and kept the late bottle-fed lambs alive till Gert should be able to take care of them again, along with all her other multifarious duties.

There was great rejoicing in the little grey house in Harrow-on-the Hill, and when the news of the fateful Battle of Jutland filtered through to her, Winifred felt that it was all as it should be. Her child had surely been destined to commemorate the struggle. All the omens pointed to it. Was she not descended from a long line of seafarers, even if they had not actually been in the Royal Navy? Was not the baby's father a clerk in the Admiralty, prevented from doing his duty at sea only by his C_3 physique and colour blindness? Was not the new baby's patronym Blake, that of one of England's great admirals? And had she not been attended at the birth by Dr Fisher, whose given name, for all she knew, might well have been Jackie?

There could be no doubt about it. Her precious little one must be given a name that would keep him in mind always of his destiny to further Britain's rule of the waves. After she had searched through her own memory and what information her husband could supply for a euphonious combination, the local vicar a month later was required to christen the child. He scooped the water over the grizzling baby, and recited sonorously, 'I baptise thee, Beresford Collingwood, in the name of the Father, and of the Son, and of the Holy Ghost.'

Winifred declared that his first given name should always be used in full, waging battle, in due course, with the headmaster of the prep school whose irreverent pupils had shortened the august cognomen to 'Berry', unnecessarily pointing out the difference between an illustrious admiral and the ubiquitous, occasionally poisonous objects to be found growing wild in any common hedgerow.

There was no such heart-searching with regard to Gert's child. She had long ago given up any interest in what her offspring should be called. All that was required was that he should be given a tag that would distinguish him from the four brothers he already had, and the others she feared he would inevitably have in the course of the next few years. She called him Fred – not Frederick, or softened into Freddie. He was plain Fred Wood, and that was that.

Beresford and Fred did not, of course, know of each other's existence, which was just as well. If by chance they had happened to meet while still young, they would have found nothing in common. Beresford, slight, dark, over-clean and over-polished, as precise in his manner as he was in his speech, would have needed an interpreter to make sense of ragged-trousered Fred's broad dialect. As for Fred, he would have regarded Winifred's young hopeful only good for kicking with his broken-toed boots, or as a legitimate target for a well-aimed handful of squishy sheep droppings.

Fate did well to keep them apart, until . . .

When Roger Spencer went to work in Sheffield, he had a problem, in the shape of a mother-in-law who was being difficult in every way. She was averse to the move, as she was to everything that concerned Roger – but they were stuck with her, and her wheelchair. She would not consider living in Sheffield, where once, in her youth, she had visited Tinsley. To her, Sheffield and hell were synonymous, full of raging fires, sulphurous smoke and black smuts.

There was only one thing to be done. They must find a house outside Sheffield, in the glorious countryside of hills and dales in which the city of steel is set. They tried – but hills mean houses with steps, and steps and wheelchairs are not a good combination, at least if the occupant of the wheelchair is as determined to be as obstructive as Roger Spencer's mother-in-law was.

Very well, they must build a house, with no steps. A bungalow, she insisted. Roger was beyond arguing. He found a plot and a builder, and put his faith in Time to work something out for him. The bungalow rose, with the usual spate of difficulties, until the great day came when they all moved in.

The old woman 'took agin it' from the outset. The hills frightened her, she said. To everybody else, the views from the windows of the bungalow were breathtaking – that is, if you were strong-minded enough to look at them instead of the devastation of mud, stone and builder's rubble lying immediately outside. The new bungalow stood in a quarter of an acre of ground from which every tree and bush and plant and weed had been ruthlessly torn out. A flimsy post and wire fence marked the boundary of the property, and between the concrete raft on which the dwelling stood and the temporary fence there was an expanse of ground dotted with large boulders, speckled with hundreds of stones of varying sizes, and spatchcocked with orange patches where in the course of construction the builder's sand had lain. In some places the contours of the garden resembled in miniature those of the surrounding countryside, with hills and valleys; and here and there were deep holes that reminded Roger continually of the bottomless pit into which he longed to consign his aged mother-in-law.

Roger had never been a gardener, mainly on the grounds that he hated the feeling of earth on his hands. His wife, Jill, didn't mind it when all she had to do was pull up a few weeds or snip off a few rose heads; but she was as cowed as he was at the prospect of ever reducing the wilderness outside the new bungalow to anything resembling a garden. They had already overspent on the building by yielding for the sake of peace at every point to Grannie's personal demands. A landscape gardener was obviously the answer, but from what source was the sort of money that he would ask ever likely to come? As summer drifted towards autumn, the stalemate continued. Then one day a saviour appeared, unheralded, at the back door.

It was a Saturday afternoon, and the atmosphere in the Spencer household was somewhat stormy as a result of a particularly virulent bout of obstinacy and perversity on the old lady's part. The sun shone gloriously over the hills, and Roger had suggested a ride out to Monsalhead, or somewhere – anywhere as long as they did not have to sit inside and view their immediate surroundings. Grannie refused either to go, or to be left. Defeated, Roger turned on the television. Grannie said it made her head ache. Roger turned the set where she couldn't see it, and the volume down so that she couldn't hear it, whereupon she entered into a loud-voiced conversation with Jill which soon turned into a rasping argument. Roger had just stood up to turn off the telly and join in when a knock came at the door. Gratefully, he went to open it, hoping for a diversion.

Standing on the slab of concrete that served as a doorstep was a short, spare, clean and tidy elderly man in working clothes. He was lean and wiry, and had a distinctly humped back, as Roger could plainly see because it was turned towards him as he opened the door. The stranger's head was covered with a large peaked cap, and his hands were deep in his trouser pockets as he stood, nonchalantly regarding the wilderness and taking his time before turning towards the opened door. He touched the peak of his over-sized cap, and looked up to Roger towering a good eighteen inches above him. Roger saw a weatherbeaten face dominated by a pair of twinkly blue eyes.

'Afternoon,' said the man. 'I'm Fred Wood, as lives down t'croft in t'village. I 'eered tell as you was looking for somebody to tek on t'job o' mekkin' this mess into a garden. I'm yer man.'

Relief and doubt alternated in Roger's bemused mind. Could this be help at last? What would the price be? And could this little specimen of a man really tackle that biblical job of creating order out of chaos? It was too good a chance to be missed for want of investigation, all the same.

'Come in!' he said. 'Let's talk it over.'

Fred removed his cap, revealing himself to be a man of sixty-plus with thin greying hair. He wiped his boots with care, and followed Roger into the sitting-room, where the altercation between Jill and her mother ceased abruptly as they took in the cause of its interruption. He stood in the middle of the room and smiled at Jill, while Grannie lowered her crackling newspaper and eyed him up and down like a mean housewife appraising a fillet of cod.

When she understood Fred's errand, Jill turned on all her charm and Fred responded. Roger saw at once that whatever he might have thought about the proposition, given time to consider it properly, was already irrelevant. The conclusion had been reached between Fred and Jill in that one smile.

At this point, Grannie dropped the ball of red wool that she insisted on keeping on the table at her elbow, though within living memory she had never been known to knit or to crochet a stitch with it. It was part of the impedimenta she insisted on carrying from room to room with her, and which also included such oddities as a bottle of aspirins that she never took, copies of the Bible, the Book of Common Prayer, *Culpepper's Herbal* and *Little Women* that she never opened, an alarm clock that told the wrong time, and a peeled banana that was replaced morning and night (because she never ate it) but which continually managed to fill the room with its sickly aroma.

The little ball of wool rolled across the floor, and Frabjous, Jill's Siamese cat, sprang after it, tossed it into the air and caught it, then dribbled it neatly with his forepaws between the goalposts of Fred's big boots.

Fred looked down at him with childlike delight. 'Ee!' he said, 'that wert best goal o't season, so far! Happen they doan't knaw about thee at Derby County!'

He stooped, picked up the ball of wool and wound it up, stepping lightly to the side of the old lady to replace it. She was watching him with her head cocked over to one side and a gleam in her eye, like a fat thrush listening for a worm. He blundered happily into the danger, and Jill, awaiting the pounce,

noted with relief that somehow or other he had managed to
come up on the right side of the belligerent old woman. He
tidied up the table to make room to put the wool down, and in
doing so picked up the clock.

'Yon clock's a liar,' he said. 'Wants to get theer afore all
t'others have set off!' He turned the hands till the clock showed
the correct time, checking it by his own battered pocket-watch.
Jill held her breath. Such interference from herself or Roger
would have set off an avalanche of wrath. All Grannie said was,
'Put it where I can see it. Thanks.'

It was Roger who smothered a gasp of astonishment this
time. He looked at Fred with admiration. A man who could
evoke a word of thanks from his awkward in-law was in Roger's
experience a new breed.

Fred and Grannie had continued to eye each other, and
suddenly both smiled, while a sort of holy silence descended on
the room. Then Fred broke it. 'Dost'a plaay dominoes?' he
asked.

'Not for years,' she said. 'It takes two.' (She cast a reproachful
glance over the top of her spectacles at Jill and Roger. They had
not played dominoes with her – but they had endured countless
hours of excruciating boredom every week playing Canasta,
which they both hated, particularly as Grannie cheated all the
time, and then accused them of doing so if she didn't win in
spite of it.)

'Ah, well – happen you and me could 'ave a gaame or two
some night when t'rest o' t' family's out. You'd be safe enough
wi' me.'

Jill really could not believe her ears. She hardly remembered
the last time she had been able to go out in the evening with
Roger.

Fred turned back to them, putting on his cap with long-
fingered brown hands. ''Appen we'd best tek a look at your
battlefield out theer,' he said. He touched his cap to Gran, again
to Jill, and fondled Frabjous, who made up his mind on the spot
not to let Fred out of his sight ever again if he could prevent it,

and strode to the door, with a dazed Roger behind him. Half an hour later the bargain was struck, and Fred peeled off his jacket to begin on his Herculean task.

'He's Puck,' Jill said to Roger, when her husband came back inside. 'A Derbyshire hob – or is it Yorkshire that has hobs? Robin Goodfellow, anyway. A household brownie. I don't believe it. He'll be gone tomorrow, vanished into thin air.'

Roger had taken her words more seriously than she had intended them. 'I always hold that folk beliefs have elements of truth behind them,' he said. 'If Fred Wood is typical of the Yorkshire or Derbyshire good-natured chap who can turn his hand to anything and will do so willingly for people he takes a fancy to, he and his kind are probably at the bottom of the belief in hobs and brownies. So we know what we have to do – the secret, if I remember rightly, is never to grudge them their wages, and never to pry into their private lives.'

'Done,' said Jill. 'Whatever Fred asks, he shall have.'

What he did ask was to be treated as a man, a friend, and not as a servant. It was more than easy. Gran and he were soon the best of cronies. He rarely came to the house without a posy of flowers, or an apple, or a geranium cutting in a pot, for his 'old lady'. His pockets also usually contained titbits for Frabjous, who ran wailing greetings to the door as soon as Fred's footfall reached his ears. Frabjous sat in dignified superintendence while Fred worked a miracle in the garden. By the time the first snow fell on the hills, order had been restored and a few bulbs planted against the spring.

Roger had misjudged the nature of winter in the hills, and without Fred to dig him out of his garage, warn him of black ice at certain spots, carry in the coal and do errands for Jill, their first winter there would have been hard indeed. But Fred was as faithful in attendance as the legendary hobs of the dales. Best of all was his soothing, pacifying, sweetening effect on Grannie. His visits, and his attentions to her in the way of playing dominoes or cards with her, alleviated the boredom that was the main cause of her obstreperousness. Mollified, she became a reasonable old woman again.

True to their resolve, they did not pry into Fred's private life, but little by little most of it was revealed to them through his conversations with Gran. He was a widower, who now lived with one of his sisters. He had been many things in his time – a farm labourer, a quarryman, a shepherd, a ganger for a construction company. At present he was a sort of general odd-job man, looking after one or two gardens, taking his turn at the petrol pumps, acting as cellar-man at the hotel in the tourist season, standing in as roundsman for the milkman – and generally waiting for his retirement at sixty-five. He had had his ankle broken by falling off a load of hay, and his foot crushed by a falling boulder in the quarry. A recalcitrant Ford Model T had broken his wrist for him and falling from a roof had broken his pelvis. None of these injuries seemed to diminish his ability to work. Neither did his humped back. As there was never any explanation forthcoming from him as to the cause of that, it was concluded that he had been like that from birth, so it was never mentioned by either side.

The garden took shape and blossomed under his hands. In the fourth spring of their sojourn among the peaks, Roger and Jill felt that their desert had been changed to Paradise. Even Grannie approved, and Fred beamed with pleasure and gratification at her praise, and worked all the harder. He had become one of the family. Then the blow fell. Roger was transferred – to Haywards Heath, in Sussex.

It would be difficult to decide which of the four of them was the most distressed. Roger had worries of his own with regard to his new job, and all the business of finding another new home. Jill faced a future without her household brownie, and his tranquillizing effect on her mother, who was now eighty-seven. Fred was utterly devastated, the tears trickling silently down his weathered cheeks as the full realization of the news went home to him. Grannie sat glum and resigned, as if the will even to argue had suddenly gone out of her.

Philosophically, it was Fred who recovered first.

'Ah thowt it were too good t'last,' he said. 'But mebbe there's som'at else round yon corner. One day at a time, Gran. One day at a time.'

Grannie could not and did not respond to his brave optimism. She was too old to face another upheaval, and began to decline. Then one evening when Fred was sitting with her she asked him to make her a cup of tea, and when he came back from the kitchen with it, she was still smiling in her wheelchair, but dead.

The relief that Jill, as well as Roger, felt had to be wholly dissembled in the face of Fred's overwhelming grief. For the rest of the time it took to sell the bungalow and organize the move, Fred went about his work wearing a grim carapace of resentful acquiescence to the inscrutable ways of fate. As he told Jill on one occasion, it had seemed to be so all his life. As soon as he had been handed something good with one hand, fate's other hand snatched it away from him.

'But Fred,' said Jill. 'Doesn't that mean that you have really always been a winner? After all, you've never let anything down you for long, have you? Who knows what may still be in store for you? Besides, let's remember how happy we have been together for the best part of five years. You made my mother's last few years happier than Roger and I could have ever thought possible. We'll keep in touch, you know – and if ever you feel like taking a holiday with us, just let us know.'

Fred brightened. Jill could see that she had hit the nail right on the head. It was the finality of parting with his new family that Fred had feared. The prospect of still being welcome to them was all that he needed to restore his faith in the genuineness of their feeling for him, now that his immediate usefulness to them was over.

'Aye!' he replied, suddenly smiling his old smile again. ''Appen I will tek 'oliday down south, one o' these days, if somebody else'll tek on lookin' after Lil fo' me for a spell.' Lil was the sister with whom he lived, but whom Jill had never seen. She had a weak heart, and never ventured abroad.

'You've got other sisters and brothers, haven't you?' Jill asked.

Fred settled his cap firmly on his head while considering the answer. 'I 'ad fower sisters and six brothers, all told,' he said. 'Two o' me brothers was killed down t'pit, one was blowed off rock face at t'quarry, and the oldest one went off t't 'fust war and were never 'eered on no more. The other two, as were twins, were both killed in t'second war.'

Jill was appalled at the note of fatality in his voice. 'And your sisters?' she said.

'One married a Yank – we doan't know wheer she is. Jinny married Bob Farrer, an' died 'eving 'er sixth, so Bob took an' married again an' went to live Manchester way. Then theer's our Lil. She allus been a bit simple, like, so I 'ave to look after her me'self. An' that only leaves Foxey.'

'Foxey?' Surprise jerked it out of Jill.

'Ay, Foxey-faace. That's what I allus call 'er, though her neame's Clara, b'rights. She'd 'ev the skin off your nose if she could sell it for a 'apenny, Foxey would. I doan't own her as no kin to me, an' never shall. So as long as Lil needs me, I'm stook 'ere. But mebbe there'll coom a day.'

Jill reported the conversation to Roger. It somehow high-lighted the image of Fred as a marked man, a Job-like target of misfortune who nevertheless had somehow managed to dodge the worst, and still come up with his twinkling eyes looking forward and anticipating better things.

They said goodbye to him in real and honest sorrow, leaving him standing bareheaded with tears flowing, while Jill sobbed openly into Frabjous's fur as the car finally took them round the hill that cut off their last sight of him.

Their new home over the border between Kent and East Sussex was very different from the bungalow. The elegant Edwardian house stood in a huge formal garden, with conservatory and greenhouses, a water garden, a croquet lawn, a walled rose garden, an orchard, a fruit garden, a vegetable patch, acres of lawn, miles of yew hedges, and a forest of trees and shrubs of such variety that Jill had never known existed. It was in the rhododendron belt: and it was in the rhododendron/azalea season that Jill first saw it. She had not been able to leave Grannie to go house-hunting herself, and had agreed to leave it to Roger. After the old lady died, Roger had wanted to keep his surprise for her, till the day they moved in.

Jill was enchanted, both with house and garden. She was also utterly appalled. She knew that Roger had stretched his financial resources to the limit to buy the property, leaving them all too narrow a margin to live on. Trust Roger, she thought bitterly, to take everything at face value, and not calculate the consequences. That breathtaking garden needed – had surely had until now, and would need in the future – the full-time services of a professional gardener, plus all the equipment he would require. 'Cutting the lawn', a nice half-hour of exercise on a suburban Sunday morning for a man with a sedentary city job, bore as much relation to the task of keeping the grass in this garden down as kicking a ping-pong ball about for Frabjous to play with bore to a cup tie between Arsenal and Manchester United.

What were they to do? How on earth could they ever hope to cope with it? Jill allowed Roger the pleasure of getting them straight before she dared broach the subject to him.

'I'm not so stupid,' he said. 'Of course I thought about it. The agent assured me that we could get a man from a local gardening firm one day a week. That ought to be enough, surely? Don't worry. I'll cut the lawns, and you can look after the rose bed and the herbaceous borders. The man can do the rest. We'll ask the neighbours.'

He put on his pipe, and puffed happily. He had not yet got used to his freedom from the incubus of his mother-in-law, and was more than usually light-headed and optimistic.

'But this isn't just a garden,' Jill said. 'It's an estate.'

'I thought you'd *love* it,' said Roger, looking hurt and crestfallen.

Jill's pleasure was dimmed with anxiety. She knew quite well the limit of Roger's capacity when it came to cutting lawns.

The neighbours proved to be a rather strange and unhelpful collection. There were two largish dwellings within a hundred yards. One was a farm, run by a successful indigenous farmer to whom land was meant for any and every use other than gardening. The second house, of similar style to their own, contained a retired diplomat who had reduced his garden to proportions he could manage single-handed, and was in any event inclined to hold himself aloof from newcomers.

That left one more near neighbour, who lived in a tiny, four-square little modern bungalow that was tucked in the shadow of the high yew hedge bordering their own garden at the back of the house. The roof of the bungalow could be seen from Jill's kitchen windows, but most of it was hidden by huge overgrown rhododendron bushes and the dark, heavy branches of an enormous macrocarpa that gave Jill nightmares on blustery nights.

After a month, the grass in their new garden was six inches high everywhere, and the yew hedges had sprouted yellow shoots that made them look like ancient chorus girls coming in after a night on the town – old, tired, dishevelled and in need of beauty treatment. Roger found an odd-job man whose one-day-a-week tiffling about only served to exaggerate the size of the difficulty they had got themselves into. He was expensive and lazy, and certainly knew as little as they did about coping with formal gardens the size of the one they now owned.

By September, things had begun to get seriously out of hand, and Roger had to admit that he had made a large and expensive mistake. The remedy, the only one they could foresee at all, was to sell again before time had made too many depredations on the beautifully laid-out surroundings to their house. The local hairdresser disclosed to Jill that the previous owners of Kenilworth House had been retired tea-planters who had kept a married couple as cook and full-time gardener. (Fancy Roger not finding out such a detail before he bought!)

'Oh!' said Jill, suddenly seeing the light. 'I suppose that accounts for that horrid modern little bungalow shoved in almost under out kitchen windows. I suppose they had it built for them.'

'Oh no, I don't think so,' said the girl. 'That's been there as long as I remember, though I believe it was once part of your property. They didn't live there – the couple I told you about, I mean.'

'Who does?' asked Jill. 'We've never seen anybody about there, but smoke comes out of the chimney, so I suppose it must be occupied.'

'Some queer old man who lives by himself – came here about five years ago. Nobody ever sees him, so they say. The tale is that he is a bit queer in the head. The milkman delivers milk and veg and finds the money on the doorstep once a week. The kids have made him into a sort of bogey-man. You wouldn't get either of my two down the Little Twitten after dark, for all the tea in China. But you know what kids are – they love to be scared. I should think he's just a harmless old chap who likes to be alone.'

'I shall keep watch,' said Jill. 'How intriguing!!'

Kenilworth House itself fronted a main road, though since it was set back in its own extensive garden and well screened by trees and bushes, the proximity of the road was never noticed. The gates to the property, however, were set facing a narrow, winding lane that ran between high-banked hedges, in true Sussex twitten style. The little bungalow next door had its tiny gate high up on the bank of the Little Twitten, and thick bushes of overgrown hazel and hawthorn practically obscured the rickety steps that led to the gate. As Jill realized when taking a closer look, the bungalow itself was almost invisible because of the mass of growth of all kinds relentlessly encroaching upon it.

'It must be as dark as winter in there, even in midsummer,' she said to Roger. 'The light can't get in anywhere.'

'Certainly not on our side,' Roger said. 'That yew hedge is at least twelve feet high – higher than the eaves, I imagine. And it can't be more than four feet from the windows on this side – but there are some windows because occasionally I've seen lights in them at night. And of course our great macrocarpa overhangs the bungalow anyway, as well as that mass of huge rhododendrons. You'd think he'd demand to have 'em cleared – but I hope to God he doesn't think of such a thing yet.'

'What are we going to do?' asked Jill.

Roger didn't know, and that was quite plain to both of them. 'Sell, I suppose,' he said at last. 'If we can find anybody fool enough to buy. The trouble is that it's the wrong time of the year, now. Remember I saw it first in spring.'

'With every blade of grass in apple-pie order, and not a weed to be seen,' added Jill. Roger looked so miserable that Jill decided to change the subject. She told him more details of her conversation with the hairdresser about their eccentric neighbour.

'I've seen him, once,' said Roger. 'I was up in the attic bedrooms, and you can see the end of his garden over the hedge from up there. Did you say he was a vegetarian? I think that perhaps accounts for what I saw. I was a bit puzzled.'

'What?' said Jill, eagerly. She was beginning to have an eerie, fascinated interest in the bogey-man next door.

Roger appeared a bit hesitant. 'Well – there's an ash sapling at the bottom of his garden, close to our hedge. You must have noticed its top branches from the lawn. When I looked out of the attic window, there was this old man tying things to the branches he could reach – an old cocoa tin, and a bit of red rag, and what looked like an old sock. But if he grows his own vegetables, no doubt he puts things up there to keep the birds off.'

'At this time of the year?'

'Oh yes, probably – after all, things like sprouting broccoli stand through the winter, and there's enough pigeons round here to strip a monastery garden, by the row they made in the mornings in summer.'

'They're ring doves,' said Jill knowledgeably. 'And collar doves, newly returned to these parts. I read about it.'

Oh, does it matter?' snapped Roger irritably. 'Anyway, I've

seen our cranky neighbour, that's what I was saying. Only I don't think he's cranky, if all he's doing is to keep the blasted birds off his patch.'

They let the subject drop. Any mention of the garden was now likely to produce the same sort of atmosphere as Grannie had been liable to do in the past. When the leaves began to fall and lie ankle-deep over the long grass, the gloom inside the house matched that outside. Their one-day-a-week man's efforts dwindled to utter futility against the magnitude of nature's dogged animosity. Yet Jill loved the house; its lovely, elegant proportions gave her immense pleasure, and just to move about in it was joy. The trees, seen from bedroom windows, were pictures in their own right, the evergreens a display of colours from misty blue to golden yellow, and the huge deciduous skeletons more graceful and grand than they had seemed to be in full leaf. In the afternoons, as the dusk fell and she sat before a huge log fire in the beautiful sitting-room, awaiting Roger's return from work, Jill felt that she had never been so happy. She racked her brains for some way to overcome the problems outside. The house itself welcomed her. It had seemed to open its arms to her the moment she stepped over the threshold. She loved it, and it loved her. The thought of leaving it was almost more than she could contemplate. She was glad, in spite of her worry, that there could be no question of putting it back on the market till the spring. After all, they had been through this all once before, and had not a miracle happened? Fate had sent them Fred.

Christmas had come and gone, and the dark time of the year was upon them all. Fog lay thick outside the windows, blotting out the ruin of the garden, and inside the huge logs of oak blazed in the handsome fireplace. Jill sat one afternoon with Frabjous on her knee, and knitting idle in her lap, just revelling in the warmth and beauty of the room while she yet had the chance. The ringing of the front doorbell sent a start of surprise through her, so unusual was a visitor at all, let alone in the dusk of such a day. Her first thought was of bitter resentment at being disturbed. Should she bother to answer the bell? It was probably only the lady delivering the church magazine. Then Frabjous unwontedly cocked up his head, listened intently, and leapt like a salmon from Jill's lap towards the door, wailing in high-pitched excitement. Goose pimples ran up Jill's arms as she followed Frabjous, thinking that he must have scented the bogey-man from the hungalow. She opened the door about six inches, leaving it on the chain while she peered into the fog-filled dusk.

A man in a trilby hat and a top coat too big for him stood outside, with a large suitcase in either hand. Jill was just about to utter the ritual 'Not today, thank you' dismissal, when Frabjous went through the door like a streak of liquid cream. The man dropped his suitcases and gathered him up, in doing so knocking his hat to the back of his head, and revealing himself. It was Fred.

'Fred!' said Jill, starting to cry as she fumbled to undo the chain. 'Fred!' She couldn't think of anything else to say.

'Ah. 'Ow do?' said Fred. 'Ah've coom for t'oliday as you promised me. Our Lil's 'ad to go t'old folks' 'ome – 'ad a stroke, like, an' doant knaw nobody. She'll niver coom out no more. So I coom, like I said I would. 'Appen you'll keep me for a week or two?'

By the time Roger got home through the fog, Fred had been warmed and fed and made much of. Then he and Jill had gone to work, and transformed the three attic rooms in the roof into a self-contained flat. One room was big enough to be a sitting-room; another had space enough, just, for a single bed; and miracle of miracles, the third was an old but still functioning bathroom.

'As long as you like,' Jill kept saying, still tearful, even after they had installed the bed and made it up, and set oil-filled radiators and fan-heaters to work to air the place (quite unneces-sarily – the central heating system reached the attics).

As soon as it was daylight next morning, Fred appeared in his working clothes, and stepped out into the garden. He had never before seen one anything like it. It was as if his dream of Paradise had suddenly materialized. He wandered up and down, with Frabjous at his heels, bemused by happiness and amazement. As if in sympathy, the sun came out, and showed him everywhere signs of the coming spring: aconites under rhododendron bushes, lilac buds swelling, snowdrops hidden in the long grass, and, wonder of wonders, the first camellia just showing its delicate pink petals. Jill was sure they had not been there the day before. They had come out, all of them, like the sun, just to greet Fred.

Then Fred set to work. He and the hired man had what Fred called 'a bit of a bargy' on the first day the odd-job man came, and Fred ended by ordering him off the premises. He twinkled as he recounted the story to a somewhat dismayed Jill.

'You see what yon means,' Fred said. 'Ah've coom to stop.'

Jill in turn recounted the day's happenings to Roger.

'It's all very well,' said Roger, 'but you know as well as I do that we can't afford to keep Fred and pay him a full-time gardener's wages. He can't stop.'

'Oh yes he can,' said Jill, bridling and ready for a fight. 'Don't you remember? He's our household brownie. He's been sent to us, and we mustn't refuse. What's more, we must never grudge him either food or wages.'

In the event, it was not necessary to quibble. Fred had turned sixty-five, and had his pension. He owned the house he had left in Derbyshire, and soon let it with ease. According to his lights, he was a well-off man. All he wanted for the privilege of being with 'his' family, and of being allowed to work in 'his' garden, was the roof over his head, his food (which turned out to be so little and so simple that Jill said it was like feeding a harvest mouse) and five pounds a week, which is what they had had to pay the odd-job man for one day. For a second time, a miracle had happened, and for the second time, the miracle was Fred.

Every hour that it was light, Fred worked in the garden, wet or fine. He, too, had never been so happy. The rose garden was his special delight, but little by little the whole estate responded. In early May, the yew hedges once more had sprouted new and yellow tufts. Armed with the latest thing in shears, Fred attacked them till they all stood again trimmed and demure, as orderly and precise as a row of uniformed schoolgirls. All, that is, except the huge one between the house and the bungalow. Even Fred quailed a little at the size of that. In the first place, he could only reach the top of the hedge from the full height of a pair of household steps, because the hedge, thick as it was, would not support a ladder. Secondly, the hedge had grown wide as well as high, never having been trimmed at all on the bungalow side. No way could he reach the whole width from his own side.

"Appen I shall have to ask to take steps round into yon garden,' he said to Jill.

Jill looked dubious. She had already told him what she had heard about their strange neighbour.

'Aye! I know,' Fred went on. 'I 'eared about him in t'pub. And Ah've seen 'im, a few times, like, from my bedroom window, skulking down his garden and standing under t'little ashling. 'Armless as a kitten, I should think. Just a bit odd, like.'

'Well, don't approach him till you must,' said Jill.

Fred gave the matter some thought. 'Won't hurt if t'hedge is left till July,' he said. 'You shouldn't trim yew till then, b'rights. 'Appen I'll clear the patch outside t'kitchen window – cut down some o' the rubbish, prune them rosydendoms, an' tek a few o't lowest branches off that big dark tree, an' let some light into t'kitchen. Didst'a knaw theer's a lily pond under all that muck?'

'No!' said Jill, unbelieving. 'Really?' The garden was always yielding surprises. Jill half-believed Fred magicked them into being for her delight.

'I'll find it fo' tha,' said Fred, and set to work.

'Coom and see,' he said to Jill one morning, and she followed him out of the kitchen door. There were no lilies in the pool, because there was no water, but the possibilities were great. At the back of it, between its further end and the hedge, was a huge dark rhododendron bush, at present a towering mass of blood-red blooms.

'Ah'll not cut yon bush till t'flowers are ower,' Fred said.

Frabjous was behaving strangely, poking about under the bush. Then, with a yowl that broke the peace as the whistle of a falling bomb might have done, he streaked away at full speed to the open kitchen door. They watched his ignominious retreat with amused astonishment, and Fred said, 'Must be summat alive under yon bush,' and went to investigate.

'Well I never!' he said. 'Coom 'ere.' Jill went, and peered down through the bush down the hole he was making for her. Close to the main trunk of the bush, a snarling black and white cat was guarding a brood of equally ferocious-looking kittens, six in all. They were about five weeks old, a mixture of all sorts of colours, beautiful as all kittens are yet, as Jill could see at a glance, wild and quite unapproachable. Their terrified mother, still spitting and snarling, turned great green eyes of terror upon the intruders, but refused to abandon her offspring. She was so thin that she could hardly stand, and her bones stood out round a scraggy little neck with an almost non-existent ruff that she was still bravely attempting to erect as a warning.

Jill was distressed. She loved cats, and the thought of the hunger just outside her own over-filled kitchen was more than she could bear.

'Leave them alone,' she commanded. 'I'll go and make some bread and milk for the kittens, and get some of Frabjous's cat food for the mother.'

'Best send for t'RSPCA to put 'em all down,' advised Fred. 'They're wild, anyway. An' mebbe full o' worms. We doan't want Frab to catch anything from yon lot, do we?'

'No,' said Jill. 'But he won't. Let 'em stop wild. But I shall feed them.'

Fred never argued with Jill. He helped her to set the food out for the brood day after day, and brought in empty plates after washing them under the garden tap. The kittens grew rapidly, but seldom left their shelter under the bush. Meanwhile, having cleared everything else around the bush, Fred had revealed the truth that the yew hedge at that point had succumbed, years before, to the tangle of dark undergrowth. It gave out in a straggly fashion at the spot where the bungalow began, perhaps having been broken in the first place during the construction of the dwelling. The boundary between the two properties for about twenty yards consisted of nothing more than a tangle of hawthorn, which Fred attacked with vigour and reduced in an hour or two to a respectable hedge. Next day, a spring gale brought down a large branch from the macrocarpa. It missed the bungalow, falling on to the Kenilworth House side, where the only casualty was a neglected azalea bush. Fred's efforts and the wind between them had, however, now bared the side of the bungalow to full view, and it was not exactly a pleasant sight. There were two windows on the side facing Jill's kitchen, one mercifully still hidden by the red 'rosydendom' bush. The other was such a terrible eyesore that Jill wished heartily that Fred had let well alone. The window had obviously not been cleaned within living memory. A tattered rag of a curtain that had once been orange hung across it from one side, not quite covering the whole of the glass, in fact leaving about twelve inches undressed. Through this aperture it was possible, occasionally, to see an unshaded electric bulb swinging, and now and then a movement inside.

The kittens grew fat, and played about under the bush. The mother was rarely glimpsed, but even she now appeared to have put some flesh upon her bones, and was less defiant.

Jill was busy in her breakfast-room one morning, and Fred was cutting the croquet lawn, out of reach, when the front door-bell sounded. Hastily taking off her apron, Jill went to open the door. Standing where Fred had stood three months before was an old man, dressed very neatly in a worn and slightly grubby suit, with a white shirt, also very dirty around the collar, and an old-fashioned trilby hat.

He doffed the hat, and stood with it in his hands. 'Mrs Spencer? I hope I have the name correct. I am your neighbour, upon the lane side. I live in the bungalow.' The voice was firm and well modulated, the diction precise, and the tone educated. Jill was frankly astonished.

'I am pleased to make your acquaintance,' she said. 'Do come in. I'm afraid I don't know your name.'

'My name is Beresford Blake. Thank you, madam, but I will not come in. I have come to register a complaint – indeed, two complaints.'

'Indeed?' said Jill, slightly adjusting her welcoming attitude. 'In what way have we offended you, Mr Blake? I assure you it was not intentional.' (She heard herself with some surprise adopting his own mode of speech, or so it seemed.)

'I respect the privacy of others. I do not spy upon them, and do not wish them to spy upon me. I have until now managed to maintain the sort of privacy I desire. You have robbed me of it, exposed me to the gaze of all in your house or your garden. You had no right to do so.'

'Oh come, Mr Blake,' said Jill. 'We had every right to do so. As you must know, the boundary hedge is ours, so we have an absolute right to keep it trimmed. And as for the branch of the tree, that came off in a gale. You should be as thankful as we are that it did not crash down on your roof. I'm sorry if it upsets you to have your windows exposed, but really, there is nothing we can do about it.'

'That I shall make it my business to see about,' he replied.

Jill was by now thoroughly nettled. 'And your other complaint?' she asked, coldly.

'Yes. I believe you have been feeding the kittens that were born under the rhododendron bush. You have no right to do that, either. They are my cats.'

'But they're wild!' exclaimed Jill. 'And they were starving. How do they become yours?'

'The father was my cat, my only companion. He was killed by a lorry on the main road. I can see by the colour and markings of some of the kittens that they are his offspring. I therefore claim them as mine. I shall appreciate it if you will cease forthwith from enticing them to your side of the hedge by giving them food.'

'I will – providing you feed them yourself,' said Jill icily.

'Then good morning, madam,' he said, putting on his ancient hat again. He turned his back on her as if he might have been a soldier on parade, and marched off.

'Well!' said Jill. 'The old so-and-so! Nasty old man.' She was quite upset about the cats, suspecting that they would now go hungry.

But surprisingly, Fred said it was a good thing. 'Cats has got to have somewheer to scratch,' he said. 'When I get seed-bed properly going, one cat in't garden'll be plenty.'

They had a family conference about the whole matter that night, Fred included. Roger was irritated by the old man's complaints, but in his usual manner prepared to take the course of least resistance. Fred was furious because Jill was upset, but said that at least it solved one problem. There was obviously no way the silly old fool would ever let him get to the other side of the big yew hedge. He'd have to find some other fashion of getting it clipped and lowered.

'Leave it alone,' said Roger. 'It doesn't really matter, does it? We don't want to antagonize him any further. If you lower the hedge, you'll rob him of more privacy, because we could then see into his garden. Let's leave it as it is.'

Fred usually took advice, though never instructions. He gave in very reluctantly. It vexed him to the core that he had to leave one side of his precious lawn and rose bed bordered by such a dishevelled untidy hedge. He had all the true gardener's passion for neatness.

'Well, theer's one thing,' he said. 'If I let yon big hedge be, Ah'll keep the bit in front of his mooky winders free o' every twig as grows. An' if I see one of his damn cats on my seed bed, I'll kill it wi' t'hoe.'

Jill did not take the threat seriously, knowing Fred's soft heart. All the same, the friction that had been set up between the occupants of the house and the bungalow gave her an uneasy concern, like finding a tiny lump on her person that might one day prove to be malignant.

It was not long before developments began. Fred, true to his declaration, made a special point of keeping clear the area between the kitchen windows, even trimming back the rhododendron to half its size. While he was doing it, the face of Beresford Blake would occasionally lurk in the shadows behind the dirty glass. Then, one morning towards the middle of June, a couple of the now half-grown cats came through the hedge in search of the food they appeared badly in need of. Fred picked up a clod of earth, and aimed it well enough to hit one. They skedaddled away, and Fred thought no more about it. Next morning, however, he came in to fetch Roger, it being Saturday.

'Come an' look 'ere,' he said, and led Roger to a view of the bungalow's window. Inside the glass at the place where the ragged curtain did not cover, two pieces of paper had been pasted. One was a page from a tabloid paper, showing a very nude girl in an extremely sexy attitude. The other was a crudely drawn picture of the devil, with two enormous horns and an evil expression.

'What dost mek o' that?' asked Fred.

'Well, it's obviously intended as an insult,' replied Roger. 'But I'm afraid it does rather prove that the old man's a bit touched. Just try to take no notice.'

Fred tried, but found it difficult. Jill didn't try, and found it sinister. When, the next day, she went down with a mild migraine of the kind she thought she had grown out of, the image that floated insistently before her throbbing eye was the evil face of the devil, with Beresford Blake's features.

The morning of midsummer day dawned bright, crisp and fair. In these long days of daylight, Fred was up with the lark, grudging every hour that he could not spend in the garden.

When Jill came down to breakfast, Fred had a strange tale to report. 'Ah were gettin' dressed, up in t'attic,' he said, 'and Ah loooked out t'winder, across to old Blake's garden. And theer' 'e wa', halfway up yon little ash-tree, 'anging all sorts o' things on it, like. It were still a bit misty wi' t'dawn, an' I couldn't see proper what t'things were, but I could see as 'e were putting 'em high enough to show over our hedge, an' all on our side. So I makes up me mind to go and tek a look as soon as I'd 'ad me breakfast. He'd got a rickety old pair o' steps up against tree, an' I watched 'im close-like till 'e got down safe, in case 'e fell off. But he folded the steps up, and laid 'em under hedge. And then 'e started going round tree, bowing to it, like – right down t't'ground, wi' his 'ands clasped together. An' when e'd done, he walked back'ards away from it all the way back to t'bungalow – well, as far as I could see 'im. Every now and then he'd stop, and bow down, and then go on again, back'ards, like I said.'

'Did you go and see what the things were?' asked Jill. She was uneasy at further proof that old Blake was really mad, and worried about the effect it was having on Fred. It was beginning to get under his skin, this antagonism with their nearest neighbour. She had observed him several times, just lately, eyeing the yew hedge, waging war upon the seven cats, and generally retaliating in a way unusual to one of his placid, contented, tolerant nature. She began to sense in Fred a very tough streak indeed, once his ire was aroused. She remembered his remarks about his sister, Foxey.

'Oh-ah! I went t'look all right. Blooody old fule.' (Jill had never heard Fred swear in her presence before. It was a sign of his deep perturbation.)

'There's a lot o' red rag – looks as if it's dipped in red ink t'make it loook like blood. Then there's several bits o' wood nailed together in queer shapes, and an old biscuit tin, big and shiny like. And right over on our side, there's a chamber pot, an' next to it summat as I doan't want thee to see. So keep away till t'boss comes back, an' when he's 'ad a loook, Ah'll tek it down, in t 'dark, tonight.'

'OK,' said Jill, half relieved at not being asked to inspect the pitiful signs of Blake's madness, and yet undeniably curious. As soon as she was alone with Roger, she asked to be fully informed.

Roger looked as if he didn't know whether to laugh or be angry. 'The object was a phallic symbol with a vengeance,' he said. 'A sort of pagan, midsummer orgy phallic emblem, made out of a rolling-pin with a couple of onions nailed to it at the base. Fred's so blazing furious that it worries me what he may do. My instinct is just to ignore the silly old man and his ju-jus. They can't do any harm.'

Jill shivered. 'I don't know about that,' she said. 'Why did you call them ju-jus if you don't think they are intended to harm us? They make me uneasy, and they are upsetting Fred. That horrid old man's just spoiling things for us. Taking the shine off. Is he mad, really? Ought we not to report it? Is he safe to be left, for instance? Suppose he set his house on fire – ours would probably go up as well!'

Roger answered her seriously, to her relief. 'I don't think he's mad in that way,' he said. 'He's just extremely eccentric. I think that tree is his ju-ju tree, or clootie-tree – they're both the same thing. Sort of devil worship.'

'That's right! Fred said he was bowing to it,' Jill exclaimed.

'Well, devil worship's nothing new, is it?' said Roger. 'It can only do harm to you, or us, if we let it.'

'It's Fred I'm worrying about,' Jill said.

Roger laughed. 'He's the one least likely to be affected,' he said. 'All it'll do to him will be to make him lose his temper. He doesn't know about ju-jus. That saves him from any consequences.'

So, for the time, it proved. Fred cut off the offending articles in the dusk that evening, and threw them back on old Blake's side of the hedge. He expected them to be replaced, but they were not. Apart from constant war against the cats, peace reigned. In the early autumn, the mother cat produced a new litter of kittens, among them a half-Siamese that had only one eye, the other being a hollow socket.

'Now, Frabjous, what has thee bin oop to?' asked Fred disapprovingly of his companion.

'Not guilty, Fred,' said Jill. 'The spirit, I'm sure, is willing, but the flesh in this case is weak.'

'Shaame,' said Fred, twinkling. 'But Ah'm glad 'e 'ad nowt to do wi' young Nelson ower theer.'

Jill, however, had a very soft spot for Nelson, who often came through the hedge for the scraps she secretly fed him. He was woefully thin.

'I wonder if I ought to send for the RSPCA,' she said. I don't think Mr Blake feeds the cats properly. There's a lot of them, now. Twelve cats take quite a lot of keeping.'

'Thirteen,' said Fred.

'How come?'

'He's took in another mangey old tom, a black 'un, half wild, as used to be at the farm. A real devil-cat, Tom is. That meks thirteen on 'em.'

At Hallowe'en, objects as before reappeared on the 'clootie tree'. Fred removed them. Next morning he looked to see if they had been replaced. Only the red rag had been restored, but stuck into the hedge near the sapling two broomsticks had been erected. On the top of each was a man's shoe, with the soles turned towards Kenilworth's garden. On each of the shoe soles was painted in white a grinning, snarling face. That on the left shoe was adorned by a pair of horns.

Fred allowed it all to 'set his hackles up', and did his utmost to remove them, but in vain. The broomsticks were held firmly in the hedge well over towards Blake's side, and too high for Fred to reach. All he succeeded in doing was to knock them somewhat askew, which added menacingly to their leering, baleful presence. After a couple of days Fred gave up his efforts to remove them, and did his best to ignore them by working harder than ever. On the third day, the local log man arrived with five tons of oak logs, to last them through the winter.

'Give us a hand, mate,' he said to Fred, who willingly went to stack the logs as the other man threw them off the truck. The load slipped, and a particularly heavy log landed on Fred's left instep. His foot swelled like a balloon, and the pain made him sweat in tight-lipped endurance. Once Roger was home, they took him to the nearest hospital.

'No bones broken,' the doctor said cheerfully. 'But it's going to be a fair time before you're on that foot again. It's just caught a nerve that happens to be particularly painful.' Fred said he knew that, already. He accepted the casualty as he had done every other that had happened to him. He fretted at the inactivity it caused him, but otherwise took it philosophically. He did not appear to connect it in any way with Blake's ju-ju shoes, but Jill did, and said so to Roger.

'Nonsense!' said Roger sharply. 'You are getting a thing about it You'll make yourself ill. Forget it.'

She tried. Nelson still came to be fed, and one day he actually allowed her to stroke him. She had a feeling that she was being observed, and was correct in thinking so. Next day, the shoes had gone, and the mop-head had been re-employed. On the mop this time was a hat – a perfectly good tweed hat such as is worn by either men or women in the country. The mop had been given a crude pair of Cupid's-bow lips, a round blob of paper for a nose and raddled cheeks. The mop-head face also wore a pair of spectacle frames through the left empty socket of which was thrust a spike of wood.

Jill was frightened. There was now no denying the truth of it. 'It's meant for me, this time,' she said to Roger. 'When he put the shoes up, Fred hurt his foot. Now it's my eyes he's aiming for.'

'Don't be so silly,' Roger retorted. 'Don't you see, you are playing directly into his hands? He's took agin us and is clever enough to try this way of making us quit. He knows perfectly well that if he keeps it up long enough, coincidence will come to his aid. How could he possibly have known that Briggs was going to deliver logs that week? We didn't know ourselves. Well, we are simply not going to let him win. He can't if you don't take it seriously. He can, if you let him drive you into a state about it. Come on, darling. This really isn't like you.'

He went to her, and made her look at him. She was sitting with her embroidery in her lap, and the spectacles she wore only for close work hung on her chest by a chain round her neck. Roger bent down, but she anticipated his desire to comfort her, and stood up, depositing Frabjous and the embroidery in a heap on the floor.

'Darling,' said Roger, putting protective arms around her, 'this is just a battle of wills, you know. There's nothing spooky about it. Don't be frightened. Just laugh at the silly old man. Remember Axel Munthe, in *The Story of San Michele*. We've often quoted it before. "The devil himself can do nothing to a man so long as he can laugh!"' He kissed her, gently, and she put her head down on his chest, thinking.

'But Munthe himself believed in the supernatural,' she said. 'Goblins and presentiments and miracles. He'd have been just the one to take notice of old Blake's threats!'

Roger realized that she really was frightened. His arms closed round her, at first protectively, and then passionately, tightening with love and the anger surging through him that she should be so unnecessarily disturbed. She put up her face to be kissed – but a crack and the sound of breaking glass stopped the caress in mid-air. Jill's spectacles had taken the brunt of the embrace, and the left lens lay shattered on the carpet.

As they took in what had happened, their previous roles were reversed. Jill began to laugh, partly in hysterical surprise, partly in relief. The old devil had only got her glasses, not her eyes! Roger, on the other hand, found goose pimples on his arms, and a sensation of cold water down the back of his neck. He pulled himself together quickly.

'The arm of coincidence is really very long, obviously,' he said wryly. 'I suppose in a way he did cause the accident to your glasses. But if he intended anything, it wasn't as innocuous as that. Blast him.'

'Don't worry,' Jill said. 'I'm all right now.'

Roger gathered up the broken glass, thinking hard.

They talked about it with Fred, Roger putting his serious thought into words. He felt that he could deal with Jill's fears, but considered Fred's reaction, the anger of a simple, uncomplicated man, a more serious threat. Fred might be a natural philosopher, but he was not accustomed to reasoning in words.

Roger explained his own theory that old Blake was a man with a kink, and that unwittingly they had got across him.

'But he can only cause serious trouble if we let him,' he said. 'If he wants to stick obscene things up in his hedge, he will. We could, I suppose, call in the police – but that would make us ridiculous. You would probably have got that log on your foot if the Queen had lived next door. And people break their glasses every day. We are just going to ignore him. Can we rely on you, Fred, to do it too?'

Fred looked dubious. 'Ah'd sooner knock his block off,' he said, belligerently.

'Please, Fred,' said Jill, and the battle was won.

'Tha art t'boss,' said Fred. 'But if theer's monny more 'appenings like yon, mebbe Ah'll act fust and let thee knaw later on.'

He grinned, and put on his cap. They felt they could trust him.

'Till next time,' said Jill.

'There won't be a next time,' said Roger.

'Oh yes, there will. Things always go in threes.'

'Aye. That's what Levi Ollerenshaw said when his wife had their third set of twins. But 'e were wrong. They turned out to be triplets,' said Fred, stumping off into the garden.

The rest of the winter passed in comparative peace. Then spring came round again. Fred now had his vegetable patch under control, and began to sow seeds. The old tom cat next door was far less under control, and did his duty manfully. By the time Fred's seeds were sprouting well, the tally of cats and kittens next door had risen to thirty-seven. As Mr Blake's garden was nothing but an overgrown wilderness of long grass and rubbish, the whole brood the other side of the hedge regarded the vegetable patch as a heaven-sent feline convenience.

Fred was at his wits' end, and at the end of his patience, too. He piled up a heap of missiles – clods of earth, bits of wood and stones – and became expert at aiming swiftly and accurately at squatting cats. One day he managed to take young Nelson fair and square on his blind side as he sat in exquisite satisfaction with his other eye closed. Nelson gave a leap and a yowl that advertised his Siamese ancestry far and wide, and bolted, unhurt, through the hedge.

Next morning, a pair of gloves adorned the hedge, mounted on a pair of broomsticks. They were of expensive brown leather, in perfectly good condition, except that the middle finger of the right hand had been unpicked, so that the fourchettes hung away from the back and front, giving the whole finger the appearance of a peeled banana.

'Now what's he after?' asked Fred, pointing the adornment out to Jill. 'Silly old b— — silly old fool! There's monny a chap in t' pit as 'ould like a pair o' gloves like them for Sundays.'

'Don't let's bother about them,' said Jill. 'They're not offensive, after all.'

Two days later, her comment was no longer true. The left glove had been rearranged, and was now standing up stiffly in the position of insult recently euphemized as a 'Harvey Smith'. Roger refused to be rattled, and for the time being succeeded in calming Fred. Jill's attitude had changed. She had begun to realize that the situation had its humorous side, and when, peering out of her kitchen window, she saw the glove, it found her funny bone. She let out a peal of laughter that Roger was extremely glad to hear. She said she had begun to feel sorry for the mad old man next door, and very sorry for Fred, besides being most concerned about the plight of so many underfed cats, but she wasn't frightened any more.

Roger was worried, all the same. The cats were beginning to present a greater threat to their stability than ever Blake himself had done. Fred was grumbling, and making veiled threats, not against Blake, but against the futility of trying to garden under the conditions posed by Blake and his cats. He had even hinted once or twice that he might as well be tending his own garden back in Derbyshire.

Without Fred, they could not remain at Kenilworth House.

Something had to be done – but what? If thirteen had increased to thirty-seven in one year, how many cats would there be by next spring? It was no use calling in the police, because there are no laws relating to cats as trespassers. The RSPCA? Roger examined the cats for obvious signs of mange or ill-treatment. Apart from the fact that they were all thin and wild-looking, they seemed healthy enough. He doubted if he could make stick a statement that the cats were starving, and he did not now underrate the intelligence, however warped, of their neighbour. He was irritable because of his frustration. It was unbelievable that he was afraid of being ousted from the house of his dreams by one senile old man and a clutter of cats! He was in such a dour mood on the next Saturday evening that he and Jill had one of their very rare quarrels, and she took herself off to bed in a huff, leaving Roger to get his own bedtime drink. She knew him well enough to predict that he would also make hers and bring it up, using the opportunity it gave to 'make it up' with her. She set the bedroom door wide open, and kept her ears alert for the sound of his footsteps crossing the wide hall towards the kitchen. When she heard them, she sat up and prepared herself to be as contrite as was necessary, and as welcoming as she knew how.

Then she heard Roger's voice, loud and raised in pent-up anger. 'What are you doing there, you old black devil?' he shouted.

Jill had no idea who it could be downstairs. She leapt out of bed, and as she did so, pandemonium broke loose in the kitchen – such a confusion of thumping, cursing, screaming, banging, wailing and clattering that it defied all explanation. She stopped, terrified, and even more so when the noise stopped as suddenly as it had begun, and was followed by ominous silence. Willing herself forward, she went towards the kitchen. Roger was hanging over the sink, his face very white and his hands very red. He had his right hand under a running tap, and it took Jill only a split second to see that the middle finger had been ripped open from the top joint to the bottom.

She phoned for the doctor before she went to Roger's assistance, pouring him a stiff whisky to drink while she plunged his hand into a bowl of Dettol. It required five stitches, and the doctor insisted on prophylactic injections when he heard what had happened.

'I went into the kitchen,' Roger told them, 'and there was that old black tom cat of Blake's standing on the draining board, licking the plates. I shouted at him, and opened the door. But instead of going out that way, he leapt at the window and started clawing up the curtains. So I grabbed him by the scruff of the neck, and he turned on me. He ripped my finger and I had to let go – after knocking the saucepans down and smashing the crockery in the sink.'

'You never heard such a row,' said Jill. 'What with the cat yowling and Roger swearing, it sounded as if a battle had begun.' She was cheering up fast, having decided that if anybody could be of any assistance to them, the doctor might be that man.

He was peering at Roger over his half-spectacles, while putting the finishing touches to a most professional-looking bandage and sling.

'Now,' he said, 'that should be all right. But I don't like the sound of that mangy old cat. If there's any sign of trouble with that finger, don't delay. We can't take chances.'

Jill took the bull by the horns. She put their case to him briefly and succinctly, and he listened without interruption. 'He's quite mad, obviously,' she concluded. 'Surely he ought not to be left alone there? And all those cats – the place must be filthy! Surely there's some sort of health regulation about such things?'

The doctor shook his head, sympathetic but professionally unmoved. 'He is a patient of mine,' he said, 'so of course I can't discuss him medically with you.' He paused, and stood up, as if to leave, but seeing Jill's stricken face, he sat down again. 'On the other hand, you also are my patients, and perhaps if I try to explain a bit we may head off further trouble for everybody in

CAVAN COUNTY LIBRARY

the future. He is not mad – clinically, that is. A year or two ago, he was found unconscious by the milkman, and had to spend some weeks in hospital with pneumonia. He hardly ever eats, you know – it took some time to get him built up again to the state where he could be discharged. In the end, he discharged himself. But while he was in there, the police traced his only relative – a cousin who has since died. She averred that he was a perfectly normal young man until they lost touch with each other during the war – clever, intelligent, ambitious, a civil servant of some kind who had spent some time in Africa. That's all she knew. We got a psychologist to see him – a friend of mine. His opinion was that as a child Mr Blake had probably been over-protected, kept over-clean and over-restricted – typical of a middle-class only child in suburbia between the wars. Something had unhinged him a bit, some time – probably some pretty terrible happening during the war, perhaps in the London blitz. He's quite sane, though eccentric, according to medical standards. If he's as offensive as you say he is deliberately, I suppose your only comeback is via the police. I'm afraid it isn't a medical problem, so far. The cats, as far as I know, are a recent development; but again, provided you feed them, I don't think there's any law about the number of cats you can keep. You could, I suppose, try a civil action against him for nuisance, but that would be an expensive business. Cheaper to buy your vegetables, I'd say.'

He got up to go.

'The silly old man's just "took agin us",' said Jill.

'Let your hedge grow up again. Give him back his privacy.'

Jill let him out. It was no use trying to explain about Fred, or about the uncanny coincidences. That would only result in them all being branded as loony as their neighbour.

It was three weeks before Roger could go back to work, and the long scar down his finger remained for the rest of his life. Somehow the summer passed, with constant battles between Fred and the cats, which continued to produce kittens of every colour and variety. Odd things went up in the hedge and on the ash tree, but for the moment, at least, they seemed harmless enough – a lavatory brush and a cocoa-tin, a pair of odd socks, a string of potatoes threaded on to a wire, a cardboard hat saying 'kiss-me-quick' across the front. Jill felt ashamed of her foolish fears. She had allowed herself to be rattled by a string of coincidences. She felt that now they had all begun to live with each other with a certain amount of tolerance, even from Fred.

One thing Fred would not do, however, was to let the screen between 'his' garden and the bungalow grow up again. He kept every twig that grew ruthlessly pruned, while on his side old Blake erected boards, corrugated iron, blankets and anything else he could think of against his windows. Jill was angry with both of them, but said nothing.

Spring had produced the usual yellowish-green fringes on the yew hedges, and Fred had clipped them all off again on every inch except for the huge divide between the two gardens. Then one September morning, the local hardware shop delivered to Kenilworth House a brand-new aluminium ladder-cum-steps, addressed to Mr F. Wood. His eyes twinkled as he stripped off the wrappings.

'Bin wantin' one o' these sin' Ah first saw it advertised in t' local paper,' he said. 'Yon hedge 'as got to coom under shears for 'aircut now. See – I can lift 'em wi' one finger! Beautiful, they are.'

Jill could no more have forbidden him to erect them against the hedge than she could have taken a toy from a child on Christmas morning, but all the same she watched him go whistling down the garden with foreboding. She noted with relief that he attacked the hedge at the very far end, away from the bungalow, where their own property ran both sides of it. The results were amazing, and Fred worked with a zest and joy quite heartening to behold, if it had not been that his efforts were taking him nearer and nearer to the junction with Blake's garden where the ash sapling stood adorned in a new crop of miscellaneous objects, including a colander filled with ancient tennis balls, hung carefully by its two handles so that its contents should not spill. The very nature of the exhibits confirmed the doctor's theory of eccentricity in the extreme as opposed to insanity. She prayed silently that Fred's eccentricity with regard to neatness would not cause an explosion.

On the morning of the third day, Fred rose earlier than usual and was out with his ladder and his shears soon after it was light. By the time he came into breakfast, the ash tree was exposed from its tip down to its lower branches, Fred having taken about two feet from the top of the hedge.

'Can't mek a proper job on't,' he said regretfully over his toast, which he ate by dipping it deep into a mug of tea so strong that it resembled sepia ink. 'I kin reach over t'top, but not down yon side. Mebbe I'll creep over afore 'e's up termorrow morning.'

'You'll do nothing of the kind,' Jill said, quite sharply. 'That would be trespassing.'

Fred looked dour, and said nothing, so Jill turned on her charm and pleaded. She knew she had won, and went off to her chores feeling fairly confident. It was about eleven o'clock when she heard raised voices, and rushed to an upstairs window to look out. Fred had been snipping away happily, gathering up his clippings at intervals into neat heaps on the path. He was about to climb the ladder again when a whole armful of clippings descended from above on his head.

'What the bloody —?' he said to himself, and proceeded to climb the ladder.

Standing on an identical ladder on the opposite side of the hedge was the neighbour, his arm full of the clippings that had fallen his side of the hedge.

The paths of Beresford Collingwood Blake and plain Fred Wood had crossed at last, and there they now stood, face to face with only a yew hedge between them.

Blake hurled another batch at Fred with more strength than in his precarious position would have been deemed possible. Looking like a medieval green man, Fred clung to the ladder and began to hurl the clippings back.

'You silly old bugger!' he said. 'What do y' think you're up to! Get down afore thi fall!'

'Don't you dare speak to me like that, my man,' said Blake in a tone of command. 'If you drop one more sprig of yew on my side of this hedge, I'll have the law on you! I'll fetch the police!'

'Fetch bloody p'lice!' said Fred. 'Tha can fetch Owd Nick and all his hellions for owt I care, you cracked ole loony! See if they can stop me!'

He gathered up an armful of yew from the top of the hedge, and threw it over Blake. They were both thus adorned with greenery, each clinging to the top of a ladder with one hand and shaking the other clenched into a fist in the adversary's face, when Jill looked out on them. She could not decide what to do, so she stood still and watched, as the battle raged on.

'Do that again, if you dare, you oaf!' shouted Blake.

'Aye I dare all right. But if tha does it again, I'll knock thi block off!' retorted Fred.

They both promptly gathered up armfuls of twigs, and re-decorated each other afresh.

'I'd like to see you try!' said Blake, baring a skeleton-like arm by pulling up his jacket sleeve.

Fred laughed, exposing his own equally spare but brown muscled arm to Blake's view. The old man the other side of the hedge was white and trembling, fatigue and passionate anger fighting for supremacy in his frail body.

'Get down afore thi falls down an' breks thi bloody neck,' said Fred. 'Saave me the trouble o' brekking it fo' thee, that would.'

Blake began to retreat backwards down his ladder, hurling bits of yew as he went.

'I'll have the law on you,' he said again. 'If one more twig falls on my side, that will be trespass. Tell your master so. I shall deal with him only in future. I refuse to bargain with such a low-class idiot as you, my man! You shall be taught your place!'

'I knaw my plaace, fair enough, ye loony! Up heer, it be, cutting this 'ere 'edge!' He felt marvellous as he watched Blake's retreat, noting that his adversary had not removed the new ladder from his side of the hedge.

Fred reported the exchange verbatim to Jill and Roger, still excited by the event. They listened and laughed, and hoped that the explosion had taken some of the pressure out of both sides of the argument. They did what they could to mollify Fred by agreeing that he had got the better of the duel of words, since Blake had been forced to get down first. Then they did their utmost to ensure that Fred would not deliberately provoke their neighbour again, but it was a case for treading with the utmost delicacy. As Jill reminded Roger later, a brownie that turns nasty can do a lot of damage. If they did have to flit, they didn't want an ill-disposed hob flitting with them against their wishes. For the first time ever, they half-regretted the existence of Fred.

Next morning, Fred came in to breakfast in a mood they had never experienced before. His face was set and pale, and the twinkle had gone entirely from his cornflower-blue eyes.

'I shall give thee me notice,' he announced, 'unless tha agrees to let me deal wi' yon bloody old fule in me own way! Tek it or leave it.'

'Why? What's he done now?' asked Jill, weakly.

'Coom an' see! Meant for me, this time, an' that's what!'

Jill and Roger followed him down the garden, impotent against his anger. He led them to the ash tree. Hanging from one of the lower branches was a coat-hanger surmounted by a crude head made of crumpled newspaper, on which was stuck a devil mask, complete with horns. On the hanger was a man's shirt, waistcoat and jacket, of fine, expensive cloth and in a perfect state of repair, as though it might have been taken from a wardrobe to wear at a wedding. Through the left side, just below the breast-pocket on the jacket, was thrust an assegai. The hole torn was enlarged to approximately the size of a human heart, and the area around it had been plentifully doused with red ink.

Jill shivered, and turned for comfort to Roger. 'It's horrible!' she said.

'It's murder,' said Fred. 'Ah tell thee, ah'm goin' t'get my blow in fust. Ah'm not sitting about to wait till the magic that old devil can work catches up wi' me, like tha did! Ah tell thee, I'm goin' to do 'im when 'e cooms out, even if I swing for it.'

'Get the police, Roger,' whispered Jill.

Roger shook his head, drawing her back into the house. 'I think we must,' he said, 'to old Blake – but not till Fred's calmed down. We don't want to make Fred the culprit. I don't think he's the man to do the old chap any real harm. Leave him to simmer down, and we'll keep watch so as to be ready to act if Blake does venture out again.'

They took turns at spying on Fred, as after a few minutes he erected the ladder and took a few snips at the hedge chosen to ensure that the cut-off pieces fell on Blake's side. But as it was Saturday, he had a routine of weekend tasks to see to, and came down from the steps again almost at once. He came in to lunch as usual, quiet and a bit morose, and put on his cap again as if preparing to go back to the hedge.

'Do stop work for today, Fred,' said Jill. 'It's Saturday afternoon, anyway, and you said you wanted to watch the cricket.' Fred nodded, but said nothing. 'Besides,' Jill went on, 'you can't go up that ladder again today – it's too windy. Look how the wind's got up while we've been having lunch.'

The relief in her voice told both men that she was telling the truth. From somewhere a wind had arisen that was bending the branches and shaking the leaves of every tree in sight. On the ash tree the suit with the spear through its heart swung and twisted grotesquely stiff, and the Michaelmas daisies and golden rod in the herbaceous border bowed low and curtsied towards it. The light breeze of the morning had turned itself into a full-scale autumn gale.

'Aye. Ah'll go an' tek me steps in,' said Fred, in his normal voice. 'No sense in askin' for trouble. Besides, Ah left shears on top of hedge.'

'Thank God!' said Jill, as Fred got out of hearing. 'Gosh, Roger, I was scared.'

'So's Fred,' said Roger. 'That's what's the matter with him. If it comes to that, so am I. The whole thing's so *silly*. Because of all the things that have happened before, we're expecting Fred to be killed somehow. But how can we prevent it? Besides, it's ridiculous! We know perfectly well that old Blake can't kill Fred by magic. Nice fools we should look telling the police a tale like that!'

They went to the window, drawn by a mutual desire to keep an eye on Fred till he should be safely back in the house again.

The wind was so strong now that they watched him leaning against it as he trudged down the path towards his ladder. They saw how carefully he resettled the ladder against the hedge before he mounted and, once at the top, how he straightened up and reached across the hedge for his shears, peering over the other side as he braced himself against a particularly strong gust.

Jill screamed, then gasped. 'Run, Roger! I'll get the police!' She sped towards the telephone as Roger's long legs took him towards the scene of action.

Jill dialled 999 and waited for the cool voice the other end.

'Which service?'

'I don't know,' said Jill, trying to control the trembling in her hands and voice. 'Oh, police, please. And an ambulance.'

She gave the address and then rushed out to join Roger. One second, Fred had been calmly retrieving his shears. The next, he seemed to have gone crazy. He had left his own ladder and was scrambling across the width of the hedge, shears in hand, struggling against both the wind and the difficulty of walking across a hedge top six or seven feet wide. Then he disappeared over the hedge.

There was nothing Roger could do but follow him, in the same undignified fashion. He discovered Blake's ladder still in place, and went down it, as Fred had done, but not before he had taken in the scene on the far side.

Blake lay spread-eagled on the patch of concrete at the back of his house, about five feet away from his back door, his head towards the yew hedge. Fred was bending over him, shears in hand. As Roger looked, he saw Fred fling the shears away, and bend as if to lift his adversary to his feet again. Then there was a rending, tearing sound like that of a huge bomb falling, followed by a crump that shook the earth where Roger stood at the foot of the ladder. The tip-ends of the huge branch that had split from the macrocarpa swept across him and felled him to the ground. Both the old men lay under the branch itself. Roger was helpless to lift it. The police found Jill gibbering with fright and worry. She led them round to the front steps, mumbling what seemed to be utter nonsense about ju-jus, clootie trees, assegais, best suits, Fred and Roger and old Blake. But the urgency in her voice impressed the experienced policeman, and he decided to look first and seek sensible explanations afterwards. Once round the side of the bungalow, the situation was plain to them.

'Go back, Jill, and get the kettle boiling,' commanded Roger, adding his strength to that of the two policemen to raise the branch.

'Fred!' wailed Jill. 'Oh Fred!' She had no doubt that he was dead, and that once the branch was removed it would be discovered that his own shears had pierced his heart.

'Do as your husband suggests,' said the policeman. 'And get an ambulance, quick!'

'I have!' said Jill, but she obeyed, with a long, sobbing look at the crumpled back of her dear household hob lying under the blanket of green macrocarpa feathers.

It was not really long before the branch had been lifted and the ambulance had sped away to hospital, with two unconscious old men lying wrapped in blankets, one on either side of it.

Roger came into the house accompanied by the two policemen. It was the senior policeman who answered her agonized look of enquiry.

'Both unconscious, but alive,' he said. 'That's all we can say at the moment. The branch got 'em fair and square, though luckily not the heaviest end of it. There'd have been no hope if they'd been three feet nearer the trunk. Now – who are they, and what can you tell us about them? What was all that about new suits and spears and the rest? Looks to me like a straightforward accident – though one that might have been foreseen, I think. Macrocarpas are always treacherous – it certainly shouldn't have been allowed to get to that size, especially so close to that bungalow.'

Roger shot Jill a reproachful glance. If she hadn't blabbed about the quarrel, there would have been no need to explain.

'My wife has had an awful shock,' he said. 'Will you allow me to give you the details? We can't tell you anything about Mr Blake, except that he was very eccentric and resented any intrusion into his privacy. If you take a look at the bottom of his garden you will see what my wife was trying to explain to you in her fright about me and Mr Wood.'

'And who is Mr Wood?'

Roger explained the domestic situation, but turned to Jill for details. They discovered that they knew little more about Fred than they did about old Blake. The policeman stood up to go.

'I'll let you know, as soon as there is a report from the hospital,' he said.

Jill let out a sound that was almost a wail. 'The cats!' she said. 'What about the cats?'

The police turned to Roger for explanation, by this time under the impression that the old man next door was not the only eccentric in the neighbourhood.

'You'd better go and take a look in the house next door, to see if you can see any sign of cats,' he said to his young and junior colleague. The youngster went off, while Roger once again outlined briefly the saga of the feline horde.

The young policeman reappeared within minutes, wiping his mouth and still retching. Jill silently conducted him to the nearest toilet, without comment.

'Well?'

'You'd better go and take a butcher's for yourself,' the constable said. 'Sarge, I've never seen anything to touch it!'

'You haven't seen much, yet, son.'

'Maybe not – but you'll have to see to believe it. The whole place is alive with cats — like maggots on a dead rat! And the stink's about the same.' He retched again, at the remembrance of it.

'A few of 'em bolted out o' the door as I opened it,' he went on, 'but I shut the rest in again so that we could find 'em. I'm sure we shall have to get the whole lot put down. I reckon it's a good job the old fellow fell outside the house, 'cos they'd have eaten him alive if they could have got at him. They're ravenous, and the stink —'

'That's enough. How many do you think there are?'

'Well, counting those already dead, I'd say about fifty!'

'*Fifty*?' The sergeant's voice broke, and squeaked in incredulity. He glanced towards Roger.

'We told you he was eccentric, and that we'd had trouble about the cats.'

'Yes, but fifty's coming it a bit too strong,' he said, with a superior scorn of his young colleague's judgement. 'I'll go and take a dekko myself.'

They waited with some interest and veiled amusement for his return.

'Let's get back to the station,' he said brusquely. 'The RSPCA should be here before dark. The decision about what to do can be theirs.'

It was an hour or so after the police left that news from the hospital came through. Roger came back to report to Jill.

'Fred's OK. Nothing more than concussion and a couple of cracked ribs. He's quite conscious, and asking to see us. Old Blake's still out, though he doesn't seem to have anything more than cuts and bruises and a big lump on his head. Of course, they didn't tell me much about him, being no relation. Perhaps if we explain, they'll tell us more at the hospital.'

They found Fred sitting up in bed with a bandage round his head that gave him the appearance of a Gilbert and Sullivan pirate, under which his blue eyes twinkled in their customary wry fashion.

'Aye, Ah'm champion,' he said, as Jill bent down to kiss him.

'Well, Ah am now – by my reckoning, that's the first kiss anybody's gi' me for at least twenty year. Ah's'll do nicely, now.'

'You had us worried,' said Jill, trying to control her voice.

'What happened?' asked Roger. 'One minute you were up the ladder, and the next you were lying out cold on the wrong side of the hedge.'

'We thought you'd gone over to "do" him, as you said,' added Jill.

'Sh!' said Fred, in a hoarse whisper. 'That's 'im, int' next bed, behind them theer curtains.' Then he looked reproachfully at Jill.

'Tha knows me better'n that, surely! Mebbe I bark a bit, but I doan't bite – well, not at such bits o' creatures as that silly old fule is! I went oop t'ladder to get my shears, and I see as his ladder were just wheer 'e'd left it, on t'other side. So I thowt mebbe if I give it a shove, like, I could knock it down wheer it wouldn't come to no harm till he could get out to put it away. So I reached across hedge, and theer he were, laying on the concrete wi' his arms flung out. Ah thowt poor old divil 'ad 'ad it – dropped down dead, like. So I scrambled over t' 'edge an' went down his ladder to see what I could do, but just as I bent over him I 'eard that branch comin' awaay from tree. I can't remember nothing else. I dunno whether I 'ad managed to drag him away or not – you see, as soon as I 'eered that creaking sort o' row, I knawed straight awaay what were going to 'appen. I've 'eered wood splintering, afore now. So I dragged 'im – I think – about four yards further up path afore it got both of us.'

'You probably saved his life,' said Roger.

''Appen. We shall never know, so it doan't matter.' He looked worried. 'What's going to 'appen to all them cats of his while 'e's in 'ere?'

They told him – they hoped the RSPCA would have dealt with the matter before they got home again.

'Aye. It 'ad to be, sooner nor later,' Fred replied. 'But who's going to tell 'im?' He jerked his head towards the silent, curtained bed. 'That'll kill 'im, even if t'branch ha'n't managed it. Mebbe it'll do for 'im anyway, when 'e finds out who's in t'next bed.'

Jill had already thought about that; but somehow fate had taken things out of her hands. She tried not to think about what was going on in the bungalow while they were at the hospital. That it would be wholesale slaughter there could be no doubt. She hoped the savage black tom had not been allowed to escape a painless death.

'We'll come again tomorrow, and tell you the news,' she said.

'Aye! Mebbe 'e'll 'ave coom round b'then,' Fred said.

Jill agreed with Roger, on the way home, that it would be the happiest outcome for everybody if the poor old man could slip away before he had to cope with the knowledge of the massacre of his feline family; but she had caught a glimpse of drip feeds and all the rest of the medical paraphernalia designed to keep life in him, whatever it was worth. She very much doubted that he would be allowed to glide so easily into oblivion, and was proved right next day.

Fred had a tale to tell. He beckoned her close, and whispered. He was obviously about to enjoy himself.

''E coom to, in t' night,' he began. 'Then this morning, along cooms young doctor to see 'im. They pulled curtains round o' course, but I could 'eer everything, 'cos doctor seemed to think 'e were deaf, and bawled at 'im.'

Jill grinned. She had often noted the habit of people, even the intelligent and professional among them, to shout louder when fearing not to be understood, as if increasing decibels had a similar effect on understanding.

'"Morning, Mr Wood," he says. "How are you feeling now?"

'So I calls out, "Morning, doctor. Me, I'm champion." Then doctor puts his head through curtains, looking vexed like, and says, "I'll be with you in a minute. I was speaking to Mr Wood."

'"Aye. I 'eered tha," I says. "So I answered." He were right put out, I could see, so I says, "Fred Wood, that's what they calls me. Not that I ha'n't been called worse things in me time."

'They pulled the curtains back, then, and the nurse coom out looking right put out. She coom an' took a look at the papers 'angin' on t'end o' t'bed, and then went and mumbled to doctor. He leaned over old man next door, and bawled louder'n ever.

'"Can you tell me your full naame?" 'e asks.

'Well, old fellow reeled off a great long string o' names. They asked 'im o'er an' o'er again to repeat 'em, but they couldn't mek nowt on it.'

'"He's delirious," says young doctor. "That theer boomp on 'is 'ead's mebbe doon more damage than we thowt."

'Then t'owd man 'eaves 'isself oop in t'bed, and yells, "I am not delirious! Tha asked my name, an' Ah've told tha! Admirals all!"

'"Admirals all?" says pretty young nurse. I could 'ear as she were 'aving a job not to laugh.

'"Aye. Admirals all," he says. Then he strung out another long list o' names, only they were different from first lot. All Ah could get were that it started wi' Nelson – sounded like "Nelson, Colin Wood, Effing'em, Blake". So I calls out, "Them's the naames o' cats 'e keeps, mebbe."

'"Who is in that next bed?" asks old Blake. But they didn't answer 'im. Mebbe b'this time they thowt they 'ad two loonies to deal wi'. I decided to keep me mouth shut an' let 'em get on as best they could.'

'Go on,' said Jill. 'So what happened then?'

'"Your name is Nelson, Colin, Wood . . ." the nurse began.

'"No! No! No!" says old man. "You ignorant, half-educated idiots. My name is not Nelson!"

'"But you just said . . ."'

'It's a line of poetry,' Jill put in, 'from a poem called "Admirals All". It begins with four names – *Nelson, Collingwood, Effingham, Blake*. He thought they'd be sure to know it. But it does sound as if he's crazy, I must say.'

'Aye. The old fellow let 'em know what 'e thowt about 'em. Then 'e says, loud an' clear, so as I could 'ear everything, "My name is Beresford Collingwood Blake, Sub-lieutenant, RN. As I told you at first, admirals all."

'"There must be some mistaake," says nurse, cooming out again an' grabbing paapers from end o' my bed.

'"Aye. Tha's got us moodled oop," I says. "Ah'm Fred Wood, an' they call 'im Blake, though I knaw nowt about admirals."

'"That'll do, thank you," says doctor, looking as if 'e'd like to shrivel me oop wi' is 'aughty luke. By this time, though, the old devil from t'bungalow 'ad got 'isself into such a rage they 'ad to gi' 'im something to calm 'im down. They drawed the curtains close, and I should think they must have give him an injection. He stopped shouting an' went to sleep, and so far 'e ha'n't coom round agin yet!'

'Poor old man!' said Jill.

'Aye. He'll be reet oopset about them cats.'

'Nelson escaped. He must have got out when the policeman opened the door. I found him in our kitchen, eating Frabjous's cat food.'

'Ah'm reet glad,' said Fred. 'But ah can't 'elp thinking 'as 'e is barmy. 'E told 'em 'e were in t' Naavy! As if they ivver 'ev sooch as 'im in t' Naavy!'

'I don't know,' said Jill. 'Dr Crouch told us he'd been in the war. He's just lost track of time, perhaps, with that bang on the head.'

After she'd left, Fred had other visitors – the ward sister, the young doctor, the nurse and a registrar.

'Now,' said the sister, 'let's get this question of identity straight. You say your name is Frederick Wood.'

'Nay, that Ah nivver,' replied Fred.

'Now look here . . .' began the doctor, but Fred interrupted him. 'Ah said they call me Fred Wood. Joost plaain Fred!'

'I see. And do you know who this is?'

'O' course Ah do! Weren't we browt 'ere together, both on us being copped by same tree? 'E lives next door, an' they call 'im Blake, though I know nowt about t'other string o' names.'

'Beresford Collingwood Blake,' said a voice, clearly, from the next bed. The curtains were drawn back.

'Ah. You've come round again, Mr Blake,' said the doctor, going and feeling his pulse with a professional air that helped hide embarrassment for all the visiting party. 'Now we can perhaps get it all sorted out.' They were looking at the papers. 'Beresford Collingwood Blake: date of birth, 31 May 1916. Is that correct?'

'Nay!' exploded Fred, indignantly. 'Tha's got that moodled, an' all.'

'Don't interfere, Mr Wood,' said Sister, sharply. 'Mr Blake has been in hospital before, and we now have his records here.'

'Tha can 'ave all t'records in Soomerset House,' said Fred, 'an tha's still got it wrong. That's mah birthday tha's got on 'is paapers.'

'It is not. It is mine, quite correct,' said Blake. 'I was born on the day the Battle of Jutland was fought. That's why I was given the names of famous admirals. I am quite capable of answering your questions myself, now. There is no need to let that yokel speak for me.'

'Or that loony to speak for me,' said Fred, sitting up. 'Yokel I may be, but I still 'as enoof sense to knaw day I were born on: 31 May 1916!' He glared at Blake, who glared back.

'What an extraordinary coincidence,' said the sister, soothingly. 'You are almost twins, in that case. Leave the curtains drawn, Nurse. Mr Blake seems much better, now. As he and Mr Wood know each other, they can perhaps chat a bit.'

They lifted Blake into a sitting position, from which he glared accusingly at Fred. As soon as the medical party had left, he opened the attack.

'What cheek, to claim Jutland day as your date of birth! Done to annoy me, I suppose. I won't put up with it.'

'Saave thi breath,' said Fred. 'Tha'll need it, mebbe, to tell soom more lies with. Just as if they'd ivver have anythink like thee in t' Naavy!'

'How *dare* you!' growled Blake. 'I'd have you know that I was an officer on active service while you were clodhopping in Yorkshire.'

'Mind what tha's saaying, thee old loony,' hissed Fred, keeping his voice low enough not to attract the attention of a passing nurse. 'Ah coom from Derbyshire, not Yorkshire.'

'I might have known,' retorted Blake.

> 'Derbyshire born, Derbyshire bred,
> Strong in the arm, weak in the head.'

Fred began to throw off the bedclothes. 'Tha'll find Ah'm strong enoof to knock thy block off, if tha' says another word,' he said. 'Tek back what tha says about bein' in t' Naavy, or I will!'

'I shall not. It is the truth,' said Blake, albeit quailing a little.

'Then tek back what tha said about me bein' clod'opping,' said Fred, doubling a lean brown fist and showing it above the bedclothes. ''Cos if tha wants to knaw, it were me, not thee, as were in t' Naavy, an' that's truth on it, an' all.'

They glared at each other, pathetically ferocious under their ludicrous bandages, while it occurred to each that there was no valid reason why the other should not be telling the truth. At last Fred said, challenging, 'If tha wert in t' Naavy, tell us summat about it, to convince me, like.'

The other old man picked up the gage with pride. 'I was a sub-lieutenant on the *Aconite*, a corvette of the Flower Class, when she was bombed in the North Sea off Grimsby, and sunk.'

Fred forgot to keep his voice down. 'Now I knaws thee for a liar!' he growled. 'That tha nivver were! Tha must ha' read on it in t' paapers.'

Blake was shaking with anger, his thin face white and tense.

'Sister!' he squeaked. 'Sister!'

'Shut oop, thee,' commanded Fred. 'We doan't want no women-folk to settle this, do we? Two men o' t' senior service?'

'Then stop calling me a liar! Who are you to doubt my word? Tell me that? How could you possibly know?'

'Ah'll tell thee 'ow I knaws! 'Cos I were on t' poor old *Aconite* meself when t' bloody Junkers got 'er wi' t' bomb! So there!'

The two bandaged heads drew closer together, each listing over the side of the bed towards the other, while their eyes met again, searchingly, peering into the fading mists of memory for something tangible to cling to, like blind men trying to identify a half-recognized object by touch alone. It was Blake who spoke first. 'You tell me, then,' he said. 'You try to convince me.'

'I were on t' deck, wi' t' gun crew,' Fred began, his voice losing some of its belligerency as his mind leaped backwards over thirty-odd years. 'We fired on t' bloody Junkers till the bomb got us – got the ship, I mean. We was all knocked sideways, and t'gun knocked out of action, but none of us 'ad more'n a few bumps and cuts. We was pickin' oursel's oop when order coom t'abandon ship. I'd picked meself oop, but I'd only been aboard *Aconite* for two days and didn't know her very well. Besides, I were dazed like, but I started follering oothers forrard, towards boats. I nivver got to the boats, though.' Fred paused.

'Why'? What happened?' The voice was that of command, and Fred looked up again, surprised.

'Ah'll tell thee what 'appened,' he went on, grimly. 'Ah were stoombling along, when soodenly me 'ead cleared, an' I see that daft beggar of an officer going t'wrong way. It all 'appened so quick then as I don't knaw t'rights on it. Theer 'e were – a bloody silly young sub . . .' Fred lifted his head, and gazed into the long-ago distance, and at his listener, merging the two images till they became one. His voice petered out, and a look of utter incredulity spread over his face as his mouth dropped open. The blue eyes and the faded brown ones locked on to each other, and held. Fred found a husky voice at last, overawed by what he knew.

'It were *thee*,' he said. 'Ah knaw thee now!' He fell back on his pillows, grinning. 'Well, Ah'll be boogered! Just wait till I can tell t'missus that!'

'What do you mean?' said old Blake tremulously. 'Finish your tale.'

'Why – doan't tha remember? When t'bomb fell, it blowed up t'bridge?'

'Yes, that's correct. I was on the bridge. I was blown off.'

'Aye. Ah knaws tha wert. An' stid o' getting out t'way as fast as tha could, tha went back t'pick oop captain's cat, as 'ad got pinned under summat. As daft about cats then as thou art now!'

'Old Satan was a friend of mine – about the only one I had aboard *Aconite*. He was really more my cat than the captain's. I couldn't just leave him.'

'Well, I sees tha reach down an' 'eave oop whativver it were atop of 'im, an' pick 'im oop. Then some more o' t' bridge collapsed, wi' thee and t'cat underneath lot.'

'He was dead,' said Blake.

'Ah didn't knaw or care about 'im,' said Fred, 'but I could see as thee soon would be. So I fell out, an' got me 'ands under that theer bit o'plate, an' 'eaved wi' all my might. It coom up, all right, but I 'eered me back go "crack" right up atween me shoulders. Then poor old *Aconite* give a great lurch, an' down comes t'rest o' t' bridge on top o' lot of us. That's last I remember, till I found myself in hospital ashore. I never got back to t'Navy no more, 'cos b'that time I'd got this 'ere 'oomp on me back. They didn't want such as me, then. I warn't good enoof to be blowed up no more, seemly. So I went back to Derbyshire.'

Blake was shaking his bandaged head, dazedly trying to comprehend it all.

'I don't remember anything after finding that Satan was dead,' he said, sadly. 'I didn't return to the service, either. I had a long time in hospital, and then was discharged as unfit for further service. A great disappointment . . . and a great blow to my dear mother. She never got over it, you know. She had set her heart on me doing well in the service.'

He turned away, hiding his face, and they lapsed into silence, each lost in his own world again. If Blake understood that he owed Fred his life, he seemed unprepared to acknowledge it. Fred felt no resentment – indeed it never occurred to him to think about it. He was still bemused by the coincidence, and lay thinking about the way life played such queer tricks on folks; but mainly he was high with blissful anticipation of being able to tell Jill the incredible tale.

They had taken Blake to be X-rayed when she came that afternoon, leaving the coast clear for Fred to tell it all after his own graphic fashion.

Once her astonishment was past, Jill wanted to go over it again, detail by detail.

'You actually lifted the great steel plate off him?' she said, wonderingly.

''Ow dost tha think I got this 'eer 'oomp?' he asked.

'You never told me,' she said.

'Tha nivver asked, didst tha?'

'You saved his life,' she said. 'Does he realize that?'

''Ow should Ah knaw? He's not said a word, sin' we 'ad that talk. Mebbe there's a reason for that, though. Officers don't 'ob-nob wi' ordinary seamen, tha knaws.'

'Don't be silly. It's over thirty years since he was an officer and you a rating on the same ship. Besides, things have changed.'

'Not wi' t' the likes of 'im,' said Fred. 'He's proud enoof t'outstare a peacock, even if he does lack eyes in tail.'

Jill grinned, but her mind was busy putting two and two together.

'Fred,' she said. 'You know when the cat clawed Roger's finger, we had to get Dr Crouch in to stitch it. We talked to him about Mr Blake. He said then that they believed that Mr Blake had had a shock or an accident of some kind that had turned him queer. Now he told you himself that he was discharged as unfit for service, but didn't tell you why, did he? He doesn't appear to have any injuries physically. Maybe it was that awful experience that made him like he is. Perhaps we ought to try to understand him a bit better, and put up with him when he has those queer fits.'

'Aye. Ah've thought about that meself, laying 'eer. Theer's

another thing. If yon doctor is right, then t'very last thing as 'e ivver see while 'e were in 'is right mind were my faace, leaning over 'im like, just after 'e'd found out as t'cat 'e'd gone back for were dead anyway. That's why 'e took against us from beginning. Seems to me as if 'e got idea into 'is 'ead as I'd got summat to do wi' all that 'ad 'appened to 'im, though o' course 'e didn't know me, or why 'e thowt like that. It accounts for 'im being so set on them old cats, an' all. Dead cat in 'is arms, an' my faace looking down at 'im.'

'And that bit about his mother – again that ties up with what Dr Crouch suggested. She let him know how much he'd disappointed – failed her in everything. Poor old man!'

'Nay – poor young lad. He were nobbut twenty-fower-year-old then. Ah knaw, seeing as 'ow we're twins.'

They brought Blake back after Jill left, and silence reigned between the two beds throughout the rest of that day, and well into the next. Fred pondered on the future, and the best way of coping with it when the time came. Both of them were recovering, now. Fred's injuries were the worse, but Blake was still weak, though making quick progress with all the food and attention he was receiving. They were both told, that morning, that in future they could make their way to the toilets themselves. Towards evening, Fred decided to take advantage of the privilege, and put on his hospital dressing-gown. He had reached the end of Blake's bed on the way back when he saw the other old man struggling feebly to rise. Cleaned up, he seemed to Fred thinner and frailer than ever, so Fred paused, and waited. After what seemed to Fred an embarrassingly long time, Blake got to his feet, and Fred moved on; but before he got to the end of his bed, Blake had tottered and stumbled. Quick as the elf Jill called him, Fred reached his side before he fell, and helped him back into bed. The thin face quivered into the first semblance of a smile Fred had ever seen on it, as his white, skinny hand held on to Fred's bony brown one just a fraction longer than was necessary.

'Thanks,' said Blake, 'for everything.'

Fred nodded. He went back to his own bed, full of thought, but instead of getting in it, he turned, and padded back again to the other side of Blake's.

'Dost plaay dominoes, Admiral?' he asked.

A Question of Sex

Lavinia Derwent had maintained all her long life that she didn't like women. Somewhat naturally in consequence, other women didn't care much for her. At the age of seventy-nine, she found her fast-diminishing circle made up mainly of the sex she despised and disliked. True, she still had her two sons, but they were not without female attachments.

This curious prejudice could hardly be said to be her fault. It had been grafted upon her when she was a small child at the end of the nineteenth century. She was the fourth child in her family, either an unfortunate accident or a very belated afterthought. She also had the misfortune to be female, while the other three were all vigorously male.

Their father was a lovable rogue of a man who teetered on the very edge of middle-class respectability, played at radical politics and continually disgraced his family by always being on the wrong side, whatever the issue at stake.

His wife, well aware of her own unimpeachable pedigree, bore with her husband's vagaries and eccentricities, and set herself to retain their precarious hold on the social ladder and to prevent her volatile husband from actually falling off his knife-edge on to the wrong side of what was upper-middle-class. In the long process of her struggle, she became a bossy, managing sort of woman who always knew best, and believed absolutely in her own infallibility.

She idolized her three beautiful boys, and it was mainly on their account that she tolerated, only barely, the daughter she could have done quite well without. Not that she didn't love the child, though it was not quite the same sort of love as that she lavished on her other three idols. It was the practical difficulties of having a child of a different sex that bothered her, and the fact that there were now four to bring up and educate instead of three.

Her object in life was to turn her boys into men according to the public-school, far-flung-empire-maker model that then prevailed in top circles. She could not afford, however hard she scraped and saved, to send them to public schools, so they attended private establishments that aped the great ones, and she supplemented their education herself, especially where physical courage and 'manliness' were concerned. She positively encouraged them to use their fists, on each other, on their peers who needed teaching a lesson, and on any 'cads' whom they found contravening the code of gentlemanly conduct she had instilled into them. This code's first clause was that women existed mainly to give men something to protect.

So Lavinia, being female, had had no choice but to be 'protected' from the very beginning. As there was not enough money to send her, also, to a good independent establishment for girls, and there could be no question of her attending a board-school with the tradesmen's children, her mother caused it be known early in her infancy that she was 'delicate', too delicate in fact to cope with the rigour of any school. Her mother would undertake Lavinia's entire education herself.

Lavinia accepted her mother's dictum that she was 'delicate' without the least understanding of what it meant. She was, in fact, as tough a little girl as they come, in spite of being 'petite' – like the royal French princess from whom her mother believed herself to be descended, or so she averred. When the three boys, romping in some manly pursuit in the house, needed an 'extra', they simply yelled, 'Come on, old girl,' and Lavinia went, joining in as any other healthy child might have done, as strong and hardy as the brothers she was obliging. But even they 'protected' her from other youngsters, even from their own friends, partly because of the code, and partly because it had been laid down as an unbreakable rule by their mother. Consequently Lavinia grew from a baby into a little girl, both 'delicate' and 'protected' by order, as it were.

The boys had grown into men – Lionel, always known as Leo, was twenty and Edwin eighteen – when their father once again lost a good job because of his unabated political radicalism and his temperamental inability to keep his mouth shut about it in places where it mattered. The boys would have to get work themselves – but they were not well enough educated to be empire-builders, and too well educated to take ordinary wage-earning jobs. Both were handsome, mischievously light-hearted charmers with a lot of real character and sturdy British pride. Leo showed a considerable talent for journalism and, under his mother's guiding hand and eye, began to have some success; Edwin, not to be outdone, went out one morning and came back later wearing the uniform of an ordinary matelot in Her Majesty's Royal Navy. James, the third son, had never quite matched up to his brothers, so his mother decided that he should leave school at sixteen and get a job in a bank.

Lavinia, who by this time already felt the gap between herself and her adventurous brothers widening, thereafter had only 'Motherdear' to look to for anything whatsoever.

Her mother eyed her growing daughter with maternal anxiety combined with disappointment. Though daintily made, Lavinia was no match for her brothers in the charm and beauty stakes. Even James, dull though he might be compared with Leo and Edwin, had 'more about him' than their sister – or so, at least, their male-orientated mother judged. She did not hide her conclusion from its object.

'You are not pretty, Lavinia,' she said, 'and you never will be. But you may be *interesting*. You must always remember that. You cannot make yourself pretty, but you can take trouble to make yourself interesting.'

'Yes, Motherdear,' said Lavinia, accepting this verdict from the infallible oracle as she had always accepted everything else. How she was ever to become 'interesting' while being insulated by layers of protection from everything and everybody outside her immediate family, nobody explained to her. Her education had been of the sketchiest, consisting mainly of lectures from her mother on ladylike behaviour, and political tirades from her father when nobody else would listen to him any longer. The effect on her character was paradoxical. She inherited from her forceful mother a determination always to believe herself to be right; and from her father she imbibed the belief that if you once expressed an opinion on anything, you never changed it. As nobody at all ever expected her to think for herself, she didn't; so to the end of her life she made statements without thinking, let alone knowing, anything of the subject under discussion, and then stuck pig-headedly to them, however stupid they were – though always in the most ladylike manner, of course.

Of any matter concerning sex, she was entirely ignorant. Though her brothers had for the last year or two been bringing their male friends home, they took no notice of the pale, shy, 'delicate' little girl, and in her turn she admired the godlike creatures from afar, because they were 'men' and Motherdear so obviously approved of them. That men were superior and in some way different was all she knew.

On the day that Edwin came home in naval uniform, both his parents nearly burst, one with pride at her 'manly' son, and the other with anti-establishment fury. Then tragedy struck. The ship that Edwin was on blew up when some fuses fired spontaneously in the magazine, and was lost. Edwin, it was learned afterwards, might have saved himself, but went back to drag a wounded shipmate from the flames, and perished with him. He died a hero's death, but that was poor consolation to anybody. His father's bombast drained away, and his mother, consumed by grief, just sat still and stared into vacancy. But the one who suffered most was Leo, to whom Edwin had been as near and dear as if he had been a fraternal twin. He could not bear to stay in the home that had once contained his so beloved brother, so he left. After a wild spell in London, during which he found out what it really meant to be a man, he tried to put as many miles as possible between himself and his grief, and left for the United States, with only his charm and his gift with words to support him.

Lavinia's life was then reduced to the company of an irascible father, a listless, grief-dazed mother, and, in the kitchen, the little maid-of-all-work, Annie.

When her mother at last made the effort to take up the thread of living again, she had no one but her 'delicate' daughter to dominate. The teenaged girl submitted more than willingly, it being the only thing she could do to help assuage her mother's searing grief. She was, as her mother had predicted, by no means pretty. She made the most of her tiny hands and small feet, but the rest of her had grown too large to be any longer classed as 'petite'. Her mother decided that she was too pale to be even interesting, and gave her a demonstration on how to make up her cheeks with a little of the colouring preparation that had been popular in her own youth. Religiously thereafter, to the end of her life, Lavinia placed a circular spot of rouge on her cheekbones and patted a little kiss-curl into place on her forehead. (At seventy-nine, she had had at last to find a substitute for her mother's Victorian cosmetic, but the kiss-curl, now quite white, was still there, held in place by the nylon net which now covered her primly permanent waves.)

At seventeen, she knew no more about sex than a newborn kitten, but she had learned to play the piano, and very occasion-ally went (on a complimentary ticket) with her music teacher to a concert. True to the training of her upbringing, she felt that these excursions into the great world of art gave her the authority of a seasoned critic to pronounce upon artiste and composer alike – and then stick doggedly to her opinion. Therefore Beethoven was good; Bach was not. Chopin was marvellous, Schubert was rubbish. (She had not changed her mind at seventy-nine.)

When Leo reappeared with an American wife who was notice-ably *enceinte*, Lavinia was extremely puzzled by it all. Leo was fast making his name as a journalist, and had come back to London with a good chance of a job on the best of the establishment's papers. He took his wife back to Motherdear, nevertheless, till he could get himself established.

Marie was half French, truly petite with ash-blonde curls and eyes so blue that they made her expression doll-like in the extreme. Motherdear hated her on sight. She had her reasons, which were based mainly on the fact that she was no longer first lady in her son's life; that Marie 'was not a lady' at all; that she, Leo's mother, had not been consulted; and that Marie was pregnant. She had forced the date of his hasty marriage out of her son, but her practised eye told her that the pregnancy was too far advanced to comply respectably with it. Either he had been guilty of ungentlemanly conduct, or he had been hood-winked by a scheming girl who was not British on either side of her mixed parentage into fathering another man's child. As the former explanation was not acceptable to her, she chose the latter. Lavinia, nearing eighteen, heard everything that was said, and understood not one word of it.

On the day of the birth, she was exiled to the kitchen with Annie. Motherdear let it be known that Marie had been brought to bed of a seven-month child.

'Seven-month child?' Annie had scoffed. 'Who's the missus think she's having on? Not me, she ain't! I've seen too many not to know a full-time baby when I see one. Me mam's had six since I fust come to work here, and my sister's had four. Seven-month donkey anybody'd be who'd believe the missus on that one!'

Lavinia was terribly shocked by Annie's outburst, which appeared to be directed against the Household Goddess. She had no idea of what it was that should make Annie doubt Motherdear's word. So she replied primly, 'You must say "isn't", not "ain't", Annie. Motherdear is always telling you.'

Annie sniffed, offended, and Lavinia lost the one chance she had ever had of being enlightened on the subject of sex. But she knew that her mother disliked her new sister-in-law intensely, and so did she. By the side of Marie, she felt like an English carthorse. And when Leo found her in the kitchen helping Annie one day and said cheerily to her, 'Time you smartened yourself up a bit you know, old girl. Don't want to be left on the shelf, do you?' she was miserably jealous of Marie. Later that night, she said openly, as if she were propounding a very serious theory that she had long been cogitating over, 'I don't like women, you know, Motherdear.' As the Goddess made no reply, Lavinia took it that she concurred. Lavinia did not like women. She had said so, and never thereafter changed that opinion.

Ten years passed, and Leo became a famous editor. He moved in higher circles, and did his best to introduce Lavinia to some of his male friends and colleagues. They were not the kind of men of whom Motherdear approved, though she was beginning to get a little bit anxious on her daughter's account. Even Lavinia began to wonder how she could make herself more interesting to the small circle of men of whom her mother did approve, because though still utterly innocent, she had begun to apprehend a few of the things she had never been given the chance to comprehend. She made no protest when her mother somehow or other engineered a marriage for her with a young man who had come to the house to sit at Leo's feet, and who was no match for the matriarch who had decided to make him her son-in-law.

Hubert's own Forsyte-like family were more than a little dismayed; Lavinia found at once that she did not like her strong-minded mother-in-law, nor her husband's sister, to whom he seemed very attached. Her new family circle had done nothing to change Lavinia's mind. Apart from Motherdear, who could do no wrong, there were no women she could like.

It pleased her enormously that both her children turned out to be male. She said so to Motherdear on the day her second son was born. 'The dear Lord knows I don't like women. That's why He has given me two boys.'

But it was only a matter of months before the dear Lord saw fit to remove the one and only woman she did like, and love, and revere. Motherdear was dead, and in her own grief Lavinia failed to see how lost and heartbroken her father was without his strong-willed wife. Hubert had taken on the task of protecting Lavinia the day he had married her, and wrapped round in her own safe little world she barely gave her father a thought. Hubert was a gentleman by birth, education, profession and, most of all, by instinct. He, too, had literary pretensions of a modest kind, and belonged to the rather curious literary set that included Kenneth Grahame and others of his ilk who preferred nature outside the home to natural instincts inside it, especially with a wife whose intellect in no way matched his own. He was fond of her, but the last thing she was to him was interesting. He found that he generally preferred a good long walk in the open air to the joys of marriage. Yet he realized that his own peace of mind lay in protecting his wife's way of life and thought. When she transferred to him the homage she had previously given to her mother, he accepted it. He cocooned her, even from the strictures of his own family, and she continued to grieve for Motherdear to the exclusion of everybody else but her two young sons. When, after only a matter of a few months, her charming old reprobate of a father appeared at her door with the news that he was about to marry again, her fury knew no bounds. She refused absolutely ever to meet or acknowledge the awful woman who had the effrontery to try to take Mother-dear's place. Hubert attempted to make her see reason, but she would not listen.

'I dislike all women,' she said. 'You know that I do not get on with them. Least of all a woman like her! Anyway, I do not want women. I've got you, and my dear boys. I never did like women, and I never shall!' It even irked her that some of her neighbours were female, and that Hubert insisted that at least she should be polite to them. 'I can't help it, dear,' she said. 'I don't like them. That's why the dear Lord gave me only boys.' Hubert didn't argue. He, too, was more than satisfied with his two boys, and gave her little chance thereafter of ever conceiving anything that might possibly turn out to be female.

In her strange way, she was, for a short time, happy, especially as Leo went on from strength to strength, becoming not only well-to-do, but a household name. As Marie had long ago left him, Lavinia felt she had every right to reclaim him as one of her 'men', and simply dismissed as non-existent the number or character of the females he always had in tow. That Leo could do no wrong was another of her opinions that was as immovable as the Sphinx.

Unfortunately, Time and the dear Lord between them allowed her two sons to grow up and, while still quite young, follow their uncle's precedent and take unto themselves wives not of her choosing. If the dear Lord had sent two of His angels to take up the positions, they would barely have reached Lavinia's criteria; being merely mortal women, they were both an anathema to her. Regarding it as her duty to follow Motherdear's example of training Marie to be what a good wife should be, she did her best to teach her daughters-in-law what she didn't know, what they had no desire to learn, and in any case could not possibly make use of in war-torn London. She was not particularly welcome in either of her sons' homes, and in consequence bitterly resented the two women who had stolen her boys from her. Before the war was over, the dear Lord had also removed not only Hubert, but Leo as well. For the first time in her life, there was no man close at hand to protect her.

She turned, as of right, to her sons; but even if she had ever endeared herself to their wives, her case would have been hopeless. One son's wife had been maimed in an air raid, and was taking a very long time to die; the other marriage had been put under too many other strains to stand up to having two widowed mothers as part of it. One was already installed. Lavinia suddenly found herself *femme seule* with a vengeance, a woman alone in a world at that time disproportionately female.

In this extremity, the streak of natural pride and hardihood her brothers had always found in her when they had included her in their pursuits, and because they did so it had not been entirely repressed by Motherdear, reasserted itself. Somebody, surely, must both want and need her. Her mind followed well-worn lines, and she concocted the person in need of her services in her imagination as male, of course, supremely healthy, very wealthy, gentlemanly to the core (with nothing in his moral attitude to women of which her mother could have disapproved) – a sort of composite of Hubert and Edwin but with all Leo's panache thrown in. Sadly for her daydream, the war had removed paragons of this variety if there had ever been any; and even Nature sees to it that if such men be, they do not outlive their marriage partners any more than Hubert had outlived her. It was their widows, not they, who had need of her services – as companion, nurse, housekeeper, or all combined. Women! All the same, having said that that was what she would do, she stuck to it. She became a companion – help to a rich old lady whom she despised, resented and, of course, disliked.

As Motherdear would have wished, she faced the world with pride, comforted by the knowledge that Edwin of blessed memory also, and even Leo, would have approved of her resolution. Without male protection among other elderly women, she endured several somewhat sorrowful and uneventful years. She was not bitter about it; instead, she lived more and more in the past with her memories, polishing those of her happiest days till the rest gradually faded into pale wraiths hovering in the shadows. She kept in touch with her sons, of course, but even they did not please her. Long before his first wife had died, Donald had become friendly with 'another woman', which she felt was most reprehensible in one who was descended from Motherdear and was related to the godlike Leo. Moreover, as soon as his wife did slip mercifully away at last he had actually married the other woman. She disliked her new daughter-in-law much more than she had Donald's first wife. But that blow faded into insignificance against the next, when her first-born, Tom, committed the unforgivable sin of leaving his wife and family, and setting up house with his 'other woman', *unmarried*.

Lavinia was now seventy-five. She was still 'at work' in her capacity as companion–help. She had a legal right to holidays – but where could she spend them? It came as something of a surprise to her to be invited not only to Donald's home, but also to Tom's new domestic if unhallowed ménage. She would go, gratefully if not altogether happily to the first, and considered long the warm letter of invitation from Tom and his 'mistress', Mary. After much consultation with the dear Lord, she decided that it was incumbent upon her as a duty to visit the sinful couple, and censure roundly if she found it necessary – that is, if she had real, undeniable proof that they actually shared the same bed.

She took the month's holiday that was due to her, and went to stay, reserving the right to return to her work whenever she so desired – just in case what she regarded as 'the worst' should materialize.

Instead, it seemed that heaven had opened to her. Whatever else she was forced to think of Mary, this female had one great redeeming feature: she could listen, and listen she did, hour after hour and day after day, to Lavinia's precious memories of Motherdear, of Edwin, who was well on the way to becoming a saint, and of Leo. Lavinia had found, at last, one other woman that she actually liked. It was plain, moreover, that Tom's new whatever-she-was also quite liked her, and enjoyed her company.

Lavinia spent a fair amount of time in silent converse with the dear Lord about it, because by all the tenets of her upbringing, this woman was not, and could never be, Tom's wife while the one he had made vows to in church still lived. Then, one day, she came to a sort of compromise agreement with the dear Lord about it.

Her son had passed behind Mary's chair, and in doing so had leaned over and dropped a kiss on her nose – unashamedly, in front of his mother! She was shocked and prepared to be very disapproving at such a brazen show of adultery, and opened her mouth to speak. But she shut it again with a distinct snap, making her look for a moment very much like a pink and white fish gaping at the side of its bowl. She did not want to be sent packing before her holiday was over, however sinful the atmosphere. Especially as there were dinner parties of the kind Leo used to give in the offing, besides other pleasant company.

Tom, however, had registered her reaction, and the snap as her mouth had closed.

'What's the matter, Mother? Something wrong?'

'No, darling, not really. As you know, I do not care to see people petting each other in public. I am sure I never brought you up to do such things as you have done, either of you – but especially Donald. But there, the dear Lord will punish him.'

Her son was bridling, showing his irritation. Mary caught his hand, but her warning was too late.

'Don't talk such rot, Mother! What's poor old Don done that he has to be punished for?'

'Marrying that brassy woman almost before dear Peggy was cold in her grave! And I am not at all sure that he actually waited till she died. *He once went away for a holiday with Jean.*' She had dropped her voice so that the cat and the curtains and the hearthrug might not hear such villainy expressed in words.

'And what about me, then? Good God, if Don's for it, for what he's done, I suppose I'm also a candidate for hell fire any minute now!'

'Don't joke about such things, darling. And don't swear at me! Motherdear would never allow a word of such blasphemy in her house. She would tell Leo so. "Leo," she would say, "if you must swear, find a swear-word that is not blasphemous." I have never taken the dear Lord's name in vain in all my life.'

Tom persisted. He was appalled by her silliness, and angrily afraid that she would upset Mary. He ranged himself physically by Mary's side, sitting on the arm of her chair, and glancing apprehensively down at her. She looked up, and wickedly drooped an eyelid at him. He relaxed at once. Mary was positively enjoying this, as she did most of the others of his mother's ridiculous foibles.

'So what about me and Mary, Mother? Are we to burn everlastingly in the Bottomless Pit because we can't help loving each other?'

'No, darling – I did not say that. I said He would punish Donald, because of what happened – and I fear there *is* no real love there. With Donald it is all —' She stopped, and looked around her, searching the furthest corners of the room to make sure that no hidden listener could possibly be lurking there. Her rouged cheeks burned with a brighter hue that spread down to her collar and up to her kiss-curl. She dropped her voice to a low, sepulchral whisper.

'It is all "*sex*",' she said.

She had never before to her knowledge used such a dreadful word in the presence of a man, if ever at all. Not even to Hubert.

'Then what about us?' Tom asked, taking Mary's hand and rubbing it against his cheek, as near to an intimate gesture as he dared go without giving his mother a heart attack.

'The dear Lord knows what He is doing,' she said firmly. 'He arranged that you and Mary should meet, and love each other. It was all His doing. I thank Him every night in my prayers for sending you a woman I could love.'

Mary gurgled, but turned it neatly into a cough. Lavinia having got the dear Lord where she wanted Him, all things were possible. She could see, though, that Tom was not going to be so easily appeased, and sought to lead them all into gentler waters.

'You were married yourself, you know, dear,' she said to Lavinia. 'I expect you and Tom's father had some good times together when you were younger. Don't be too hard on Don and Jean.'

'I had wonderful times with Leo,' the old lady replied wistfully. 'And with darling Edwin, before he was killed. Leo used to take me out with him into the country, on our bikes, just the two of us together, you know.'

Tom's face was registering a bewildering variety of emotions, and Mary was having more or less to hold him down. His mother always irritated him beyond endurance, but he had never heard anything like this before. He considered her liking for Mary a very mixed blessing, if it meant that it was likely she would come again for anything longer than three days. The

growing intimacy between the two women was already beginning to reveal aspects of his mother that he had never even
glimpsed before. In the first place, she was incredibly more
stupid than he had ever realized till now. She had brought him
up on advice gained directly from the dear Lord, or so he had
been told; but he now wondered how, even as a very small
child, he could ever have been gulled into obeying her silly
diktats, encompassing as they did only her own wishes and
desires, without protest just because she averred she was only
acting as a medium for some sort of mystical control she called
'the dear Lord'. Or, if it came to that, her spirit guide's code of
conduct for growing boys. He was having doubts at this moment
about just what the code had included. What extraordinary
revelation was contained in that last utterance of hers? He
glanced at Mary, but she would not meet his eye. It was all very
well for her to laugh at his mother's oddities, but this was
something different – an unease menacing his memories of a
happy childhood and loving home life in spite of his mother's
quirky character. If Mary wouldn't make her be more explicit,
then he would.

'Mary was talking of Don and Jean, and what you object to
about them,' he said. 'Not your childhood bike rides with Uncle
Leo. She meant your married life with Father.'

Lavinia looked up at him reprovingly through her thick-lensed
spectacles, as if he were still a curly little toddler who must be
corrected.

'I heard what Mary said,' she replied. 'Now let me see, Tom
dear. Who was your father?'

Tom was incapable of taking any more. He turned away,
making a sound in his throat between a growl and a hiccup. He
heard the quiver of laughter in Mary's voice as she strove to
speak to put things right, and was momentarily furious with her
for finding it funny. She spoke soothingly, though, the salve
meant for him as well as for the old woman.

'Your husband, Hubert, dear,' Mary said. 'You and Hubert
must have been quite like Don and Jean, or Tom and me, once.'

'Oh, yes, *Hubert*,' she said. 'Of course I remember Hubert. He was very good to me, very kind. We were married, you know, Hubert and I. Motherdear always liked Hubert better than any other of the young men in the Church Social Club. That is how he first came to our house – Leo met him, and liked him, and Hubert thought the world of Leo. He admired Leo so much, you see. He always did, though I do think he was just a tiny weeny bit jealous of Leo's success. They both used to write things, you know, and Leo's were always being in the papers, but they always sent Hubert's back, or nearly always. Leo was so successful.'

Tom left the room.

Later that night, in bed, he exploded his pent-up wrath to Mary. 'Silly old fool!' he muttered, clenching his teeth. '"I remember Hubert", indeed! They were married for over thirty years, and all she can remember of him is that he was jealous of her precious Leo. Poor old Pa. No wonder he just gave up and died. I should have committed suicide.'

She soothed him, stroking his face and letting him know that she took his anger seriously. 'Don't let her upset you, darling. She is a very old woman now. Like all old people, she has to go further and further back in memory for comfort. But I think there is more to it than that in her particular case. It came to me when she hissed "Sex" the way she did. She's never understood anything about it. She's spent all her life terrified of it. First being kept in utter ignorance, which she has retained – on principle. Then your grandmother's distress at Leo's peccadilloes, which again she didn't understand. She told me the other day that she knew nothing at all until the night before she was married, when her mother gave her a sort of sanitized account of what she might possibly find her husband expected of her; but even so, she held him off till they got home from their fortnight's "holiday" as she put it – she had no idea what a "honeymoon" was meant to be. And now, she is subconsciously suppressing all memory of the fact that she was ever a party to any physical sex. She can't help it, darling – really. You should be sorry for her, not angry with her. Think of all she's missed.'

'But her precious brother was an absolute pirate, sex-wise, all his life! He had affairs galore. She must have known about them, whatever she told you about her own wedding night. I don't believe in her innocence. You should have seen the way she used to flirt with any man who came to the house to see Pa. I can remember it. It used to embarrass us all.'

'I think that proves my point. Her mother told her she had to make herself "interesting" to men – her brothers' friends, for example. She didn't know what it was supposed to lead up to. Motherdear would have been jolly careful not to leave her alone with any of them long enough for her to become enlightened! By the time of her marriage she had been so completely brain-washed that she was quite incapable of responding to your father's advances. I'd like to bet that what she was told was simply not to be shocked because "men were like that", and that it was the dear Lord's way of giving married ladies babies. She accepted it like she accepted all her other lessons, as something to be remembered like – like – well, the date of the Battle of Waterloo. What her mother disclosed didn't in any way make her a party to it emotionally – or even physically, if you ask me. If it did ever occur to her that what she was having to "endure" with your father was what Leo got up to – well, her god could do no wrong, and those sacrificed to him were only women, anyway. She's got through her whole life absolutely untouched by sexual feelings. It is still an utter taboo to her, in every respect. You may "love" me as much as you like – that's the dear Lord's arrangement for her comfort. But you mustn't do anything to force her to think of us in bed together. Once she believed that, I should be as despised as Jean or any other woman. She thinks of us as "unmarried" in every way.'

Tom spluttered. 'But what about poor old Pa? What was he made of? You are making me out to be the offspring of a simpering fool and a plaster saint! Poor old Pa! And God damn my blasted grandmother, if you are right. But didn't Mother's own instincts tell her anything, when it was actually happening to her?'

'She was twenty-eight when she was married, so your grand-mother had had a good innings. She had been taught to regard all instincts as wicked, and sexual ones had to be suppressed altogether as both immoral and unladylike – simply not to be countenanced. I guess she was instructed to pray for strength never to give way to them. Don't you see? She had learned at twenty-eight how to subdue any sexual reaction whatever. Maybe what she needed was a sexy buck-navvy like your Uncle Leo, not a sensitive gentleman like your father. How far would *you* go without the least hint of any response? By the time he married her, it was far too late for his gentle approach to have any effect on her. Anyway, I'm jolly glad you take more after Uncle Leo than either of your parents.'

She snuggled up to him, and he pulled her closer still.

'Well, it's too late now,' Tom said.

'Too late for what?'

'Too late for her ever to find out what this is all about,' he said, and proceeded to put into practice all that his mother – lying just the other side of the bedroom wall – wanted to have his brother condemned to sizzle in hell for doing.

But as it turned out, Tom was wrong in dismissing it as too late now.

Enjoying herself as she had not done for many years, Lavinia extended her stay with them. Tom began to see her more and more through Mary's eyes, as an individual, a different person from the mother he had known and loved, though, as he now realized, had always had reservations about liking. He knew, too, that this unacknowledged dislike had been compounded of irritation at her obstinate foolishness, and his intuition that in some way she was failing his father. It was all so clear, now that it had been pointed out to him, and it hurt and grieved him for his father's sake. He was, if the truth be told, quite irritated with Mary for opening his eyes to what he would rather not have known, and he found it more and more difficult to be nice to Lavinia herself. She seemed not to have even the vaguest idea of the ways in which she got under his skin, and when he tried a courteous protest about anything, she stuck doggedly to her own line, and turned his irritation into anger. Mary found her diplomacy stretched to its very limits, trying to prevent minuscule incidents from flaring into great quarrels.

Lavinia had laid her plans to do her duty to her other son by visiting him and his lawful wife for no more than forty-eight hours before returning to her 'place', which consisted of keeping an eye on another woman even older than herself, in return for which she had her own rooms and board. 'Poor dear Mrs Weaver' she always called her employer, with a decided air of patronage. Mrs Weaver was neither the daughter of a paragon nor sister to a famous journalist as well as an heroic saint.

But, as the Bible tells us, pride goeth before a fall. The dear Lord failed her. News arrived that he had seen fit to remove Mrs Weaver to Abraham's bosom, and her house was to be sold. Lavinia had no home. Moreover, by the same post was a letter from Don, saying that Jean had had an invitation to accompany a friend to New Zealand and was leaving immediately, so that Lavinia's visit to them would have to be indefinitely postponed.

Lavinia's distress was great, and so was Tom's. He was afraid of Mary's kind heart. Lavinia herself was seeking a scapegoat, and turned her sorrow and her fear of the future into bitter anger directed towards Jean, and even more at Donald for being such a weakling as to allow his wife to please herself and put her wishes before the welfare of anybody else.

'I am his *mother!*' she said, putting into the word such reverence and holiness that in intensity it almost rivalled her one delivery ever of the word 'sex'. 'But there, the dear Lord will punish him. Honour thy father and thy mother: that is one of the dear Lord's commandments, you know.'

Tom turned on her in uncontrollable, childlike temper. 'It isn't, as it happens!' he said. 'It's one of an old Jewish patriarch's commandments, four thousand years before your dear Lord ever got a look-in! But in any case, do you know what you are saying, Mother? Do you really want your bloody dear Lord to punish your son – your "baby boy", as you always call him to me? It's downright wicked of you!'

She drew herself up to her full height of five feet nothing and looked Tom in the eye. 'I will not be sworn at by anybody! Certainly not by my own son! Leo and Edwin never swore at me in all their lives. If you do not apologize instantly, I shall leave this house at once!'

She turned with great dignity and took the stairs as if she might have been twenty-nine instead of a few months short of her eightieth birthday.

'Oh, don't upset her any more than she is already, *please*, Tom,' Mary pleaded. 'She truly doesn't know what she is saying. She is in such distress already.'

'Yes, well, she shouldn't aggravate me deliberately,' he said. 'And don't you go suggesting that she can stay on here indefinitely, because I warn you, I can't stand it!'

But he put his arms round Mary, and went obediently at her request to make his peace with the outraged old lady. Moreover, he tacitly agreed that she should stay where she was until he and Don could work out some plan of salvation for them all. It was not really all that difficult: she was not without means, and both her sons, if need be, were willing to help financially. A room in sheltered accommodation was soon procured for her, where she could still have a few treasured possessions around her. It seemed an ideal solution, though she fought it every step of the way. The dear Lord had let her down, in allowing her to be disturbed at her age when for so long she had given Him all her trust to make things go just as she wanted them. As she said repeatedly, she ought not to have to go anywhere among strangers when she had two sons with homes of their own. As she could not bear to be with Jean for more than a few hours at a time, that left only one choice, to which, to Tom's horror, Mary did not seem wholly averse. She let her very active conscience trouble her to the point of persuading Tom to agree reluctantly that if the new arrangement made Lavinia desperately unhappy, she could, at any rate, look forward to spending extended holidays with them, like this one. Tom was not to be seduced into giving this plan his unqualified blessing.

'Let's wait and see how she behaves herself tonight,' he said guardedly. 'Then I'll think about it.'

Neither he nor Mary was keen on television, and Lavinia was definitely opposed to it. But sensing tension in the air, Mary scanned the offered programmes for the evening and came up with a suggestion that they should watch the sheep-dog trials. ('There can't possibly be any sexiness in that!' she told Tom. She was wrong, of course: the presenters discussed the breeding of the prize-winning bitch. Mary came to the bitter conclusion that without the subject of sex, television's lights would all go out at once.) Nevertheless, her idea appeared to have been a good one, and Lavinia had obviously enjoyed watching the programme. Mary struck while the iron was hot.

'You must have a television set in your new room, of course,' she said. 'It would prevent you from feeling cut off and lonely.' To the relief of both, Lavinia neither burst into tears at the mention of her impending departure to her new quarters, nor rejected the thought of getting a television set installed.

Mary congratulated herself on getting the last evening over without an argument. A lot of her future peace of mind depended on it.

Time for the nine o'clock news, and up on the screen popped the face of Edward Heath.

'Such a dreadful man!' said Lavinia decidedly. 'He has done the country such harm.'

Tom was a dyed-in-the-wool Tory. He choked. 'What on earth do you know about it, Mother?' he asked.

'I know what I think,' she answered. 'And I am not a fool. He is a conceited and pig-headed man who only knows about ships.'

'Yachts,' corrected Tom, sharply. 'Not ships.'

'There's no difference. I do know that! Don't be so stubborn and rude, Thomas.'

Mary rushed in between them. 'He knows about music, too,' she said. 'You are a musician yourself, and you must appreciate how good a musician he is.'

Lavinia pursed her lips, flattered but by no means prepared to agree.

'And it was he who gave you your £10 bonus on your pension at Christmas,' Tom said wickedly.

'Oh no he did not!'

'Oh yes, he did! It was all his doing!'

'He did not give me any £10 bonus!'

'Mother! It was in your pension book. You must have had it!'

'Well, I did not. I told the man in the post office that I did not want it. He said I had to have it. So I went straight home and put it into an envelope and sent it back to that terrible toothy Heath, with a letter telling him I did not need his charity. So there! He is just ruining the country dear Edwin died for. What does a man like him know about being Prime Minister? His father was a *grocer*!'

Tom was robbed of speech altogether.

So she continued, unchecked. 'Now Harold Wilson is altogether different, you know. I would have taken the £10 from him, because he would have meant it in the right way, as a kindness. He is such a nice man.'

'*Nice* man?' Tom's voice had risen to a strangled squeak. Mary's efforts not to giggle out loud were occasioned almost as much by Tom's fury as by his mother's idiotic gaffes. 'Nice man? Why?'

'Well, he's got such a pleasant face – not all teeth, like Heath. And he doesn't push himself forward like that grocer's son – he wears a mackintosh, like a man going to work. And he smokes a pipe, too. Leo smoked a pipe. I always vote for the man who smokes a pipe, if there is one on the list. So manly, and so healthy.'

With that conversation, Lavinia sealed her own fate, as far as permanent or even long spells of residence in her elder son's house was concerned. She took up her abode in her solitary little room the very next day. Mary saw to it that a television set was installed at once. She had done her best.

During the ensuing winter, it was at Mary's urging that they paid Lavinia flying visits to make sure that she was all right. Though pleased to see them, she made it clear that they were welcome only at times that suited her. Very puzzled, they sought all sorts of explanation before a chance remark gave Mary the clue.

'She's become a telly addict!' Mary said. 'She just lives for it now.'

'When Wilson is likely to be smoking his filthy pipe on the screen, I suppose,' said Tom bitterly.

Though he hadn't hit on the right detail, Tom was on the right track. Quite by chance, Lavinia had been watching when a well-known actor of both stage and screen had made an appeal for charity. Max Pendleton showed in his voice, his mannerisms, his gestures and above all in his wide, somewhat lopsided smile a decided resemblance to Leo when young. She looked in her *Radio Times*, and found that he was, in fact, the star of a long-running series. She marked every programme in which he appeared in red, even the repeats. She had to see him, again and again, whenever it was possible. She watched both showings of each episode of the violent criminal-espionage adventure series he was appearing in, even though watching the repeat meant that she had to stay up till nearly midnight.

The intervals between the programmes began to be long and painful for Lavinia. She found that reading no longer satisfied her, even the old-fashioned novels of romance that the local librarians sorted out for her. Whatever the hero of the romance, whether dressed in Elizabethan ruffs or Regency cravats, he now always wore Max Pendleton's face. The non-explicit love passages no longer satisfied her unless she was able to identify herself absolutely with the heroine. She found herself wishing, for the first time ever, that the novelists of her youth had sometimes taken the pair of lovers beyond the bedroom door. If she was ashamed of such thoughts – and she was, very often –

she put things right with her own conscience and the dear Lord by reminding Him how old she was and that Max Pendleton was not flesh and blood, but only a moving image on the screen. Surely it could not be wicked to fantasize about a picture? Even sex – no, she could not bring herself to admit that her daydreams about him could be sexually motivated. She set her mouth firm, and switched off the set the first time such a thing occurred to her, before switching it back on 'just to the end of this programme'.

But the damage was done. She had thought about him as flesh and blood – a real man, as he must be, or they wouldn't be able to photograph him. Surely there would be no harm in writing to tell him how much she admired him, and of his resemblance to her famous and long-dead brother?

She had always been a good letter-writer. Motherdear had said dogmatically that it was an accomplishment no real lady could or should be without. She penned her letter to him with care, quite ignorant of the fact that she was one among thousands who wrote to him every week. Maybe it was her age combined with her naïveté that caused him to choose her letter as the one he would reply to in his own hand that week.

She was ecstatic. His reply was to her the pathetic aggregate of all the love letters she might have received in her youth, and never did. She unfolded it and refolded it till the paper, thick and expensive as it was, showed signs of wear. By that time she knew it by heart, so she carried it, carefully folded into a dainty handkerchief, on her person. But like any love-sick teenager, she craved a chance to talk to somebody about him – and there was no one to talk to. Her sons were men, and she had alienated all the women she knew, except Mary. The first time they were alone together, Lavinia told all.

Mary found it difficult to deal with. It was so pathetic, yet somehow disturbingly embarrassing. Could it be that in senility the old regressed gradually through all the stages till they reached their second childhood? Should she tell Tom? She felt that she could not bear him simply to deride this midwinter blossoming of emotion that should have flowered and fruited sixty years ago. But if it was a sign that his mother was becoming senile, Tom ought to know; yet there was something so innocently insouciant about the old lady that Mary felt it would be a betrayal she could not bear to be part of. Surely it could do no real harm, and might even do good if it enlarged Lavinia's understanding of her sons and her grandchildren. On the other hand, Mary's closeness to Tom forbade her not to give him a hint or two about it, especially as it tickled her funny bone.

'Blast the old fool!' he exploded. 'I hope she isn't likely to do anything dafter than usual! She's mad.'

Mary patiently explained her theory that the dam of repressed emotion had been breached by a tiny incident, like the famous leak in the dyke. The flood of feeling, now it was released, had overwhelmed her. It was beyond her control.

'Well, my domineering old grandmother has got her come-uppance at last, anyway,' Tom said. 'God, the harm she did to us all – we've all been touched by it – till now. But her training hasn't stood the strain, after all.'

'I wonder,' Mary replied. 'My own guess is that it will take more than Max Pendleton at a distance to conquer Motherdear's teaching. It seems to have held out for more than thirty years of marriage to your father – who must have been a lovely man, by all accounts.'

'Like me?' he asked. Mary agreed wholeheartedly. She had to break the news to him that Lavinia was to be expected on a visit within a few days.

'No doubt I shall hear the latest about her schoolgirl crush,' Mary said, having dealt expertly with Tom's apprehension.

Lavinia arrived, as rouged and kiss-curled as ever, but to Mary's sympathetic eye, a bit subdued. There was also a most tantalizing silence about Max Pendleton, and a reversal of any interest in the telly. Mary could do nothing but wait to find out why.

Then came an evening when Tom was out, and the two

women were left together at twilight with only the glow of a
wood fire as light. Lavinia drew her chair close to Mary's.

'My dear,' she said, 'you remember me telling you how much
I liked that young man on television? He wrote to me, you
know – in his own hand! I really felt I loved him. He was so
much like Leo. But about two weeks ago, I saw that he was
going to be in a play late one night, so of course I sat up to
watch it.' Her mouth quivered, and she held a dainty handkerchief against it to still it. Her voice dropped to a barely audible
whisper.

'My dear, in the very first scene, he was in bed with a woman!
And they were both naked!' She paused, trying to control the
horror of the memory of that jealous moment.

'So?' Mary prompted.

'Of course, you could only see their backs – so perhaps he
may have had his pyjama trousers on. But she hadn't got a stitch
on! You could see that. My dear, it was disgusting!'

Mary was silent, because she couldn't think of anything
appropriate to say.

Lavinia didn't notice. She just went on. 'I couldn't say any of
this in front of Tom, of course,' she said. 'Motherdear would
turn in her grave. But I can't tell you how badly I felt. That
dreadful woman – and he was in bed with her! And they kept
saying such terrible things – you know – well, for instance, she
threw off the covers as if she were going to get out of bed, and
he said, "Where are you going?" and she said, "To make a cup
of tea," and he pulled her back, and said, "Who wants *tea*, when
we've got this?" And he actually *fondled* her!'

The old lady's voice had sunk to its lowest register, with a
hint of tears in it. In the fireglow she looked like an ancient
child, eyes agog with avid interest even while registering the
ultimate of dismay and disgust. It seemed to Mary that Motherdear, with all her values still intact against twentieth-century
licence, had materialized in the shadows at the back of the room.

'Of course,' said Lavinia, the chance to censure bringing back
some strength to her voice. 'It was the woman's fault, you

know, being naked like that. She was tempting him so dreadfully. I never did like women. But I did use to like him. It was like having Leo with me again, just the two of us together in my little room. But after seeing him in bed with that woman, of course I realize he wasn't a bit like Leo at all. Leo would never have done such a thing. Motherdear brought us all up better than that, I hope.'

Mary had to say something. 'But it was only a play, dear,' she said, weakly.

Lavinia turned tetchily towards her, her blue eyes holding the familiar glint of stubborn rectitude.

'I know it was only a play!' she snapped. 'I may be old, but I am not stupid! If he had been a *nice* man, he would never have consented to take part in a disgusting play like that. When I first had my television, and saw him in that series I used to sit up to watch, there wasn't a single word of *sex* in it.'

She brought out the forbidden word in a tragic, despairing whisper.

'I should never have wanted to see him again if there had been, but there wasn't. The part he was playing then was quite different – a real manly part. He was only a hired assassin.'

Stained Moonlight

The new chief verger turned up his overcoat collar, and wound a warm scarf round his neck. His bachelor quarters in the medieval buildings on the north side of the Minster Close were small and cosy, and he glanced round his beautiful little sitting-room with deep satisfaction. He felt that he had very good cause to feel seasonal goodwill, this particular Christmas Eve.

His appointment had been as sudden as it was unexpected. He had been the runner-up for the job, after a lengthy selection process, and had then been pipped at the post by an older man of the typical verger variety, with a lot of previous experience. He had none. He was a disillusioned schoolmaster, a historian manqué now seeking to mend a damaged personal and professional life. He asked for nothing but to live simply in the presence of history and beauty, knowing that of all things they could heal his spirit. He had not expected to get the job when he had applied for it on the spur of the moment, and had not been unduly disappointed – indeed, he had been astonished to get as far as he had. Then the other man died on the very eve of taking up his appointment, and with Christmas almost upon them, the Dean and Chapter had taken the easy way out. So here he was.

'Come, Edward!' he said, though the command was quite unnecessary. The golden labrador was already at the door, pointing eagerly. The verger lifted its lead from an ancient hook by the door, and on impulse took down the huge bunch of keys from the next hook, and shoved them deep into his overcoat pocket. The full moon was high, a cold alabaster disc reflecting icy light on crisp grass and frosted stone. The shadows were deep and blue with cold. Across the Minster Green the outline of the building lay like a cut-out pattern, pinnacles and all. There was no breath of wind, and the murmur of modern traffic in the distance only seemed to enhance the timeless stillness of the place. Then the Minster clock bell boomed, and broke the spell. The verger closed his door behind him, and set off at a brisk pace, with the dog for company. He walked all round the moonlit building, admiring its Gothic grace afresh from every angle with a growing intensity of feeling. It was *his*. No doubt the Bishop said the same, and the Dean – but neither of them would or could ever know its every nook and cranny as he would in the future. He fingered the keys in his pocket, prouder to feel them there than he had ever felt about 'owning' a building before. His eyes imaged the interior, the glorious nave, the vaulted ceiling, the delicate screen, the peaceful effigies, the dignified high altar, even the rather battered crib that he had helped set up just inside the west door. He visualized how the moonlight would fall through the clerestories on to the stillness of the worn stone floor. He had to see it. The temptation was too great.

He put the dog on to its lead as he crossed the porch, and fitted a key into the postern of the huge west door. The little door swung gently open, and he stepped across the high thresh-old, pausing there to take in the scene before him. The long nave stretched away, barred by shafts of moonlight as it fell across ancient pillars, carved marble and hollowed flagstones. The nearest patch of moonlit floor was only a few yards distant, and he looked up to the window from which the radiance came. The beam of moonlight descended as insubstantial as Jacob's ladder, to rest on the floor at the foot of the pillars on the north side of the aisle. He let his delighted gaze come down the ladder of light. A dark, indistinct shadow, pointing vaguely towards the high altar, marred the brightness of the stones.

'Queer,' he said to himself. 'I never noticed that in daylight. Must be a stain where something was spilt, and never properly cleaned up. I must have a word with the cleaners – when I know them better.'

After only one week, he was still unsure of the personnel attached to the Minster, and afraid of making bad gaffes, especially with the clergy. The thought distracted him momentarily from the beauty spread before him. He pulled on the dog's lead. 'Come,' he said. The lead tautened, and brought the man to a halt. The dog did not move.

'What's the matter, old fellow? I know it's all strange, and you haven't actually been inside before. But I want you to get used to it at night, because that's when I can bring you in.' He put his hand down to the dog's collar, and tried to urge him forward.

Reluctantly the dog stepped across the threshold, and they proceeded a few steps towards the stained moonlight. On the edge of the bright patch, the dog suddenly crouched, and began to whine. The eerie noise echoed round the aisles and beat down from the vaulted roof. Then the dog stood up, stiff-legged and with raised hackles, and the whine turned into a howl.

The man peered at the floor in front of him. From where he now stood, there was no sign of the strange shadow he had previously noted, and his dog's behaviour seemed quite incomprehensible. He unclipped the lead from the collar and, thus released, the animal sped back through the postern and into the porch, where it sat down in anxious obedience to its master's stern order, keeping up, nevertheless, a low, miserable, grumbling whine. The verger was annoyed. The very last thing he wanted was for a late passerby to call the police and involve him in a long explanation. It must be getting on for midnight, and he wanted above all to have the Minster to himself for the first few minutes of Christmas Day. All the same, he went back and did his best to calm his silly companion, standing in the postern and fondling Edward's ears while he spoke soothingly. Then he turned again towards the nave, and stepped back to the edge of the moonlight.

He froze into immobility as a human voice spoke almost in his ear.

'Queer, isn't it? I've never yet seen a dog that would cross this particular spot, day or night. Even in broad daylight they skirt round it, or bolt back like yours did a moment ago. I hope I didn't startle you.'

The verger didn't want to admit to being startled, though he certainly was. They still stood in shadow, but he could see the speaker reasonably clearly in the reflected light on the edge of the floodlit patch. A cleric, tall and well made, with a long black cloak down to his heels and a white head bared. It was too dim to distinguish his features, but once the initial shock of his appearance began to wear off, the verger's mind began to tick over normally and supply explanation. It must be the Dean – he also had keys. Did any others have keys, too? Or had the man, like himself, merely been taking a midnight stroll and, attracted by Edward's howling, come to investigate? If so, he must have stepped through the postern while the verger still had his back to it.

'I apologize for my dog,' he said. 'I'm the new verger, incidentally. I was just passing, and yielded to the temptation of seeing the nave in the moonlight. I'll lock up again now, and get off to bed. But that is interesting – about the dogs, I mean. Have you any idea at all why it should be so?'

'Oh, there's the usual sort of story to account for it, of course. A place like this germinates tales as April showers sprout seeds.'

'Please tell me,' said the verger. 'I want to know everything there is to know about the Minster.'

'You are a very unusual verger, if I may say so,' said the cleric, amusement sounding in his deep, musical voice. 'They don't usually come quite so – er – receptive as you to the aesthetic and imaginative side of their duties. The tale is approximately two hundred years old. They were doing some restoration to the gallery just up above here. There had been a lot of internal bickering about it, with the Dean on one side and most of the Chapter on the other. The Dean had the last word, of course, and got his own way. If the rest of them hadn't opposed him so openly, he wouldn't have been half so stubborn, I dare say, but there it was. He became obsessed with the work, in case there should be any underhanded interference as it progressed.

So one moonlit night he let himself in, and went up to the gallery to inspect the work that had been done during the day. The verger found him next morning, spreadeagled on the flag-stones. It must be quite forty feet.' A shiver ran down the verger's spine as he remembered that strangely shaped stain. But his companion was speaking again. 'There have been those throughout the years who swore that in some lights they could still see the outline of his body. And certainly dogs seem to find the spot uncanny.'

'I wonder what really happened,' said the verger. 'I mean, did he fall, or was he pushed? He must have known every inch of the tread up there, even in the dark, and of course he must have been well aware of the danger. Even in broad daylight it takes a cool head to stand on an unprotected narrow ledge, and look down forty feet. He wouldn't have gone up at all if he hadn't had a good head for heights.'

'Oh, it was an accident. There's no question of that. That's where the dog comes in. He had left his dog below, just inside the postern, and it had begun to bark. He didn't want it to draw attention to the fact that he was there yet again — any more than you want yours to call attention to you now. So he leaned over to speak to it, and lost his balance. That's all.'

The tall man stepped out into the patch of moonlight, upright and dignified, with an unmistakable air of authority in every line of him. He turned his face upwards in the radiance, and the aristocratic features showed clear for the first time. The verger felt vaguely uneasy, and a bit embarrassed. 'Who is he? I ought to recognize him, and I don't. He certainly isn't the Dean. I saw him this morning. Surely it can't be the Bishop?' The dog set up another spine-chilling howl, interspersed with sharp, terrified barks. The verger turned away to quieten him.

'Stop it, Edward! That's enough, now.' When he turned back to his companion, the question he had decided not to ask was already on his lips.

'I don't mean to be rude, but how can you be so sure what

really happened? I mean, how could anybody know for certain? He was dead, wasn't he?'

'How do I know? I certainly ought to. You see, it was I who fell.'

The tall cloaked figure sank from its erect posture and folded into the floor, a shapeless blur with its right arm outstretched towards the altar. Then it faded, and faded, till it was only the faintest of outlines of a stain on the moonlit flagstones. The bell above tolled for midnight, masking both the dog's frantic howling and the verger's involuntary cry.

Long Journey

He was ahead of me in the queue waiting at the ticket barrier, conspicuous because his grey-capped head stood clear above those of the huddle of tourists between us. They were all laden like caravan camels with huge bulging back-packs, besides being hung about with bags, bundles and bits like over-decorated Christmas trees. Every one of them seemed to possess as many arms as a Hindu goddess, all very much in evidence as they gesticulated to aid communication with each other in a farrago of foreign tongues. The foyer of our little railway station rang with the sound, which grew louder and shriller every second, like an engine with its bearings running dry. The whole lot of them appeared to be intent upon lifting the ancient curse of Babel by the power of mere decibels alone. I supposed that our ancient little city might have reason to be grateful to them for stopping off for a canter (between trains) round the nave of our glorious cathedral, *en route* for an even more furious gallop round Cambridge, but all the same, I found both the noise and the back-packs more than usually irritating and hackle-raising, especially the back-packs. As their yelping owners turned and twisted, constantly reversing like Viennese waltzers, any unfortunate behind them in the queue was more than likely to get a quick one-two in the chest, if not occasionally one on the chin. Only the young, the agile and the very alert were likely to escape unbiffed. In that privileged group I could hardly hope to be included. A large and well-filled plastic carrier-bag making a sweeping parabola on the end of a long male arm lifted one of my crutches neatly off the floor from under me. Since my weight at that moment was resting almost entirely on the other crutch, it did no more than make me stagger.

However, my struggle to maintain my equilibrium had a

startling effect on the tangle of tourists. They turned as one, and stared in silence, as if, Zachariah-like, they had all been struck dumb upon the instant. No murmer of apology was attempted in any language, nor any tacit acknowledgement made of the fact that one of their party had, however unintentionally, very nearly caused the downfall of a large, elderly, disabled female speciment of the genus Brit. The cessation of noise inside the confined space was so sudden as to be uncanny, and it was in that moment of otherwise shattering silence that the tall man, already at the ticket barrier, spoke, his voice wafted towards me by the resident station draught.

'Ninety come next Saturday,' he said.

The ticket collector put out a hand that had nothing to do with inspecting a ticket. 'So long, then, mate. Good luck!' he replied.

The sound of a train approaching, albeit in the far distance, broke the spell. It galvanized the bag-bedecked febrile foreigners into instant action, as if triggering in them some conditioned reflex that drove them, Ulysses-like, forward. They surged towards the barrier with heads lowered and noses pointing like hounds on the scent. The old man was swept through the barrier in front of them.

I let them go, because I knew there was no need for haste. The 'up' train was not due for at least another twenty minutes. I always allowed myself plenty of time to negotiate the long downward slope of the underpass, a hazard even to the able-bodied after a little rain made the going a bit slippery. By the time I actually entered the tunnel at one end, the scramble of sightseers were emerging from the other, the split-splat of their 'sneakers' and the echoes of strident excited voices still reverberating around me, making it clear that they had all taken the underpass at a steady trot.

The old man was standing to one side of the upward gradient to let them pass, so that when I rounded the bend, he was not far in front of me. He kept his tall figure erect with an old-fashioned walking stick cut to match his height, while in his left

hand he carried a modern aluminium walking aid of the same
sort of NHS issue as my own elbow crutches. It was one of the
kind that could be opened out to provide a seat-support in an
emergency. Both his hands being thus full, he, too, wore a back-
pack, though both he and I would have called it a haversack.
Compared with the others, it was of extremely modest dimen-
sions, its khaki colour almost the same as that of his well-worn
raincoat, and the shoulder-strap of it was carefully arranged so
as to hold the collar of the coat up round his long neck against
the brisk, cold wind blowing off the fen. He moved with the
slow tread of a man who knows well where he is going, but is in
no particular hurry to get there.

There was a fair sprinkling of people already on the 'up'
platform, waiting to change trains. Because of the rain, they
were all herded together in a most un-British-like fashion under
the short length of sheltering canopy; but being British, they
had all disdained the seats provided by BR and stood in resolute,
resigned patience facing the rails. Not so the tourist group.
They made straight for the unoccupied seats and off-loaded on
to them their combined array of extraneous impedimenta, which
afforded them a welcome chance of free hands with which to
adjust their heavy pack-loads as well as their damp, skintight
jeans. Then they, too, turned to face the rails, but with the backs
of their legs touching the seats so as to be able to keep a close
eye on their accumulated souvenirs.

The ninety-year-old paused by a cluttered seat, leaned his
modern contraption against the back of it, and prepared to
scotch his weight on the six inches or so of green iron slats that
had been left free. Then he caught sight of me. Touching the
peak of his cap with the handle of his walking stick, he rose and
offered me the only available resting place. The hubbub of a
train just leaving the 'down' platform made any spoken reply
inaudible, but I indicated by a gesture with my hands that his six
inches would hardly accommodate my own broad behind. He
smiled and sat down again, while I, my fen-tiger blood rising in
protest, raised one of my crutches and with it pushed the

offending baggage along till I had cleared a space wide enough
for me to sit down beside him. He turned his face towards me
then with an appreciative smile at my audacity, and gave me my
first good look at it. It did not betray his great age, except for
the paleness of eyes that I guessed had once been intensely blue,
and were now the pearly grey colour of the sky behind the
cathedral tower on a misty summer morning. The lower lids,
too, had a rather weary droop, but the rest of his long, lean face
showed barely a wrinkle.

Civilities over, he placed his walking stick between his knees
and crossed his hands over the top of it, resting his chin upon
them. He turned his eyes towards the lines and gazed towards
the point at which they appeared to converge in the distance
across the wide flatness of the fen. Then he turned and gave the
short distance he could see towards Cambridge the same long,
level scrutiny. His reverie was broken by the arrival on the
opposite platform of one of the new 'Sprinter' trains. When it had
made an equally noisy departure, he spoke, as if the sight
and sound of it was more than his self-induced composure could
stand. Tossing his head backward in a gesture of eloquent
derision, he said, 'And they call that a train!' He paused, to
assure himself that further conversation would not be taken
amiss, and then shifted his position a little so as to be able to see
me. His hands, still clasped round the handle of his stick, were
now brought into full view. They were nothing less than
beautiful – lean and strong, long between the joints, the fingers
tipped with well-trimmed oval nails that most girls would be
proud of. My father's hands were just like that, and so, I
reflected, were those of Lindow Man, dug up from where he
had lain under the peat for two thousand years. But then he,
too, was a true Briton, one of the Iron Age Celts whose genes
had survived in so many of us in my own particular fen.

'Two coaches!' said my companion witheringly. 'And I suppose that's what they call progress.' The bitter scorn was almost
tangible, and led me to a swift conclusion.

'You must be a railwayman yourself,' I said.

It was as if I had switched him on like a radio.

'Only all my life!' he said. 'Till they forced me to retire.' There was no way of switching him off again, even if I had wanted to, but I didn't. His father had been a top-link driver, and his grandfather before that. He himself had been 'on the footplate' from the age of eight, because he used to sneak away in spite of all his mother's prohibitions to go and find his father, who was only a fireman then, so as to take many an illicit ride with him. 'I used to pinch half a dozen eggs from the pantry,' he said, 'so we could fry them on the shovel for our breakfast.' The recollection made him smile.

When his father had been made up to a driver, they had had to go and live in London. He hadn't liked that much, though it had meant a lot more stations to explore and the engines used by the different lines to see.

'I got my first job as a cleaner when I were sixteen, with the old London and North Eastern,' he said. 'That were in the year the first war broke out, 1914. By the time I were twenty-six, I were a driver myself. So I were back again round here when the second war started. I shan't forget them first few days of it in a hurry! Bringing trains with fifteen coaches out o' London on them hot September days, every coach stuffed up to the roof-racks, very near, with poor little kids being evacuated out o' London. Everybody expected Hitler as soon as ever the war was declared, you see.'

'I remember,' I said, but he didn't hear me.

'All the kids crying 'cos they couldn't understand what was happening, and why their mothers wanted to send 'em away. Every little tot carrying his gas-mask, and a packet o' sandwiches. Most o' them ate their grub straight off, not knowing at all that it was likely to be hours and hours and hours before they could get another bite or a drink. They couldn't put a teacher in every compartment, you see, because we'd had to fetch out every bit of old rolling-stock as could be found to meet the emergency, and a lot o' them old coaches had no corridors. They were sending trains out o' London as fast as ever they

could get 'em filled up, and that meant we had to stand in
sidings over and over again to get out of each other's way. So
them journeys took hours and hours longer than they ought to
have done. The kids coming this way was mostly from the East
End, places like Bethnal Green and Islington, slum kids, a lot of
them. You never did see anything in your life like the state o'
them compartments when the children got out o' them at last –
but we had to take the trains straight back and pick up another
lot, and there wasn't no time to be fussy about things being
cleaned up. The next lot had to get in the compartments with
whatever the first lot had left behind. You've got no idea.'

I forbore to stop his flow to tell him that I was one who did
know, because I had spent the first three days of what ought to
have been my honeymoon standing on the platform of Hunting-
don station taking the children out of the trains.

He just went on and on, painting vivid word-pictures of the
sort of details that never get into the history books. Of bringing
trains crammed with troops through all the miles of bomb-
flattened London on the morning after a bad raid; of seeing lines
like those in front of us choked with great bowsers full of high-
octane aviation spirit for the many airfields in East Anglia, while
lone enemy pilots with a buccaneering turn of mind followed
the railway lines and machine-gunned the tankers as they stood
in sidings at little stations or at lonely wayside halts.

'But it all come to an end at last,' he said. 'Like every else
does, sooner or later.' His pale eyes swept the fenscape again.
Even that ended at the horizon, where the upturned bowl of the
sky sat on the black earth.

'I were a top-link driver by that time, of course. They were
good times, once the war was over. When the Queen – well, she
was Princess Elizabeth at that time – when she got married, it
was me that drove all the continental royals as had been over for
the wedding back to Harwich after the wedding. All come up
and shook hands with me that day, they did. I shan't forget that
in a hurry, either.' He paused again, but I kept silent. I felt that
he still had more he wanted to give voice to.

'But the good times ended, same as the bad ones had. I were married then – well I had been for years – and when they told me that I had got to retire, I bought a little cottage out in the fen as close to the line as I could, so as I could watch the trains go by and very often see some of my old mates as well. And nights when I couldn't sleep, I could lay and listen to the trains going by. Then my wife died, bless her old heart. Fifteen year ago that was, now . . .

'I were so lonely that I couldn't bear it, so I got married again. She were a good woman, but it wasn't like the first. Then after eight year, she died as well, and I've managed by myself from then till now. I reckoned I could get along all right for the bit o' time as I had left, you see. But it ain't worked out like that. Now I'm coming up to ninety, them welfare buggers won't let me be. They say as I ain't safe no more. I've had enough of life, anyway – so what has it got to do with them? But there's nothing for it – I've got to go somewhere where I can be looked after, so they say, whether I want to or not. So my son's made arrangements for me to go and live in a part of his house. On the south coast. I've got a few o' my clothes on my back, and I'm on my way today. My home will be coming after me on Monday.'

'Your son,' I said, hardly daring to hope. 'Is he a railwayman, too?'

A flash of pride crossed his face. 'Was,' he corrected. 'Retired now, of course. A driver as well – but the last of us. His wife didn't want no children.'

Our train, already quite late, had come in at last. It was another of the new 'Sprinters' with only two coaches, already well filled.

By the time we two old folk had struggled to our feet and picked up our extra legs, there was another war raging for possession of the few vacant seats. Yet when all the eager backpackers were seated, one place still remained unoccupied in full view of the two of us as we stood by the door when all the others had got in. My companion courteously drew back, hold-

ing the door open for me to mount the high step. There was no
option for me but to acknowledge his courtesy by the equal
courtesy of accepting it. So I took the seat, and he was left
standing in the narrow little space between the two coaches.
Nobody other than I seemed to notice the gentlemanly old man
at all.

As the train drew out of the station, he looked out of the
window with the same intensity as I had noticed before. He
must have known as well as I did that from where he stood he
had no hope of catching even a last glimpse of the cathedral, but
I felt that in forlorn hope he was longing for just one more sight
of the wonderful lantern.

Reason prevailed, and he turned his back to the fenscape,
opening out his walking aid and perching his weight upon it,
with his other stick between his knees, and his splendid old
hands crossed over it. He rested his chin on them, and closed his
eyes.

Of necessity, he was the first one out on to the platform at
Cambridge. As the rough and tumble of the young beasts of
burden rushed through the door and began to run down the
long platform, he stood back holding the door for me, waiting
to help me down.

The London train was standing in, as I could see.

'Don't miss your connection,' I said anxiously. 'You still have
a long way to go today.'

He transferred both his sticks to one hand, so as to be able to
raise his cap properly with the free one. He smiled, a genuine
old-person-to-old-person smile.

'Yes,' he said. 'A long way, as you say. But not so far as I
hope and pray my next long journey will take me.'

Then he replaced his cap, rearranged his sticks, and turned to
walk away, still unhurried, still with the same firm, dignified
tread of a man who knows where he is going, if not when he
will get there.

Leabharlanna Conndae an Cabáin